Dear Reader,

In honor of "Labor" Day, Silhouette Books is delighted to present you with *Maternity Leave,* a sexy and fun-filled short-story collection celebrating the blessings and surprises that babies can bring.

What happens when three independent women find themselves without a partner and with babies on the way? They vow to be loving single mothers, of course! But in an ideal world, a child has a mother *and* a father, and as you'll see in these three brand-new stories, fate has a way of taking care of these three delightful mothers-to-be....

Beth, Daisy and Jane are very different women in very different situations. But while each of the three deals with her pregnancy in her own special way, they all unexpectedly find love around the corner. Obviously, parenthood is never easy...but true love can certainly make things a little less difficult.

We hope you enjoy this unforgettable romantic collection by three of the best-loved authors in romance!

The Editors
Silhouette Books

See What The Critics Are Saying About These Three Remarkable Authors

CANDACE CAMP

Candace Camp writes with "ingenious wit...."
—*Publishers Weekly*

✸ ✸ ✸ ✸

CAIT LONDON

"An irresistible storyteller whose delicious forays into love and laughter are always sheer delight...."
—Melinda Helfer, *Romantic Times* Magazine

✸ ✸ ✸ ✸

SHERRYL WOODS

"Sherryl Woods is an author who writes with a special warmth, wit, charm and intelligence."
—Heather Graham Pozzessere,
New York Times bestselling author

CANDACE CAMP
CAIT LONDON
SHERRYL WOODS
MATERNITY
Leave

Silhouette Books

Published by Silhouette Books

America's Publisher of Contemporary Romance

SILHOUETTE BOOKS

ISBN 0-373-48366-X

MATERNITY LEAVE

Copyright © 1998 by Harlequin Books S.A.

TABLOID BABY
Copyright © 1998 by Candace Camp

THE NINE-MONTH KNIGHT
Copyright © 1998 by Lois Kleinsasser

THE PATERNITY TEST
Copyright © 1998 by Sherryl Woods

CONTENTS

CANDACE CAMP

Writing comes naturally to Candace—she grew up in a newspaper family. But she didn't follow in their footsteps, at least not initially. Candace earned a law degree and practiced law before making the decision to write full-time. It was a good decision, resulting in over nine million copies of her books in print worldwide. Candace is the popular author of over forty contemporary and historical novels and is the recipient of the *Romantic Times* Lifetime Achievement Award for Western Romance, an honor well deserved by this Texas resident.

CAIT LONDON

Award-winning author Cait London lives in the Missouri Ozarks but loves to travel the Northwest's gold rush/cattle drive trails every summer. She loves research trips, meeting people and going to Native American dances. She is an avid reader who loves to paint, play with computers and grow herbs. Three is her lucky number; she has three daughters, and the events in her life have always been in threes. "I love writing for Silhouette," Ms. London says. "One of the best perks about all this hard work is the thrilling reader response and the warm, snug sense that I have given readers an enjoyable, entertaining gift." She also writes historical novels under the pseudonym Cait Logan.

SHERRYL WOODS

Whether she's living in California, Florida or Virginia, Sherryl Woods always makes her home by the sea. A walk on the beach, the sound of waves, the smell of the salt air all provide inspiration for this author of over sixty romance and mystery novels. You can write to Sherryl—from April through December—or stop by and meet her at her bookstore: Potomac Sunrise, 308 Washington Avenue, Colonial Beach, VA 22443.

TABLOID BABY

Candace Camp

Chapter 1

It was not supposed to happen like this.

Beth Sutton scanned the horizon, fighting down panic. It stretched limitlessly all around her, the flat West Texas landscape, dotted with low mesquite bushes and prickly pear cacti. The road beside which she stood bisected the empty landscape, disappearing into the distance like a gray ribbon. She had been standing here for ten minutes, and there hadn't been a car yet.

Another pain gripped her, and she leaned against her crippled car, trying to breathe as she had learned in Lamaze class. *Why hadn't they taught her what she really needed to know now: what to do when you're having labor pains and are stranded in the middle of nowhere?*

The worst of it was, she knew that it was all her own fault. She had been utterly, hopelessly stupid. She had felt two pains this morning, about thirty minutes apart, but after that there had been nothing. She had assumed it was like last week, when she had had a few false labor pains one day and nothing else had happened. Of course, she realized now that it had been foolish to assume it was false labor—and even more foolish to decide to drive into town to get the eggs that she needed for muffins. She understood now—too late—that her sudden burst of energy and the urge to start cleaning and baking were part of the nesting instinct the Lamaze teacher had told them about.

She should have stayed home, should have waited to see if the pains began again. Instead she had driven into town, but as she was returning to the ranch house, a sudden pain had struck her, so much sharper and more severe than the others that when it hit, her hands had jerked on the wheel and the car had wound up in the ditch. So now here she was, miles from anywhere, with her car half in the ditch and one tire blown. Not only that, her water had broken during the accident, soaking her dress. Only a few minutes later, she had had a second pain.

Tears battered at the backs of her eyes. Beth blinked them away. *She had to be strong.* She was all alone, but she told herself that she was used to that. She had always been an independent woman. It was, after all, why she had moved away from the ranch when she was nineteen. She had felt as if she was being smothered by the small town, where everyone knew everything everyone else did, and by her father and three doting older brothers, who were convinced it was their duty to protect her from all life's little bumps and scrapes. She had been living alone in Dallas and taking care of herself for ten years now, and even if she had come back to her dad's ranch for help when she found out she was pregnant, it had been a purely practical move. It did not mean that she was any less capable of taking care of herself.

She drew a calming breath and made herself think. She obviously could not stand there dithering beside an inoperative car and wishing she had brought the cell phone with her. The fact was that she didn't have it; Dad and Cory had taken it when they went out to work on the other side of the ranch today, so that she would be able to get hold of them if she had an emergency. Another fact was that no one had come down this road in almost twenty minutes, and she could easily stand here for another hour before someone did, since it was only a side road.

She took her purse from the car and slung it over her shoulder. Then she set off down the road in the direction in which she had just come. Though it was a good deal farther to the town of Angel Eye than it was to the ranch house—ten miles instead of five— at least in another mile or so she would reach the main highway. While it was not exactly heavily traveled, her chances would be much better of flagging down a ride. She trudged along, refusing to think about the horror tales she had heard about hitching rides. She also tried not to think about how hot the sun was or how thirsty she had become or how far a mile was when one was heavily pregnant and being blasted by pains every ten minutes.

Suddenly there was the sound of a car behind her. It was so faint, and she was concentrating so hard on walking, that for a moment she did not recognize the sound. When it finally dawned on her that she was hearing the purr of an engine in the distance, she whirled and looked behind her, shading her eyes. Sure enough, there was a dark shape on the road. Relief flooded her, leaving her knees so shaky she almost sank onto the ground. She hadn't realized until that moment how tensely she had been holding herself.

As the car drew closer, she could see that it was a large, dark, expensive car, a Mercedes, in fact. In one way, that was reassuring; a Mercedes seemed like the car of a solid citizen, not a psycho serial killer who preyed on hitchhikers. On the other hand, it also meant that it was not anyone she knew. She could not think of a soul in or around Angel Eye who drove a Mercedes. Just then another pain hit her, and she almost doubled over with it.

The car screeched to a stop beside her, and she heard the car door open and the sound of running feet. She could not look up, could not even open her eyes. It was difficult enough just remembering to breathe right.

"Ma'am? What's the matter?" It was a man's voice, deep and with the faintest tinge of the South in it.

She could see his feet. They halted a few feet from her, then came forward more slowly. "Ma'am?" he repeated, and now, as the pain began to blessedly recede, she could hear the wariness in his tone. "Do you need some help?"

He was close to her now, and the pain was beginning to be almost bearable. She uncoiled from her defensive posture, and for the first time she looked up at him—and found herself staring into the most beautiful blue eyes she had ever seen.

She knew she must look like a fool staring at him, but she could not help it. This was a man who did not belong in Angel Eye, Texas. He wore loafers, off-white linen trousers and a collarless shirt of the same color. It was the sort of casual outfit she had seen on male models in *GQ*, and the clothes suited him to a T. His hair was black, thick, excellently cut and just a fraction too long, giving him a hint of the rebel. His lips were modeled and firm, his jaw strong and his nose straight. A slash of a scar, about an inch long, cut through one of his dark eyebrows and saved his face from perfection.

"Who in the world are you?" she blurted out.

His brows went up at her words, and he replied coolly, "The man who stopped because you looked as if you were in a great deal of pain."

"I'm sorry. That was rude. I was...just so surprised. I—yes, I was in pain, and I'm extremely glad you stopped." Her hand went instinctively to her swollen stomach. "My car broke down back there."

She turned and pointed and was surprised to see how short a distance she had walked from her automobile. It had seemed like forever. She looked back at him. Those cool blue eyes were still on her assessingly, and Beth realized, embarrassed, how awful she must look: sweating and dusty, her curling red hair, never tame, now blown in every direction by the wind, her stomach huge and pressing against the cloth of her dress.

"I'm sorry. I know this must seem bizarre. But I—you probably guessed. I seem to have gone into labor. Could you possibly take me into town?"

"Of course." He took her arm and guided her toward the car. Beth decided that she must have been wrong in thinking he had been wary a moment earlier. No doubt it had merely been the surprise of finding a woman in this situation.

"Thank you," she said, as he opened the passenger door for her. "This is very kind of you."

He came around and got in on the driver's side. The car started with a smooth purr, and he took off. He glanced toward her and said, "My name is Jackson Prescott."

"I'm Beth Sutton. It's nice to meet you," Beth responded politely. His name sounded faintly familiar, and she wondered if he was someone she was supposed to know. "Have you moved into the area recently?"

His eyes lit up with amusement, and he let out a bark of laughter. "No. That is, well, I was just looking around. Checking the place out."

"I see." She didn't, really. She supposed he must be considering moving here, and she had the uneasy feeling that his face was one she had seen before. Perhaps he was some politician or well-known businessman or something, someone she should have recognized. It was obvious from the clothes and the car that he was wealthy. A trial lawyer? She supposed he might even be a sports figure—he was tall and well-built, although he didn't have the thickly muscled frame she associated with football. Tennis, perhaps? A swimmer?

At that moment another pain seized her, and she forgot all about Jackson Prescott. Fingers digging into her palm, eyes closed, she concentrated on her breathing.

Prescott glanced over at her. She was in obvious pain and struggling not to show it. There was strength in every taut line of her body. *Beauty and strength.* They were the hallmarks of a Prescott heroine. Indeed, it had become a capsule description in Hollywood to call a gutsy, intelligent female character a "Prescott woman." Looking at her, Jackson felt certain that this woman would someday, someway, work her way into one of his productions.

Her head was back against the seat, and her eyes

were closed. Her skin was translucent in the way of some redheads, pale and luminous, with just a sprinkling of light brown freckles across her cheeks. Her mouth was wide, with a full lower lip. Her nose was straight and a trifle short; he suspected that at better moments the combination of the snub nose and freckles gave her face a gamin look, particularly when she smiled. Her hair was a mass of red curls, tied in the back by a ribbon, but a great deal of it had gotten loose and tangled around her face.

Though he could not see them now, he knew that her eyes were mahogany. He had taken in the detail just as he had taken in all the other details about her. It was part of what made him good, that attention to detail. Another of his assets was his calm, the unruffled attitude that was capable of seeing him through a continual series of crises, and that soothed the frazzled nerves of studio executives and insecure stars alike. It was rare that anyone saw him lose his temper on the set or give way to the gut-gnawing anxiety that dogged every director at one time or another.

But that calm was certainly being tested at this moment. Prescott was accustomed to daily film crises. He was not accustomed to crises being of the life-and-death variety.

He pressed down a little harder on the accelerator, and the speedometer moved up to eighty. It made him feel a trifle queasy to think that he had been tempted not to stop when he first saw Beth Sutton. Fifteen years of living in L.A. had taught him to be wary. Fame had made him even more so.

Of course, he had not driven past her. He could not have ignored the vision of helplessness and pain she had presented, even if it had been on the carjacking streets of L.A. instead of a deserted road in West Texas. However, as he had walked over to her, there had been a niggling suspicion at the back of his mind that this was some sort of setup, a stunt by a would-be actress to meet him, or even one of those bizarre celebrity practical jokes that had been popular on TV a few years back. Then he had seen the panic in her eyes, the remnants of pain on her face, and all such thoughts had fled his mind, replaced only by the instinctive need to help.

He reached the intersection of the highway and turned right, assuming that the sign pointing toward Angel Eye, 8 Miles was the correct direction. They sped down the road.

"I'm sorry." Beth spoke and Jackson glanced over at his passenger. Her eyes were open again and tinged with the aftermath of pain. Her skin and the hair around her face were damp with sweat.

He raised his brows. "For what?"

She shrugged. "Stopping you. Forcing you to have to deal with this." She fluttered her hand in a vague way.

He smiled faintly. "Don't worry. Don't apologize to me. You're the one who's having to go through this. I'm just driving the car."

Even in the backwash of fatigue that followed her pain, Beth had to smile back at him. There was something quite calming about him, she thought—a sort of sureness, an inner strength that reached out and enveloped her. She could count on him, she sensed, and the thought made her feel stronger.

She sat up straighter. It would be a few more minutes, she reassured herself, before she had to go through that again. "You can drop me off at the sheriff's office in town," she told him.

Her brother Quinn would not be there, of course. He was over in Hammond today, testifying in a district court case. But any of the deputies would take her, sirens blasting, over to the hospital in Hammond. She was, after all, the sheriff's sister, and besides, she had known most of them all her life. But she hated to do it. She didn't like asking favors of anyone, even one of her brother's deputies, and she particularly did not like the thought of having to ride all the way to Hammond with Darryl Hawkes, who apparently had never gotten over his high school crush on her and who, with her luck, would be the very deputy chosen to take her.

But there was little other choice. Cater was out of town, and it would take too long to phone her father and Cory to come in from the ranch and take her to Hammond. Her oldest brother, Daniel, lived just as far out of town. She knew time was of the essence. Already she was beginning to feel the first little twinges that she now knew presaged another contraction.

"The sheriff's office?" her driver repeated, puzzled. "Don't you think you ought to go to the hospital?"

"The hospital isn't in Angel Eye." She frowned and began to do her breathing in preparation for the pang. "It's in Hammond."

"Hammond?" His voice rose a little. "Is that another town? Is that where you're going?"

She nodded and gasped out, "Thirty miles from here." She pointed vaguely east as she tried to stay above the pain.

"Then that's where I'll take you."

Beth nodded again, in too much pain to argue. It would be faster than stopping at the sheriff's office and explaining. Besides, she realized that she would rather have this calm stranger with her than Darryl Hawkes, who would probably drive her to distraction with his chatter as he tried to take her mind off her labor.

"We'd better call ahead—" He reached automatically for his cell phone, then remembered. "Damn! I didn't bring it with me."

He had wanted to be by himself today, away from the people and the distractions. That was why he had insisted on coming to look at the West Texas locations himself, not bringing the assistant director or even his personal assistant. He had been feeling stifled and restless, and he had wanted a day or two of complete peace and silence. So he had left his cell phone lying in his briefcase and set out with only a minimum of clothes, a pad of paper and Kyle's memo about the possible locations for the desert scenes that he had scouted.

"I'm sorry," he said, looking over at her. But her eyes were closed and she was in the midst of her battle with pain.

The contraction subsided before they reached Angel Eye. Beth glanced at her watch to time the next contraction. "Turn left at the stoplight and keep driving till you get to Hammond," she said when they reached the outskirts of the small town of Angel Eye. "The hospital's on the edge of town—on this side, fortunately."

"Will do." His voice was as cool as if they were out for a Sunday drive, but Prescott glanced at Beth anxiously. He didn't know much about labor, but it seemed to him that there had been very little time between her contractions.

He made the turn carefully, not wanting to jar her. "Odd name for a town, Angel Eye."

"Yeah." Beth wiped away the sweat from her forehead with the back of her hand. "Comes from the name the Spanish explorers gave it—Los Ojos de Los Angeles."

"The Eyes of the Angels. Poetic. Referring to the stars, I presume."

"Yeah. They're so bright out here. 'Course, the gringos weren't about to have to say a mouthful like that. They worked the name down to Angel Eye. *Mmmph.*" She let out a muffled noise as the pain started again and glanced at her watch. "Damn! Five minutes."

They were out on a flat, deserted highway again, and Prescott floored it, nerves beginning to dance in his stomach. Five minutes apart sounded way too close to him, particularly when the hospital was thirty miles away.

The contraction left Beth panting, her dress drenched in sweat. She thought with longing of the ice chips that the Lamaze instructor had said the nurse would give them to chew on in labor. She noticed out of the corner of her eye that Prescott reached over and turned the temperature lower.

"I'm sorry," she said. "You're probably freezing in here."

"No problem." He gave her a slow, reassuring smile. "I've been colder. So tell me, how'd you get stuck in this situation?"

She gave him a wry glance. "The usual way."

A corner of his mouth lifted at her small attempt at humor. *Gutsy.* He liked this lady. "I meant going into labor by the side of the road."

"Stupidity. I was driving back home when I got a contraction, and I went off the road. Got a flat tire. I think I might have hurt the axle, too. The wheel was at a funny angle."

"Is there someone I should notify when we get to the hospital?"

"Yes, if you want to go to the trouble." She looked grateful. "My father. I can write down his number." She glanced around vaguely, and Prescott reached up to his visor, tearing off a piece of paper from a pad there and handing it to her, along with a pen.

Beth wrote down her father's name and the numbers of both the ranch house and the cell phone. Prescott plucked the paper from her fingers and tucked it into his shirt pocket.

"What about your husband?"

"No husband."

"Oh. Well, uh, the father, then. Don't you want—"

Beth let out a harsh laugh. "No, I don't want. He's in Chicago and he doesn't know a thing about it. And he wouldn't care if he did."

"Oh."

Her breathing was beginning to sound as if another pain was coming. She put her hand on her stomach and winced. He could see her whole body grow taut. "Damn!"

Prescott knew it hadn't been even five minutes this time. More like three. Surely things weren't supposed to develop this quickly. She groaned, panting. He had never felt so helpless in his life. He was used to controlling things, to making the worlds and people he created move in the direction he wanted. But here, he had absolutely no control over anything.

"I hope Dad and Cory don't come home and go looking for me," she gasped as the wave of pain gripped her.

"Don't worry about them right now. You've got enough on your mind." He looked across at her. Her hands were balled into fists.

He reached out, the only thing he could think of to help, and took her hand. She gripped it gratefully, squeezing it hard as she rode out the pain. When the contraction ended, her hand relaxed in his, but she didn't let go. It felt too good, strong and reassuring, and at the moment she needed those qualities badly.

"Cater was supposed to be my coach," she panted. "But he's gone on a book tour. We thought…we thought it would be all right. I wasn't due for another week. He'll be back the day after tomorrow."

"Your brother's an author?"

She nodded. "Mysteries. Cater Sutton."

"I think I've heard of him." *Hadn't he once optioned a Cater Sutton book? If so, nothing had come of it.*

"Damn! Why did it have to come early?" Beth was seized with panic at the thought of going into the delivery room by herself. She had counted on having Cater's strong presence by her side. "Cater's the calmest, you see. Quinn—well, he's so easy to fire up. He'll always fight your battles for you, but you can't rely on him to keep everything under control. Daniel's reliable, of course, but everyone knows he can't stand to see a woman in pain, especially his baby sister. Dad's the same, only worse, and Cory's only nineteen." Beth realized that she was babbling, but she couldn't seem to stop.

"It'll be okay." Prescott squeezed her hand comfortingly, feeling inadequate to the occasion. He watched as another contraction gripped her. Her fingers dug into his hand, and he felt her struggle.

"Go ahead. Scream if you want to." It hurt, somehow, to watch her fight her pain.

"I...refuse...to...scream," she panted out, as if it were somehow part of the battle she was waging.

"It's happening so fast," she went on when the pain subsided. "The contractions are coming so close together. I thought I would have more time in between. You know, to sort of gather up my strength for the next one. They kept talking about it taking hours and hours. Now...God, I'm hoping we can make it to Hammond."

Prescott was, too. He was driving too fast for safety. *Where were all the cops?* He would have welcomed seeing flashing red-and-blue lights in his rearview mirror right now. He could feel Beth's rising panic, and it was infectious, but he made himself push down his own uneasiness and keep his voice calm and free of stress.

It was the longest twenty minutes of his life. Beth continued to gabble between contractions, stopping abruptly when the pain seized her and gripping his hand so tightly that her nails dug into his flesh. Jackson held on, trying to impart strength and calm to her; it was all he could do to help. His own nerves were becoming increasingly jangled. It was obvious that her contractions were growing closer together at an alarming rate, until he thought there was no more than a minute between them.

The number of cars on the road increased. There were more billboards, even a building or two. Hope rose in him that they were nearing the town of Hammond. Then, blessedly, right on the edge of town, as she had said, rose a blocky, modernistic white building with the unmistakable look of a hospital.

"Here we are," he told Beth encouragingly. "Just a minute more now."

Beth opened her eyes and looked, and a sob caught in her throat. "Thank God!"

Prescott felt like sending up a few hallelujahs himself. He whipped into the driveway and surged up the long driveway to the emergency entrance. He came to a screeching halt and jumped out, running around to open Beth's door. She was leaning back in the seat, breathing hard, her eyes closed and her face shiny with sweat.

"We're here." He leaned in and unfastened her seat belt, then slid his hands behind her back and beneath her legs and gently pulled her out of the car.

She opened her eyes, murmuring a faint protest as he lifted her up.

"Shh," he said softly, smiling. "Don't spoil my big scene."

Beth gave in gratefully, leaning her head on his shoulder. He hurried toward the automatic doors, which whooshed open before him. Inside, there were three people in the small waiting room, looking bored, and they glanced up with interest at Prescott's entrance. A woman behind a raised, horseshoe-shaped counter looked up, also.

"Can I help you, sir?"

"I need a doctor!" he barked back. "Are you blind?"

"Of course, sir." She pushed a button. "A nurse will be right out. Are you admitting this patient to the hospital?"

"She's having a baby!" His voice escalated to the roar that, though rarely used, sent underlings running.

Fortunately, at that moment, a nurse hurried toward them, pushing a gurney, and he turned toward her. Gently he laid Beth down on the rolling table. The nurse began to take Beth's pulse, asking her questions in a soothing voice. "Now, honey, how far apart are your contractions?"

"If you're admitting your wife to the hospital," the receptionist went on doggedly in her flat voice, "you'll need to fill out some paperwork." She picked up a clipboard stuffed with forms and held it out to him.

"I can't fill that out! Can't it wait? She needs help immediately!"

Beth listened to the bickering, awash in pain and feeling as if she might burst into tears at any moment. She missed Prescott's large, warm hand in hers.

"And she's getting it, sir." The receptionist nodded toward the nurse, who was starting to wheel Beth toward one of the small examining rooms. Then she picked up a pen with an air of resigned patience and held it poised over the top form. "Now, if you would just give me your name, Mr.—"

"Why the hell do you care what my name is?"

"Elizabeth Anne Sutton!" Beth shrieked from the gurney as she disappeared into the examining room. "I'm preregistered, dammit!"

"Oh." The stiff-haired receptionist gave Jackson an exasperated look. "Well, it would have been much easier, Mr. Sutton, if you had simply told me that to begin with. Let's see." She began to type on the keyboard of her computer. "Yes, you are." She pushed another button, and the printer began to click away. Tearing off the sheet of paper, she handed it to him with a practiced smile. "There you go, Mr. Sutton."

"Thank you," he responded with awful politeness. "Now, could you please call this number?" He handed her the slip of paper on which Beth had written her father's numbers. "It's her father. He needs to know that she's here."

"I'm afraid that I can't use the hospital line for—" the woman began officiously.

"Lady." Jackson leaned forward, fixing her with an icy blue stare that had been known to frighten powerful stars and even studio executives into submission. "You have been a pain in the butt from the minute we walked in. Now, if you don't want everyone in the administration of this hospital, from the top down to your supervisor, not to mention the local press and my attorneys, to be told in great detail of your uncooperative, insensitive, bullheaded, down-right inhumane attitude—then I suggest you call this number and very nicely explain to this gentleman that his daughter is here having a baby. Understood?''

The woman nodded mutely. Jackson straightened, taking the hospital printout, and strode away to the admitting room.

He found Beth with a sheet draped over her and a doctor examining her. The nurse had just turned away from a phone on the wall and was saying, ''I've called your doctor, honey, and he'll be here in fifteen minutes.''

Beth groaned. ''I don't think I can make it that long,'' she growled. The pains were continuous now. She could hardly tell when one ended and the next one began. And now there was this force building in her, this thing that shoved down through her abdomen, demanding release.

She sensed Prescott's presence beside her, and she reached out for him. He slid his hand into hers, and she grasped it as if it were a lifeline. She was scared. She had never thought she would be this scared.

''Just remember to breathe.'' The nurse began to demonstrate.

The doctor cut in. ''She's fully dilated. Get her up to obstetrics. Stat.''

The nurse called for an orderly as she shoved the gurney from the room. An orderly appeared and began to roll the cart down the hall toward the elevators. The nurse rushed to push the button for the elevator.

Prescott strode beside the gurney, still holding Beth's hand, his heart pounding.

The elevator seemed to take forever to come. Beth squeezed Jackson's hand, letting out a groan, and jackknifed her legs, bracing her feet against the gurney.

"She's bearing down," the orderly commented.

"Don't push," the nurse instructed as the elevator doors opened and they rolled her inside.

"I can't stop!" Beth snapped back.

When the doors opened, they got off the elevator in a rush. Another nurse came toward them, holding out a pile of green clothing with a mask on top. "Here, you'll have to get into your surgicals quick," she said cheerfully to Jackson, "or you'll miss the show."

"What?" He stared at her blankly.

"You have to change," the nurse said patiently, obviously used to dealing with distraught fathers-to-be. "You have to wear scrubs in the delivery room. So hurry and change."

"But I'm not—"

Beth squeezed his hand tightly, and he looked down at her. "Please..." she said hoarsely. Her eyes were wide and panic-stricken.

"All right," he said and took the clothes. Apparently, he was going to attend a birth today.

Chapter 2

Beth closed her eyes to shut out the sickening movement of the ceiling above her head as the attendants wheeled her down the hall at a trot. Doors banged open, and then they were in a chilled room, bright with lights. There were people and noise around her. Everyone wore green surgical scrubs and masks. They lifted her onto a different table, this one with a back that slanted her up to a half-sitting, half-reclining position. Someone began to put an IV into her arm. A man stopped beside her, looking down at her with kindly brown eyes.

"I'm Dr. Hauser," he told her. "Sorry. Your doctor isn't here yet, but I'm afraid we're going to have to go ahead. You seem to have an eager one there."

"That's fine." Beth was in the grip of the fierce

pain again, the force that seemed to be tearing her apart. "I don't care...who delivers it...as long as you do it *now!*"

He smiled, unperturbed, and moved away. "Let's see what we have here."

Beth bore down, the pain ripping through her, panting and almost sobbing. *Where had Jackson gone?* She wished desperately that he was there. She didn't want to go through this alone. "Jackson!"

"Right here." His calm voice came from behind her head, and then he was beside her, taking her hand. A silly-looking surgical cap covered his hair, and a green mask hid most of his face, but she could still see his eyes, as blue as a lake, calm and smiling, and that made her feel much better. "It took me a while to get into these things. How are you doing?"

"I'm about ready to kill somebody." She let out a sigh, relaxing as the intense pain went away. "I'm just not sure who to start with." She took another gulp of air. "I think I'm in delivery now."

The pain was vastly different. Much better, she thought. At least for these few moments of breathing space, the pain was gone. It was not the constant, unbearable contractions that had plagued her earlier. And the pain, when it came, had a purpose; it was making her *do* something.

A nurse moved around her, handing things to the doctor and reminding her to breathe. "Bear down," she said when the pain slammed through Beth again. "Bear down."

Beth didn't need the instruction. Bearing down was all she *could* do. She clung to Jackson's hand. He murmured encouragingly to her, wiping the sweat from her face with a cool, wet rag. She couldn't really make sense of his words, but the tone was comforting, something to focus on in the haze of pain.

"All right, come on, you're doing great," the doctor was saying. "Just one more push. We're almost there."

It slammed through her again, and then suddenly there was a blessed release. Beth let out a gasping sob.

"It's a boy!" the doctor announced gleefully, and the thin wail of a newborn filled the delivery room.

"You did it!" Jackson Prescott beamed down at her, his eyes sparkling with excitement. He pulled down his mask and bent to plant a kiss on her lips. "Congratulations."

"Thank you." Beth was still holding on to his hand, half crying, half laughing in the blessed aftermath of the pain. She gave his hand a squeeze. "Thank you so much."

"Are you kidding? You did all the work."

There was another pain, which the doctor encouragingly told her was the afterbirth. By the time it was over, the nurse was on the other side of her, laying a little bundle, wrapped in a thin blanket, on her chest. Beth's arms went instinctively around the baby, cradling it to her, and she bent her head to it, murmuring gently. The baby was tightened up into a ball, legs hunched up and arms waving around. His face was scrunched up, eyes closed and mouth wide-open. When Beth cuddled him closer, murmuring to him, his tight little body relaxed, and the crying ceased.

"Look. He knows you already." Prescott leaned over them, beaming. He felt almost high with excitement and wonder.

The baby was deep red and wrinkled, wet dark hair plastered across his head, and his eyes were swollen, with bluish patches.

"Looks like he's gone a few rounds," Jackson commented, and Beth chuckled waterily.

"Isn't he beautiful?" she asked, and Jackson agreed.

"Just like his mother."

"Yeah, right." Beth made a face.

But Jackson meant what he had said. It didn't matter that she was sweaty and pale with exhaustion. Beth *was* beautiful, her face glowing as she gazed down at her child.

A nurse stepped in and scooped up the baby, saying, "Now, now, don't worry. We'll bring him back soon. There are just a few things we have to check, and you have a little more to do here." She turned toward Jackson, smiling. "You want to hold him for a minute, Dad?"

"What? Oh. Uh…" The little bundle seemed impossibly small and fragile, and Jackson felt clumsy taking it in his arms. But the urge to do so was far greater than his fear. The baby nestled naturally in the crook of his arm, he found, and he stood for a moment, gazing down into the little red, wrinkled face as if he were viewing the eighth wonder of the world.

Finally, with a smile, the nurse reached for the baby, and with some reluctance, Jackson let her take it. They wheeled Beth first to Recovery and then, since she had been given no anesthetic and was obviously healthy and alert, after only a few minutes they whisked her down to her room. Jackson stayed with her the whole time. They talked and laughed, giddy in the aftermath of the adrenaline-charged experience. They rehashed the events of the morning, chuckling now over the skirmish with the receptionist and the headlong dash to the delivery room. Jackson wondered idly what had happened to his car, left, door open, in front of the emergency room, and they giggled over that, too.

Everything seemed rosy to Beth. Problems did not exist. Even the lingering ache she felt was a minor annoyance, easily borne as she floated on a cloud of euphoria.

It was bizarre, perhaps, for this man was an utter stranger, but at the moment Jackson Prescott was the person closest to her in the world. He had been with her through the most important and intimate event of her life; he had been her rock in the haze of pain. He had shared with her that wondrous moment when they had laid her baby in her arms. It seemed only natural that he stayed with her now.

A nurse brought the baby in, swaddled tightly in a

thin blue blanket, and settled him in Beth's waiting arms. The two adults gazed down at the child in awe.

"Look at him," Beth breathed. "Isn't he absolutely perfect?"

"Absolutely."

She pulled the sides of the blanket away, exposing his waving arms and legs. Tenderly she ran her hand down one little arm and tucked a finger into his hand, holding it up to examine each astounding tiny finger and minuscule nail. Jackson bent over the bed, watching with the same kind of wonder as she inspected each finger and toe.

The baby's arms and legs moved ever more frantically. His face started to screw up; then a wail issued forth. Beth looked at him anxiously. Guiltily she decided that he was cold, and she quickly wrapped him back up in the blanket, but that did not stop his cries. She turned to Jackson as if he might have the answer, but he simply stared back at her in consternation. For a moment Beth was swamped with uncertainty. She didn't have a clue what was wrong, and it occurred to her that she was going to be a horrible mother.

Then she felt a sort of tingling in her breasts, a fullness that was not quite pain, and suddenly, she realized what was wrong. "He's hungry."

"Oh." It sank in on Jackson that she needed to breast-feed the baby. "Oh!" He could feel a flush of embarrassment rising in his throat. He almost laughed; he had thought himself incapable any longer of actually blushing. "I—I guess I'll leave now."

Beth felt a little lost. She didn't want him to go. It was awkward. He was a stranger, and yet for the last two hours they had been incredibly close. She wanted to ask him to come back, yet she knew that she had no hold on him.

"I—thank you so much. I don't know what to say." Tears shimmered suddenly in her eyes. "You were my lifesaver."

Jackson shrugged. "I didn't do anything special. I should thank you for letting me be a part of it." He reached out and ran a gentle finger down the baby's soft cheek. "I've never experienced anything like it."

It was the truth. None of the fancy premieres of his movies could even begin to compare to this. He knew studio heads and world-famous actors and actresses on a first-name basis. He had met the wealthy and the famous, politicians and rock stars and businessmen. But none of those people, none of those experiences, had ever filled him with the sense of awe that he had felt holding Beth's hand while she gave birth. Nothing had ever seemed as wondrous as this tiny scrap of flesh in her arms.

The baby made himself known with an even heartier cry, and Jackson stepped back. "I'd better go."

"Will you come back?"

"Of course!" He smiled. "You couldn't keep me away."

"Good." Beth smiled back.

He turned away and walked out the door.

* * *

A few feet down from Beth's door, the hallway was blocked by a crowd of enormous men. Jackson stopped, intrigued. There were only four of them, actually, but as tall and broad-shouldered as they were, they seemed to fill the hall. They were all glaring balefully down at one short, squat nurse, who stood, arms akimbo, facing them.

"Now, blast it!" the oldest of the men said, slapping a stained, creased Stetson against his leg. "That's my daughter, and I am going in to see her!"

"Not while she and the father are spending their first time with the baby. We will take the baby out in thirty minutes, when it's visiting hours. You may go in at that time. Until then, you can sit in the waiting room." She pointed toward a small room down the hall.

None of the men even glanced in the direction she pointed.

"The father!" one of them repeated in shocked tones.

"Yes, the father," the nurse repeated, as if they were rather dense. She glanced back over her shoulder and spotted Jackson. "Why, there he is!" Her voice was tinged with relief. "Gentlemen, you can talk to him. He will tell you all about the birth."

With that, she shouldered through the line of men and strode off down the hall. The men all focused on Jackson. They were an imposing group. Their faces were hard, their dark eyes cold and narrowed with emotions ranging from contempt to fury as they looked at Prescott. All of them were dressed in casual Western garb—boots, jeans and sweat-stained shirts—except for the one who was dressed in khaki, with a sheriff's badge pinned to his chest. Jackson was not a short man, standing about six foot one, but all of these men topped him by at least two or three inches. With the heels of their cowboy boots adding to their height, they loomed even taller. One, the youngest-looking, must have been at least six-five. They were, Jackson realized, Beth Sutton's family.

"The local basketball team?" Jackson asked lightly. "You're missing one."

"Cater's not here," the boy responded, as if it had been a serious statement.

"Don't be dense, Cory," the one in the sheriff's uniform snapped. "He's making a joke." He stepped forward, his hands clenching into fists. "No doubt he thinks this is all real funny. Don't you, you little scum-sucking, bottom-feeding, slimy son of a bitch?"

Jackson stared back at him in amazement. "I beg your pardon?"

The others moved forward, too, advancing on him like something out of *High Noon.* Jackson held up his hands in front of his chest, palms out, in a stopping gesture. "Hold on. Wait a minute, fellas. Let me explain."

"You think you can just get her pregnant and leave her stranded, then come waltzing back into her life when the baby arrives?" This came from the one with the gray-streaked hair and the most lines in his face.

"I take it you're Beth's father," Jackson began in his calmest voice.

"You're damn right about that. I am also the man who's going to shove that pretty-boy face of yours out the back of your head."

"I wouldn't—" Prescott began.

"Yeah, well, I would," said the fourth man, the only one who hadn't spoken yet, and with that he stepped forward and swung, his fist connecting smartly with Jackson's cheek.

Jackson, taken by surprise, stumbled back and crashed into the door of Beth's room. It swung back easily, and he tumbled inside, falling to the floor. Beth let out a shriek, and the baby began to cry. Jackson came up lithely to his feet as the man who had hit him headed toward him again.

"Daniel! Don't!" Beth shrieked.

Jackson punched the man with a short, hard jab in the ribs, surprising him, and followed up on the advantage by grabbing the man's arm and twisting it up behind his back. Hooking his leg across Daniel's shin, he knocked him off balance at the same time that he threw all his weight against him from behind. Daniel crashed into the wall beside the door, and Jackson pinned him there.

For a moment all the other men froze in shock. Then, with a curse, the khaki-clad one started forward. Behind Jackson, Beth scrambled off the bed, laying the baby down on it. "Quinn! Don't you dare! *Daddy!*"

She threw herself into the doorway between the men and Jackson. At that moment the squat nurse came charging down the hall and burst through the men as if she were a linebacker.

"What do you think you're doing?" she snapped. She gave Beth a quick glance and pointed a forefinger at her. "You! Get back in that bed right now. And you!" She turned to glare at Jackson. "Release that man."

Jackson did so, feeling rather like a third-grader who had been caught fighting on the playground.

"Gentlemen—and I use the term loosely—may I remind you that this is a hospital? This woman just had a baby, and I am sure the last thing she needs is to have her family brawling in the corridor like a bunch of yahoos."

"Yes, ma'am," Beth's father answered, and all the Sutton men seemed to find something highly interesting to look at on the floor.

"All right, then, any more outbursts like that and I will have to ask you all to leave."

She took the baby from Beth, cast a last admonitory look around the room and marched off down the hall, shoes squeaking, leaving a much chastened group behind her.

"All right," Beth said in a coldly furious voice. "You three get in here and close the door."

The men, looking disgruntled, shuffled into her room to join Daniel and Jackson. Jackson started to slip away, but Beth said, "No. You, too. I want you to meet my family the right way."

With a sigh, Prescott stayed. Beth folded her arms and gave each of her brothers and her father a hard stare in turn.

"I can't believe you. Attacking strangers in the hospital!"

"Ah, Beth…"

"What the hell are you doing protecting that sorry—" Quinn began.

"Shut up, Quinn." Beth shot him a look, and he subsided.

"Now." She took a long look around at her family. "I would like for all of you to meet the very kind *stranger* who stopped to help me when my car broke down and I was stranded by the side of the road. He drove me all the way into Hammond and stayed with me through the whole delivery, even though I had no claim on him whatsoever."

"You mean he's not the guy who—"

"No. He's not 'the guy who'," Beth retorted pointedly.

"But the nurse said…" the youngest one protested.

"She was mistaken, Cory. They all assumed Mr. Prescott was the father of the baby because he brought me in. We didn't tell them any differently because I was scared and wanted him to stay with me during the birth. Which he very kindly did." She cast a significant look at Daniel. "And he managed to hang in there and not faint, like some people I could mention when their son was born sixteen years ago."

Daniel blushed to the roots of his hair. "Ah, Beth…why'd you have to bring that up? I didn't faint. I just…"

"Had to leave the room," Quinn, the sheriff, put in, his brown eyes, so much like Beth's, dancing with unholy amusement.

"Shut up," Daniel told him without heat. "It's different seeing blood when it's *your* wife doing the bleeding. And screaming…damn! I'd rather take a shot to the jaw any day."

Beth cleared her throat ostentatiously. "Now, then, if you guys can conduct yourselves like adults, I would like to introduce you to Jackson Prescott. Jackson, this is my father, Marshall Sutton."

"Mr. Sutton." Jackson, suppressing his amusement at the other men's abashed expressions, reached out and shook the oldest man's hand.

"Mr. Prescott. I can't tell you how grateful I am or how sorry about that—that incident in the hall."

"It's perfectly understandable."

"And this is my oldest brother, Daniel."

Jackson nodded and shook the hand of the man who had hit him, a younger version of Beth's father. Both men were tall and lean, with an impressive set of shoulders and hands roughened from years of hard physical labor. But the resemblance went beyond the similarities of their dark brown hair and brown eyes.

There was a kind of stillness, a quiet, in them that wasn't in the other two.

"I'm awfully sorry about that," Daniel said, gesturing vaguely toward Jackson's face and looking embarrassed. "I don't usually lose my temper."

"I know," the redhead added, grinning irrepressibly. "I was real impressed, Daniel."

"The sheriff here is Quinn." Beth cast a smile that was part exasperation, part affection at her quick-tempered brother.

"Sorry. Pleased to meet you." Quinn reached out and shook hands with him. "Thank you for helping my sister."

"I was happy to do it."

"And this—" Beth smiled at the teenage boy with special affection "—is my baby brother, Cory."

"Do you have to call me that?" he protested, but he stepped forward manfully and shook Jackson's hand. "Sorry, sir."

"No problem." Jackson looked up at the towering boy and wondered if he had stopped growing yet. He glanced around at the men. "I'm glad I met all of you. But now I think I'd better go and let you all talk with Beth."

With a nod, he slipped quietly out of the room. For a moment there was an awkward silence. Then Beth sighed and held out her arms. "Oh, you guys. Come here and give me a hug."

She could never stay mad at her family for long.

It had been devastating when her mother had died

when she was a teenager, but Beth had managed to get through it with the love of these men. Hardworking, loyal, even a little rough-and-tumble, they had done their best to make sure their little girl had a good life. Their concern had sometimes made her want to scream such as when she was a sophomore in high school and had sat home alone every Friday and Saturday night because Quinn had threatened all the boys at school with the wrath of the Suttons if they tried anything with his sister. But she had never doubted that they loved her or that she could go to any one of them if she was in trouble. It was, after all, one of the reasons she had come home to the ranch when she learned she was pregnant. She had known they would take her in and wrap her around with their rock-hard love.

Finally, after all the hugging was done, her father said, "We called Cater."

"Boy, he was mad as fire about missing everything!" Cory added. "Said he was going to jump the tour and fly down on the first possible plane."

"He shouldn't do that," Beth protested. "He has two more days of it. Besides, it's already over. I'm fine."

"I know, but he's feeling bad because he wimped out and went on the tour," Cory said bluntly.

"Cory!" Beth looked at him reprovingly, but she could not keep the loving light from her eyes. She was close to all her brothers, but she knew that there was a special place in her heart for Cory. Ten years younger than she, he had been only three when their mother died. Beth, at thirteen, had been a little mother to him. The hardest thing about leaving home when she was nineteen had been leaving Cory. "I hope you didn't say anything like that to him!"

"No, but it's what he thinks. And he's right."

"For heaven's sake. He had to go. And we didn't figure it was going to happen this early." She waggled her finger at Cory. "You tell him to stay on that tour and finish it. The baby and I will barely be out of the hospital by the time he's through."

Her father shrugged. "You know Cater. He'll pretty well do what he pleases."

"Mmm." The corner of Beth's mouth quirked in amusement. "So unlike all the rest of you Sutton men."

"I hope you aren't including me in that," Quinn said, grinning. "We all know that *I* am a model of flexibility."

"Uh-huh. Right." Beth rolled her eyes. "Now, tell me. Have you seen the baby yet?"

"Nothing but a glimpse of him when that drill sergeant of a nurse whisked him out of here." Marshall Sutton frowned at the memory.

"Then you'd better get down to the nursery and look at him."

"It's a boy?"

"What else?" Beth answered. "I would probably have been drummed out of the family if my first hadn't been a boy."

At that moment the door burst open, and a sixteen-year-old boy entered excitedly. "Hey! Hi, Gramps. Hi, Dad. Hey, Cory. Quinn. Aunt Beth. How are you doing?"

"What are you doing here?" Daniel looked suspiciously at his watch. "School isn't out yet."

"They let me out early as soon as Coach Watkins heard about Aunt Beth having the baby."

Quinn shook his head in disgust. "Best spy system in the world," he said. "The CIA ought to come train in Angel Eye."

"It was on the scanner."

"Jimmy." Beth opened her arms, and the boy went to her for a hug. Daniel's son made up the last of her family of men. Daniel's wife had left when James was just a boy, and Daniel had raised James alone. Since Beth had moved back to the ranch, the boy had taken to hanging around their house, confiding in Beth about his teenage problems.

"Have you seen it?" James asked the other men, straightening up from the hug. "It's only about this big." He demonstrated with his hands. "And squalling! Hoo-wee! Raising hell already."

"It's a 'he,' not an 'it,'" Beth admonished, laughing. "Why don't you take these guys to the nursery and show him to them?"

"Wait. First I want to hear the whole story about how you got here," Quinn said, folding his arms and fixing her with what she called his "cop stare."

"Who is this Jackson Prescott guy? Don't get me

wrong, I'm grateful to him for stopping to help you. But there was something weird about him.''

"Dressed funny," Daniel concurred.

"Just because he doesn't wear cowboy boots and jeans..." Beth said disgustedly. "He dresses very nicely. He's a handsome, sophisticated, perfectly respectable—"

"Who did you say?" her nephew interrupted, an odd look on his face.

"Jackson Prescott. My car broke down, and I—"

"Jackson Prescott! You're joking, right?" James glanced around at the others.

"No. What's the matter? You act like you know him."

"Know him? Well, of course I know him. Everybody does."

"I don't," Daniel said, pointedly.

"Oh, Dad...not you. I mean, anyone who goes to the movies. Except it couldn't be him. What would he be doing in a jerkwater place like Angel Eye?"

"Oh, my God!" Beth exclaimed, her hands flying to her mouth. Her eyes grew wide. "I thought I knew that name! I thought there was something familiar about him!"

"You mean it *was* him?" James gaped at Beth.

"Him, who?" Beth's father interrupted impatiently. "What in the devil are you two talking about?"

"Jackson Prescott," Beth said numbly. She let out

a groan and covered her face with her hands. "He must think I'm a complete idiot!"

"Oh, yeah!" Cory slapped his forehead. "That's the name of the guy who made that movie you and I went to see last month, Jimmy."

"Right. *Flashpoint.* Also *The Fourth Day.* And *Pursuit.*" James shook his head in despair at his family's ignorance. "Jackson Prescott is known all over the world. He's only one of the most famous, most important producers and directors in Hollywood."

When he left Beth's room, Jackson strolled down the hall, trying to ignore the disapproving gaze of the nurse at the station. Apparently people who got involved in brawls in the hall were not popular here. He stopped in front of the nursery. Baby Boy Sutton lay in a clear crib in the center. He was awake again and obviously displeased. His little red face was screwed up, his mouth wide-open. Jackson couldn't keep the broad grin off his face.

After a moment he turned and walked down to the lobby. The same woman sat at the receptionist desk. It took a few minutes to wangle out of her the information about what had happened to his car, as well as the keys to the vehicle. He was so involved with the bureaucratic struggle that he did not notice that across the room a young woman was staring at him.

"Casey." She jabbed her boyfriend in the side with her elbow. "Casey, look at that man. Do you know who that is?"

The young man with her looked up disinterestedly. "No."

"It's Jackson Prescott."

"Who?"

"The director. *You know*...we went to see *Flashpoint.*"

Casey turned his head and surveyed her with scorn. "Yeah. Right. A Hollywood director is here in the hospital in Hammond, Texas."

"Well, it could be," she replied defensively. "I just know it's him. Don't you remember those couple of teenage movies he was in before he became a director? I used to watch them on video." Jackson Prescott had, in fact, in his younger incarnation on video, been the focus of her adolescent dreams. *And this man—well, it hardly seemed possible, but it looked like him.*

The woman got up and moved closer, peering around a pillar at Jackson. Her boyfriend, curiosity aroused, followed her. Prescott turned, and she had a full view of his face. "That's got to be him!" she hissed.

Casey, taking in the expensive cut of the man's clothes and hair, was beginning to think that maybe Janine was right for once. This man definitely didn't look as if he came from around here.

Prescott walked out through the front doors. Casey strolled over to the information desk. "Say. Wasn't that Jackson Prescott who just left?"

"No," the woman behind the desk said coldly. "I

don't know any Jackson Prescott. That man is Mr. Sutton. His wife just had a baby.''

Casey made a noise of disgust and turned away. "See, Janine? It wasn't him."

Janine grimaced and followed him. "It was so. I've seen pictures of him in the papers and magazines."

Hurriedly she thumbed through the magazines on the small table beside her chair, then moved down to the next table. Finally, triumphantly, she returned, holding up an old issue of an entertainment publication. "Here he is. This is an article from last year, when *The Fourth Day* came out. Look."

She held open the magazine, pointing with one long, hot pink nail to a photograph at the top of the article. Her boyfriend stared. "Holy—you're right. That *is* him. But what is he doing here? And why did that lady think his name's Sutton?"

"He's probably going incognito," Janine said knowledgeably. "They do that a lot, you know, famous people."

"Is he married?" Casey asked suddenly.

"No way." She pointed to the article again. "See? 'Hollywood's most eligible bachelor, Jackson Prescott.'" She looked up into her companion's face. "Casey? What are you looking like that for?"

"Just had an idea, Jeeny. Those newspapers like you like, you know, like *Scandal*, they pay for stories, don't they?"

"Oh, yeah. Tons of money." She nodded solemnly. "So they can get an exclusive."

Casey's smile turned predatory. "You know, hon, I think I'm going to go home and get my camera."

"But why?"

"Well, if a man's 'wife' just had a baby, he's going to come back here to see it, isn't he?"

"Yeah. Ooh, Casey, that'd be great, to get his picture."

"Yeah. Great. Especially since I'll have an 'exclusive' about a big shot director who doesn't have a wife but whose girlfriend just had a baby."

Chapter 3

Beth lay on her side, contemplating the vase of twenty-four red roses that sat on her bedside table. The arrangement dominated the table, out of place in the plain little hospital room. Beth had never gotten anything quite like it. The roses were long-stemmed and utterly perfect, each a deep red, and they were set in an elegant crystal vase. Since it had arrived an hour ago, seven nurses and other hospital personnel had popped in to see it. Some of them hadn't even bothered with an excuse.

She turned over the simple, elegant small card that had come with it. It said only, "Jackson." She could not keep a smile from creeping over her lips again. Two dozen bloodred roses had a way of making one smile. Until they had arrived, her day had been less than joyous. The euphoria she had felt yesterday at giving birth had ebbed, leaving behind soreness, pain and a certain sadness. It had been wonderful, of course, when they brought in the baby. There was a kind of bliss in cradling her son in her arms as he nursed avidly that was like nothing she had ever felt before.

But in the middle of the night, when the nurse took the baby away after his feeding, Beth had lain awake, unable to return to sleep, thinking about the loneliness and fear of raising a child by herself. Only a few minutes ago, when she had shuffled down to the nursery, as the nurses kept telling her she needed to, and had stood looking in the window at her baby, she hadn't been able to suppress a pang of envy when she looked at a new mother and father who were looking at their child together.

Impatiently Beth shook her head. She was *not* going to give in to feeling sorry for herself. After all, there were lots of other women who were raising children on their own, and she knew that she was lucky in having the loving support of her family and friends around her. She looked at the roses again and reminded herself that even strangers had been exceedingly kind to her.

A tap on the door interrupted her thoughts, and Jackson Prescott stuck his head inside the room. Beth's spirits rose. "Jackson! Come in."

She gasped, and her hand flew to her mouth as she got a better look at him. There was a blue bruise high on his cheekbone where Daniel had popped him. "Oh, no! I'm so sorry."

He shrugged. "It's all right. I'll live."

"My family really isn't like that usually. It's just that they're so protective of me. I'm the only girl."

"I gather they're not too fond of the baby's father."

"They don't even know him. Obviously, since they thought you were it. All they know is that I'm raising the baby alone, and that's enough to make them hate him."

"I can see their point." He smiled and walked over to the bed.

There was an awkward pause. Beth gestured toward the flowers. "Look. Your flowers came. They're beautiful."

"You like them?" He had been carrying something behind his back, and now he brought his hand around and held out a fluffy white bear toward her. "I brought something for the baby, too. Figured I couldn't leave him out."

"It's beautiful." Smiling, she reached out and took the animal. It was incredibly soft, and she rubbed her cheek against its fur.

He nodded toward a chair in the corner of the room. "I see he's already starting a collection."

Beth chuckled. "Yes." She had had a steady stream of visitors since yesterday afternoon, and it seemed as if at least half of them had brought a little stuffed animal for the baby. "I foresee some serious spoiling going on here."

"He deserves it." Jackson looked down at her. "How about you? How are you doing?"

Beth shrugged. "Not as ecstatic as I was yesterday. I've discovered a few aches and pains I didn't notice then. But I'll be fine."

"A little blue?"

"How did you know?"

He shrugged. "Just guessed. Don't they always talk about postpartum blues?"

"Yeah. But I don't think this is enough to quality for that. I think it's more sleep deprivation. I had the hardest time sleeping last night, and it seemed like every time I'd finally doze off, a nurse would come in with the baby to feed or a pill to give me. Then they woke me up at the crack of dawn to feed me." She rolled her eyes. "I'll be glad to get home so I can get some sleep."

"Well, you're looking good."

"Bless you. I've looked in the mirror today, so I know you're lying, but it's very kind of you to say so."

"No. Just truthful." He smiled.

Beth shifted a little uncomfortably. There was something in his smile that started a strange flutter in her abdomen, a feeling she was sure was most inappropriate for a new mother still lying in the hospital.

Quickly she changed the subject. "Have you seen the baby?"

Jackson nodded. "Yeah. I went by the nursery as I came in. And I stopped by yesterday evening to look at him. I came to see you, too, but you were asleep."

Beth smiled. It pleased her that he had thought of her the evening before, too. "I wanted to ask you something."

"Sure."

"It's about the baby. If it had been a girl, I was going to name it after my mother. She died when I was thirteen. So now, I'm thinking I could name it after my dad, but I always hate to have two people with the same name in a family. Everybody would be calling him 'Little Marshall,' and that's not fair. So I was thinking I'd make Marshall his middle name."

"Sounds good."

"For his first name…well, you did so much for me. I don't know what would have happened to either of us if it hadn't been for you."

"Oh, no." He looked at her with horror. "Don't tell me you're thinking of naming him after me. You don't want to saddle the poor thing with Jackson. Trust me, it's awful. It's caused problems all my life. Everybody's always asking which is your first name and which is your last. This poor kid would have *three* last names—Jackson Marshall Sutton."

Beth giggled. "You're right. That would be awful. But I'd like to, I don't know, acknowledge what you did. Honor you somehow. What about your father's name? What was it? Would you mind if I used it?"

"It was Joseph."

"Joseph." Beth smiled, and Jackson found himself staring at the way her face glowed. "That's a good name. I like it. Joseph Marshall Sutton. It has a nice ring. Would it be okay with you? I won't use it if you don't want me to."

"I'd be honored. It's a wonderful name. If you're really sure that that's what you want to name him."

Beth nodded. "Yes. It's perfect. I've been worrying and wondering what to name him. And the lady from county records has been by twice asking me what I plan to name him. Joseph. Joey. Joe." She tried it out, savoring the name. "Joe Sutton."

Jackson grinned. "I'd say it's an improvement over Baby Boy Sutton." He hesitated, then said, "Thank you. I really mean it."

He could not explain precisely the bond he felt with this baby and this woman. For a brief moment in time he had been connected to them in a way he had never been connected to anyone else. His life had been filled largely with his career until now, and people had perforce taken a back seat. He had had relationships, of course, but he had never thought of marriage, let alone raising a family.

But when he had held Beth's hand during labor, feeling her fingernails scoring the back of his hand and hearing her struggling breaths, almost feeling the waves of pain that came from her, he had been close to her in a powerful and intimate way. When he had heard the baby's cry, it had shaken him. And when the nurse had laid Joseph in his arms, he had experienced a tenderness so profound, a connection so deep, that it had seemed as if the baby actually were his own.

It had been an emotional letdown later when he had realized that he really had no business staying with Beth in her hospital room. He was not connected to her or the baby in any real or important way, not even as close as the men who had crowded into Beth's room yesterday afternoon. He had known that there wasn't any reason for him to hang around today, either, even if he had used the excuse of checking out other locations in the area. He could have looked at them and driven on, he knew, rather than returning to Hammond to spend another night. But he had not been able to leave. He had been drawn back to the hospital and to the nursery, where he had stood gazing at the Sutton baby for at least twenty minutes last night. Nor was he really sure why he had felt the impulse to find a stuffed animal for the baby or to send the roses to Beth.

He had let his assistant in Austin take care of the details of getting the perfect roses delivered, but he had tried to find the stuffed animal on his own. It had been a shock to discover that his selection was pretty much limited to the local discount store. Once he returned to the city, he promised himself, he would find one of those huge lions or elephants or bears, the kind that stood thigh high and were as soft as rabbit fur.

"You stayed in Hammond today?" Beth asked, wondering why the thought pleased her so much.

She'd had no interest in men, *any* men, not since that bastard Robert, and this was certainly not the time to start.

He nodded. "I had a few locations around here to check out."

She was aware of a certain disappointment that there was a practical reason for his staying. "Oh. For one of your movies?"

"Yeah. We begin shooting in Austin in two months. We have some 'barren land' scenes. That's why I'm out here."

"I see." She paused, then went on, "My nephew Jimmy told me who you were yesterday. I'm sorry. You must think that I'm an idiot for not recognizing your name."

He smiled, shaking his head. "Actually it was kind of enjoyable. It's good to get away from L.A., get a dose of reality. It's kind of fun to have someone relate to me as a person, not as 'a director'."

"I have seen your movies, though," Beth went on. "When he told me, I remembered. And weren't you an actor first?"

He nodded. "For a couple of years. Two teenage movies that made a great deal more money than they had any right making. But I discovered that acting wasn't for me. I wanted to be running the show. Directing, producing."

"You're obviously quite good at it."

"What do you do? For a living, I mean. You said

something about a ranch house. Is that what you do? Ranch?''

''That's what my father does. He and Cory work the family ranch. Daniel has a horse farm. He runs a few cattle, too, but it's a small operation. But I don't usually live here. I live in Dallas. And I make my living by painting portraits.''

''Really?'' He looked amazed.

She nodded. ''Yes. You'd be surprised how many people want their portraits painted—or their spouse's or their children's. I've even done a portrait of one lady's dog. It was beautiful, too.''

''So you're good.''

She chuckled. ''Of course I am. I've been able to make a living at it for several years. It was a struggle at first, but I do all right now, and it will be a good career for raising a child. My studio's right there at my house. But when I got pregnant, I decided to take a break from it. I didn't think all the fumes I breathe in every day would be good for the baby. And all that standing would have gotten pretty tiring, too. So I moved back to the ranch.''

''You'll return to Dallas?''

''Oh, yes. I rented out my house for a year. When that's up, Joseph and I will go back.''

Jackson found himself wanting to ask about the father of the baby, but he managed to restrain himself. Beth had made it pretty clear the day before that she didn't want to talk about the man.

Soon afterward a hospital volunteer wheeled in the

baby in its little rolling plastic cart. "Ready for a visit?"

"Yes." Beth held out her hands, her tired expression lightening perceptibly. She gazed at the baby for a long time, stroking his little cheek with her forefinger, letting him curl his hand around her finger, straightening the thin snap top that he wore. "I always have to check him out again," she explained sheepishly to Jackson. "Just to make sure he's still perfect."

"Understandable." He leaned closer over the bed. "You want to hold him?"

"You wouldn't mind?"

"Of course not. I'll have plenty of opportunity to hold him. They'll leave him here for at least an hour. He ought to be getting ready to eat soon."

"Okay." Jackson grinned and reached down to slide his hands under the baby. "I'm an easy sell."

"So I see."

Beth watched as he picked up the baby and cradled him against his chest. Jackson bent over Joseph, compelled, as Beth had been, to inspect every detail of his tiny face. He slipped his forefinger beneath the baby's palm and felt the miniature hand grasp his finger. Joe was frowning fiercely, his legs pumping beneath the light blanket in which he was wrapped, and his lips pursed and working as he looked all around in an unfocused way.

"What do you suppose he's thinking?" Jackson asked in an awestruck voice. "Do you suppose he thinks we're all idiots for grinning at him so fatuously?"

Beth chuckled. "I don't think they decide that until they're about twelve or thirteen."

"And nobody's grinning by that time."

Beth watched Jackson smile and talk to the baby. The baby was gazing back at him earnestly. It was a picture that made Beth's heart swell in her chest. *If only someone like this had been her baby's father!* She thought about Joseph growing up, never bonding with a father. She had thought her brothers and father would provide plenty of male role-modeling for the baby, but she could see now that it wasn't the same. There would not be a father who had shared the baby's birth, who would have the same sense of pride, awe and joy that she did.

She sighed. It was useless wishing for something she could not have, and she knew it. Robert Waring would never have been this kind of father, anyway. He was a cheating, sneaky bastard, and she had made the right decision.

Joseph's mouth began to work ever more furiously, and he flailed his arms and legs. By accident his fist landed on his lips, and he sucked it greedily.

"Time to eat, I think," Jackson said, turning and handing the baby back to Beth. "I, uh, I'll go now." No doubt she needed to breast-feed him, and the thought made Jackson feel uncomfortably warm. It was, he thought, peculiar to feel embarrassed at the thought, when he had seen plenty of actresses' bare breasts in any number of shots. Somehow, though, this was very different.

"All right. Goodbye. I'm glad you came back today."

"I have to go back to Austin now." He had stalled here as long as he reasonably could. "I'll be there for two or three more weeks, scouting locations before I go back to L.A. If you need anything, just get in touch with me. Will you do that? We're staying at the Four Seasons." He pulled out a pen and glanced around. Then he saw the small card from the flowers he had sent, and he picked it up and wrote a number on it. "This is my room number there. I'll put your name on the list of callers they should let through. If by chance they screw up and won't put you through, leave a message. I'll call you back. Okay?"

"Sure." Beth took the card, fighting back a giggle. There was something so silly about the idea of such security, as if he were the president or something.

He saw the amusement in her eyes and smiled. "Sure. Go ahead and laugh. You aren't the one who gets calls from every writer and actor anywhere in the vicinity any time you're on location—not to mention all the fans who just want to tell you what you ought to do for your next picture."

"I'm beginning to realize how lucky I was that you stopped."

"I'm always a sucker for a woman with a stomach out to here." He bent and planted a kiss on her forehead in a spontaneous gesture that surprised both of them.

He stepped back, feeling suddenly awkward. Joseph set up a howl.

"All right. I can see he won't wait any longer for his dinner." He turned away, strangely reluctant to leave. At the door he turned back for a last look. "Remember—call if you need anything."

She nodded. "Goodbye. Thank you for everything." She realized with some astonishment that she was hovering on the edge of tears.

He smiled and waved and was gone.

Of course, Beth had no intention of calling him. Jackson Prescott had done more than enough for her already. She was capable of doing things herself and, besides, she already had a father and four brothers who were eager to do everything for her.

The hospital sent her and Joseph home the next day, despite her father's protests that it was too soon. Cater, who had left his book tour a day early, was waiting to drive her home in his sparkling blue BMW.

"Cater!" Beth shrieked, momentarily startling the child in her arms into silence.

He bent to kiss her on the cheek, smiling, his dark green eyes warm with affection. "Sorry I missed the main event."

"Don't worry. I had an able substitute."

They talked all the rest of the way home, chuckling over the mad rush to the delivery room and the case of mistaken identity in the hospital corridor. The baby, ensconced in his car seat, promptly fell asleep.

However, he did not remain so. Cranky from the final shots he had received that morning in the hospital, he slept fitfully and cried often. During the next few days, Beth found herself spending most of her time rocking him, feeding him and coaxing him to burp or sleep. She gave her family credit for trying to help her, but they obviously could not feed him, and it seemed that he was already developing a preference for Beth's holding him. Besides, her father and Cory had to work during the day, and they needed their sleep at night. She blessed Cater for taking care of the cooking, cleaning and washing, as well as trying to relieve her of some of her burden with Joseph, but even so, she found herself run ragged.

They were awakened three times that first night by his cries, and though it got better as the days went by, Joseph was still crying to be fed every four hours. Beth had to catch her sleep as best she could in between his feedings. She wondered—panicked—what she would do when Cater went back home to Austin, as surely as he was bound to someday.

One afternoon the doorbell rang, and Cater went to answer it. He returned carrying a gray stuffed elephant that had to be at least three feet high. Beth stared at it, then began to laugh delightedly.

"Let me guess. Jackson Prescott."

Her brother looked at the card and nodded. "This thing's huge."

"I don't think Jackson thinks small. He told me he wanted a different stuffed animal for Joseph's room."

Beth went over and stroked the animal. It was plush and soft, even the two tusks. She ran her hands over it and picked it up, hugging it close. She wished suddenly that she could see Jackson. But she knew that was stupid. She hardly knew the man. He just took an interest in Joseph because of what had happened, and no doubt even that would fade with time.

That night Joseph got colic—or so her father pronounced knowledgeably. All Beth knew was that he cried and cried and almost nothing would shut him up. She fed him; she changed his diaper; she walked him; she bounced him; she rocked him. Cory, Cater and her father each tried his hand with him. Nothing seemed to do any good. Joseph occasionally nodded off, but as soon as she laid him down in his bed, he would start to scream again. Finally she gave up and just dozed in the rocking chair, the baby asleep on her chest, and didn't even try to put him to bed. Even that way, however, he slept only fitfully, no more than an hour at a time before his face would screw up and he would begin to wail.

Cory and Marshall went off to work. Cater made her breakfast and tried to take over rocking Joseph. But the baby sensed the change and would have none of it. Beth, bleary-eyed, took the baby back, grinding her teeth. She wondered what had happened to her much-vaunted patience. *Why had she ever thought she would make a good mother?* It was becoming clear to her now that she would in all likelihood go insane after a few more days of this and have to be locked up.

Then, miraculously, Joseph let out a little sigh, burrowed his face deeper against her chest and fell into a deep sleep. Beth sat in stunned amazement, unable to believe that his little body was actually limp in the deep relaxation of sleep. She waited a few more minutes, scared to believe it was real, then tiptoed into Joseph's room. Cautiously she laid him down in his bed, afraid that he would once more wake up and begin to scream, but he was out like a light, and he did no more than let out a shuddering breath and begin to make sucking motions with his mouth.

Beth left the room, closing the door softly behind her and leaned limply against the wall. If anyone wakened him, she thought, she would tear them limb from limb. She walked back into the kitchen, where Cater was rinsing out baby bottles and stacking them in the dishwasher.

Beth collapsed into a chair with a groan. "I'm going to go to bed and sleep for a year."

The telephone rang, and Cater pounced on it. Over the past few days they had turned off the ringers on all the phones except this one in the kitchen, since it was farthest away from the baby's room, and whenever it rang they all jumped on the nearest phone as if it might explode. The whole world now revolved around Joseph's sleeping habits.

Cater turned to Beth, his brows going up inquisitively. "It's for you. You want to take it?"

She sighed. "Yeah." Friends and neighbors kept calling to ask how she was doing, and she felt guilty for so often trying to get out of talking to them. All she wanted to do these days was sleep.

She took the receiver. "Hello?"

"Elizabeth Sutton?"

"Yes?" She regretted taking the call. It obviously wasn't anyone who knew her.

"This is Julie McCall, with *Scandal.*" The speaker's voice went up a little at the end of the sentence, almost as if she were asking a question.

The words made little sense to Beth. What was *Scandal?* It sounded like a perfume.

"I understand that you're the proud new mother of a baby boy," the woman on the other end of the line went on cheerfully. "Congratulations!"

"Thank you." Beth realized that this must be a come-on for some baby product. But what baby product would be named *Scandal?* Maybe she had heard it wrong.

"I wanted you to know that we're very interested in what happened."

Beth could think of nothing to reply to that statement. *What was this woman talking about?* She wished she weren't so sleepy. Perhaps then this conversation would make sense.

"For instance, how did you meet Jackson Prescott?"

"On the road," Beth replied automatically. "I'm sorry. I'm a little confused. Why are you calling me?"

"We're very interested in your story, as I said before, Ms. Sutton. And I imagine that you would enjoy a little extra cash to help out with some of those baby bills, too—unless, of course, Mr. Prescott's taking care of those."

"What?" This whole conversation was surreal. Beth felt as if she were one of those characters in an absurdist play, where none of the conversations made sense. "Of course not. Why would—"

"Well, we here at *Scandal* are prepared to pay you $10,000 for your story."

"My story?" Beth was sure now that the woman was insane—or she herself was. "What in the world are you talking about?"

"Why, the story of you and Jackson Prescott, of course."

There was a long silence. Beth was too stunned to speak. Finally she managed to say, "Are you nuts?"

The woman on the other end of the line chuckled. "No, Ms. Sutton. I'm not. And I'm not joking, either. We would like to publish your story."

"But there's nothing—" Beth shook her head as if to clear it. This whole conversation was making her vaguely uneasy. "No. No, thank you."

"Don't be too hasty. Perhaps I can persuade my editor to give you a little more money."

"I said, *no.*" Beth hung up the phone.

"Who was that?" Cater turned to look at her.

"I don't know. Somebody name Julie Something-or-other from something called *Scandal*. Do you know what that is?"

"Sure. You really have been out of it lately," Cater teased. "It's a tabloid. You know, 'My baby is a 310-pound alien.' That kind of thing."

"She just offered me $10,000 to tell her my 'story.'"

Cater's straight black brows sailed upward. "What story? 'My baby is a crying alien with colic'?"

A giggle bubbled up out of Beth's throat. "No. I think that's too common. Apparently she wanted me to tell her about Jackson Prescott's rescuing me from the side of the road. Can you imagine?"

He shrugged. "I guess it'd make a fairly interesting story. The human side of a famous person and all that. But it sounds a little tame for a rag like that, I would think."

"But why do they think I would want the story of my delivery in some national scandal sheet?"

"Lots of people would."

Beth shrugged, dismissing the subject. "Well, I'm going to bed now. Don't wake me up unless the house is on fire."

To her astonishment, she was able to sleep for almost six hours before the baby awoke. The awful night of his colic seemed to have been a turning point, for after that, Joseph began to sleep for one good long stretch of six hours each day. At first he had his days and nights all turned around, sleeping during the day and staying awake during the night, but after a couple of days that straightened out. By Friday, two weeks after he'd been released from the hospital, he had awakened Beth only once during the night—about one o'clock—and she had been able to get an almost normal night's sleep. She thought she was beginning to feel almost human again.

She was feeling so chipper, in fact, that after her shower, she put on a bit of lipstick and mascara and tried on some of her prematernity clothes while Joseph lay waving his arms and legs on the bed. She was pleased to find two or three casual, loose-fitting old dresses that looked all right on her. Of course, she still had a few pounds to lose, but she was hopeful that the extra calories she expended daily on breast-feeding would help to take care of that, plus she had managed to fit in the exercises that the hospital had taught her every day—or almost every day.

Beth straightened and regarded herself from every angle in the mirror, smoothing her hand down over her abdomen. She sincerely hoped that little pouch was not here to stay. The worst-fitting part of her dresses, actually, was over her bustline. Her breasts, swollen with milk now, were at least a cup size larger.

The front door slammed, making both Beth and the baby jump. He gave out a little uncertain cry, and she swooped down and picked him up, cuddling him reassuringly. He stopped the beginnings of his wail and simply looked at her.

"Hi, darling." Beth smiled down at him and planted a kiss on his forehead.

"Beth!" came Quinn's roar from the living room. "Where are you?"

"I'm in here," Beth replied tartly, going into the hall. "Would you kindly stop shrieking like a banshee? You're upsetting the baby." She turned away and went into the baby's room to put him down in his crib. Then she walked down the hallway to the den, where Quinn was alternately standing and pacing, fairly vibrating with impatience.

Quinn's face was almost as red as his hair, and his brown eyes crackled with fury. In his hand he held a thin magazine, which he shook agitatedly as he came toward her. "Have you seen this?"

"No. What is it?"

"Lord, Quinn." Cater appeared in the doorway. "What are you yelling about? I could hear you all the way outside."

"Come see."

He thrust the magazine at Beth. She could see now that it was not a magazine but one of the tabloids sold at the checkout counters of grocery stores. Across the top of the front in bright red letters, it read, *Scandal*. Just below that was a headline in bold type: Director's Secret Love Child! Beneath it was a photograph of Jackson Prescott leaving the hospital in Hammond. Beside the photo it read: "Jackson keeps secret mistress and illegitimate son hidden in Texas."

Chapter 4

Beth stared at the cover, blood draining from her face. "Oh, my God."

"Yeah. I found my secretary reading it."

"What is it?" Cater had reached them by now, and Quinn plucked the tabloid from Beth's nerveless fingers and handed it to his brother.

"Holy—" Cater let out a whistle as he perused the cover. "Well, I guess *this* is the story that woman was trying to buy from you the other day."

The phone began to ring, and Quinn went to answer it. "Hello? Yeah, hi, Tina. No, Beth can't talk right now. She's, uh, lying down. Yeah, she saw it. Just now. What? No, of course it's not true! You know how those newspapers are."

He hung up, and almost immediately the phone

rang again. "Everybody'll be driving you crazy now," he said and answered it. "Yeah? No, this is her brother. *Sheriff* Sutton. No, she doesn't have any statement to make." He put down the receiver, shaking his head. "Can you believe it? That was a TV station."

Cater opened the tabloid to the article inside and began to read aloud: "World famous director and producer Jackson Prescott is in Austin, Texas, today, following the birth of Joseph Marshall Sutton, in tiny Hammond, Texas. Local sources confirm that Prescott, going under the name of 'Mr. Sutton,' was present at the birth of the baby. Both baby and mother, Elizabeth Sutton, a statuesque redhead, are doing fine. Hollywood is all agog at the news. Apparently Prescott had kept the news of his Texas honey completely under wraps."

"Texas honey!" Beth let out a heartfelt groan. "Cater!"

"I didn't write it, darlin'. I'm just reading it." He continued, "Ms. Sutton told this newspaper that she met the renowned director while he was on a publicity tour for his blockbuster movie *Pursuit*."

"I never said that!" Beth protested.

Cater shrugged. "These guys are not known for their concern with accuracy. Didn't you say something to that lady about meeting him on the road?"

"Well, yeah. She asked me where we met, and I told her 'on the road.' I didn't say he was on a publicity tour."

"I guess they figured that was close enough."

"Where did they get this stuff?" Beth moaned. "How did they even hear about my having a baby? Or his being there?"

"Probably from him," Quinn said.

"Jackson? Don't be ridiculous! He wouldn't want something like this spread all over the tabloids."

Quinn made a noise of disgust. "He's from L.A. Those movie people will do anything for publicity. They don't care if it's good or bad, just so long as it gets their name in front of the public. Hell, they hire publicity guys just to make sure they *are* in the media."

"I don't believe it," Beth replied staunchly. "He was so nice."

Quinn pulled a cynical cop face. Beth turned toward Cater, who shrugged.

"I don't know," Cater admitted. "They got the news somehow. They certainly didn't get it from us. Who else knew that he was Jackson Prescott and that he was in Hammond with you?"

"Well, if it was him, surely they would at least have gotten the facts straight!" Beth said pointedly. "Maybe somebody recognized him at the hospital. After all, someone shot that picture of him. That had to be the day it happened or the next day."

"You think someone just happened to be hanging around the hospital with a camera who saw him, knew who he was and took a picture?" Quinn asked sarcastically.

"He certainly didn't take it himself!" Beth snapped.

"He could have called and gotten one of his guys down there from Austin to take the shot. That's probably why he hung around an extra day and came back to see you."

Quinn's words stung. Beth planted her hands on her hips pugnaciously. It had always been Quinn with whom she had the worst fights. Whenever they got into one of their flaming arguments, the others would turn away, saying, "The redheads are at it again."

"So you think that's the only reason a man would come visit me a second time?"

"I didn't say that." Quinn backtracked, realizing he was treading on dangerous ground. "But think about it, Beth. You had a stomach out to here, and you were in labor. Do you really think he came back because of your looks?"

"Not *all* men are solely interested in a woman's looks. Just macho, chauvinistic—"

"Don't start in with me on that," Quinn warned. "You know that's not what I meant."

"Oh, yeah? Just what *did* you mean, then?"

Cater chuckled and folded his arms, waiting for Quinn's reply with an air of expectation. "Yeah, Quinn, I'd like to hear you get out of this one."

Quinn cursed. "Ah, hell, Bethie, you're just too nice. You believe everybody's good. I don't know that it was Prescott who leaked it. Maybe he *is* a wonderful guy who would never stoop to getting publicity like that. But it's the most obvious choice.''

''He came back because he liked Joseph,'' Beth said stubbornly. ''I don't fool myself that he fell for me. But he did fall for the baby. You didn't see him holding Joseph. I did.''

''Okay. Okay.'' Quinn held up his hands in surrender. ''The man's a saint.''

''I didn't say that, either. Honestly, Quinn, you're as bad about twisting my words as that—that paper!''

Beth took the tabloid from Cater's hands and studied the article. There was little else there. It wasn't surprising, Beth thought, since they had so little to go on. She sighed and handed the newspaper back to Quinn.

''What should I do? Call them and demand a retraction? Threaten to sue?''

''Well…the article doesn't actually say that Joey is this Prescott guy's baby,'' Cater replied thoughtfully. ''All it really says is that he was present at his birth, which is true. It calls you statuesque—no argument there—and says you met him on his publicity tour, which is false, but I'm not sure you want to even get tangled up in a telephone call with them over something as minor as that. There's no telling what else they might trick out of you and twist around for another story.''

''But what about the front page? That says that Joseph is his. Doesn't it?''

Quinn and Cater studied the front. ''It implies it,

sure. It says director's love child right next to a picture of Prescott leaving the hospital. But it doesn't actually say that the director who has the love child is Prescott. I don't know. The thing is, they're used to being threatened all the time by pretty powerful people. They look on lawsuits as part of the cost of doing business. I don't think you're going to scare them with the threat of a suit. Are you willing to actually sue?'' Cater asked.

Beth thought of the ordeal of a trial and all the attendant publicity. She shook her head reluctantly. ''No. This is bad enough. It just makes me mad, though, to let them say stuff like this and not take any action.''

''I know. I'll call them if you want me to,'' Quinn offered.

''I don't think a sheriff in Texas is going to scare these guys.'' Beth sighed. ''I guess the best thing to do is just to keep quiet and let it all blow over.''

Days later, Beth would think back to her words and shake her head over her naiveté. The thing had not blown over at all. They had been deluged by phone calls from more tabloids and several members of the legitimate press, as well as from almost everyone they knew. Even friends of Beth's from Dallas called up to ask her if the story was true. Her father had finally had to give in and buy an answering machine, which he hated. But even worse was the fact that a reporter from one of the tabloids, *The Insider,* showed up at their front door one day.

He came back several times, until finally Beth's father met him at the door with a shotgun and a scowl and pointed out to him that he was trespassing on private property, and that the next time he did so, the sheriff would personally be out to escort him to jail. After that the obnoxious man took to sitting on the side of the road at the entrance to their land, waiting for Beth to come out. As a result, she stayed in the house until she could stand it no longer and finally decided she was going to go stir-crazy, so she set out for the grocery store. Within twenty minutes she was back, muttering imprecations on the man's head.

"I'm trapped!" she exclaimed, as she walked into the kitchen and slammed her purse down on the table. "Trapped! I can't go anywhere or do anything without that guy *stalking* me!"

She walked into the den, where Cory was sitting in the rocker, the baby in his lap gurgling and spitting. Cory was leaning over him, making faces and cooing. "Hi, Beth. I swear, I didn't wake him up. He just started hollering a few minutes ago."

Beth had accused Cory yesterday of tiptoeing into the baby's room to see if he was awake in order to wake him up so he could play with him. He wore a look now of such virtuous innocence that Beth had to smile. "It's okay. As long as you changed his diaper and didn't save it for me."

Cory assumed an even more saintly expression. "I

certainly did. It was a stinker, too." He turned his attention back to the baby. "Wasn't it, Joey?" He bent down to rub his nose against the baby's, dissolving into baby talk.

Beth turned away, smiling at Cory's obvious infatuation with Joseph. Cater, sitting on the couch, feet propped up, smiled back at her. "Looks like you've got a permanent baby-sitter."

"At least until he goes back to college." She let out a sigh and plopped down on the couch beside him.

"Rough day?"

She nodded. "That *Insider* reporter followed me all the way to the grocery store, and when I got out in the parking lot, he came running after me, asking all these questions. I realized that if I went inside, everyone in the whole store would be staring at me, with this guy pursuing me. So I just got back into my car and left."

She did not add that she had been fighting a bluesy feeling for the past two or three days—or that she kept wondering why Jackson Prescott had not contacted her since the arrival of that stuffed animal ten days before. She supposed it was foolish to feel so bereft—after all, she hardly knew the man. Sure, he had been nice when he was caught up in the emotional aftermath of witnessing Joseph's birth. But it stood to reason that he would cool off after a few days. She had no real place in his life, and it was natural that he would more or less forget about her.

Such reasoning, however, only served to make her feel even bluer.

"I'm afraid I'm not going to make you feel any better," Cater said, picking up a tabloid from the table beside him. He tossed it into her lap. "This is what you would have found if you *had* gotten inside the store."

It was yet another tabloid, this one emblazoned with the words "Family Feud—Prescott And Suttons Brawl In Hospital!" Beneath was a fuzzy close-up of Jackson Prescott, a bruise clearly visible on his cheek.

"What!" Beth sat up with a shriek. She tore open the paper and began to read. It was an account of a major brawl in the corridor outside Elizabeth Sutton's hospital room. "Oh, my God, it makes it sound like you all jumped him and beat him to a pulp."

"Mmm."

"It even mentions Quinn by name and says he's the sheriff! Oh, no! He'll be furious!"

"Doesn't look too good for a county sheriff to be brawling," Cater agreed.

"I can't believe they wrote this! It's so untrue, so unfair. Oh! I'd like to get my hands on that Julie Whatsis... Where do they get this stuff? How did they find out?"

"Probably someone at the hospital. You've seen how willing the paper was to grease palms."

"But this isn't what happened. That nurse saw that Daniel just hit Jackson once, and then it was all over."

"It sounds more sensational this way."

"Yeah—it's a lot more sympathetic to Prescott, too," Cory added.

"You're saying it was Prescott who told them? You don't know that. It could have been anyone at the hospital."

Cory just looked at her, and Beth flushed. *Why was she clinging to the thought that Prescott had not let the story leak to the press?* She jumped up from her seat. "Okay. Let's just call him and see."

"Call who? Prescott?" Cater asked.

"Yeah, right," Cory said sarcastically. "Like you can just ring up his hotel and they'll put you through."

"He told me I should call him. He gave me the number. He said he would put my name on a list." She charged into the kitchen, opened her purse and pulled out the card Jackson had given her. Then she marched to the phone and rang the number.

When the hotel operator answered, Beth identified herself and asked for Jackson. There was a moment of silence. Then the operator said, "I'm sorry, ma'am, Mr. Prescott is not accepting phone calls."

Beth's stomach clenched. "He—he said he put my name on a list of approved callers. Did you check it?"

"Yes, ma'am. I'll check it again." She spelled Beth's last name questioningly and when Beth agreed that that was the spelling, she finished, "No, ma'am, I'm sorry, but I do not have your name on that list."

"Oh." Beth hung up the phone with suddenly nerveless fingers. *He had lied to her! He had told her that she could call him and acted as if he were concerned for her, and all the time it had just been an act.*

She stood for a moment staring at the kitchen wall, then slammed her fist down on the counter. "Damn him!"

She marched back into the den, her face pale and her eyes blazing. "I'm going to Austin."

"What? Why?" Cater and Cory stared at her.

"Because I'm going to find Jackson Prescott and tell him exactly what I think of him."

"Uh, Beth..." Cater rose to his feet. He had had some experience with his sister's hot temper. "Do you think that's a good idea?"

"Yes. I think it's a wonderful idea. It is exactly what I'd like to do."

"Are you sure you feel up to it?"

"I feel fine. It's been three weeks since I had Joseph. And having a baby doesn't exactly make you an invalid."

"No, but...what about the baby? You can't just leave him here while you run off to Austin. That's at least a six- or seven-hour round-trip."

Beth made a face. "Of course I'm not leaving him. I'll take him with me."

"You're going to cart the baby around with you while you track down a celebrity?" he asked skeptically.

"Fine. You come with me if you think I'm so incapable of managing on my own. Cory, too. You all can take Joseph back to your house while I locate Jackson Prescott."

"Beth..."

"What? Are you coming or not?"

Cater sighed. "Of course I'm coming."

Cory jumped up. "Me too." He grinned. "I wouldn't miss this for the world."

They left the ranch by the back road, then drove the three hours to Austin, going first to Cater's house in a quiet old section of Austin, where Beth fed the baby, then left him with Cory and Cater, adamantly refusing to take either one of them with her. "I am *not* taking one of my brothers with me, as if I can't handle it on my own."

She took Cater's car and drove to the Four Seasons hotel. She suspected that Cater had hoped that her anger would cool off on the drive over and that she would give up on her idea to confront Jackson Prescott, but it had not. She had spent the whole time fuming over what he had done, stoking her fury with memories of his kindness toward her and his apparent affection for Joseph, which made his betrayal all the worse.

She marched into the elegant hotel and asked at the desk for Jackson Prescott. Predictably she was told he was not available. Beth had expected this, and she found a comfortable chair in the lobby from which she had a clear view of the front doors and sat down to wait for him.

She had been there almost two hours when Jackson walked through the front doors with two men and a woman, all of them dressed in typically casual Austin summer wear. Beth jumped to her feet, a ball of anger and anxiety swelling in her chest. She strode over to the group purposefully. They turned, sensing her approach. One of the men took a step forward, putting himself between her and Jackson.

"Hold it right there. We got a restraining order against you reporters. Remember?" he said flatly.

"Jackson." Beth stopped, her voice even but carrying. "Are you going to talk to me, or are you going to have your goon toss me out?"

It had taken Prescott a moment to recognize the tall, attractive redhead striding toward him. She was slender, and now that her features were no longer pale and drawn with pain, all the promise of her strong facial bones had come blazingly to life. Her hair curled riotously around her face, full of life and color. For an instant he had thought she was an actress or model hoping to talk her way into a part in his movie.

Despite the anger he had been harboring toward her since the *Scandal* article came out, he could not suppress the leap of instinctive physical appreciation inside him. Nor could he keep his lips from twitching with amusement at her words.

"He's not a goon, Beth. He's my assistant director. It's okay, Sam. I'll take care of this."

He moved around his AD, reminding himself why he was angry with her. Beth, looking at his cold, set face, wondered why she had ever thought this man was warm and kind.

"I found out how much your word is worth," she began, pulling out the card he had given her and ripping it in two. "'Just call me if you need anything,'" she mimicked savagely.

"Sorry," he replied in a voice that made it clear he did not mean the word. "I figured you had already gotten plenty out of me."

His words slammed into her like a fist, hurting more than she would have thought possible. Beth blinked back the tears that started in her eyes. "Excuse me for taking up any of your precious time just because I was in labor."

He snorted. "Don't try to turn the tables here. I'm not talking about taking you to the hospital, and you know it. I am talking about your turning me ov—"

But Beth paid no attention to his words, sweeping on in her rage, "How could you do this to me? How could you be this low? To take my life and turn it into some sideshow so you could get a little extra publicity! Quinn tried to tell me, but I thought I knew you. I told him you would never be that cold or calculating, that you weren't the sort to sell someone out—"

"What in hell are you talking about!" Jackson snapped back. He had been disappointed and unexpectedly hurt when the story came out, but he had lived too long in Hollywood to be surprised or enraged that Beth had turned his helping her to her profit. But now, facing her and her anger, he found his own fury springing to life. "If you want to talk about selling someone out, what about what you did to me? Did you honestly expect me to take your calls after what you'd done? Were you hoping to find out a few more juicy tidbits to feed the press?"

"Uh, Jackson..." The AD sidled closer, glancing apprehensively around the lobby, where faces were turning to stare at Jackson and Beth, drawn by the loud, angry voices. "This is a little public...."

"What do you care?" Beth shot at him. "I figure the more public, the better for you guys. After all, it will mean more precious publicity for your movie."

Jackson, however, heeded the other man's warning. He clamped his hand around Beth's upper arm and started toward the elevators. "We'll finish this upstairs."

"I don't want to go upstairs with you!" Beth retorted.

"I realize that you prefer to make a public spectacle of yourself." Jackson jabbed the Up button of the elevator furiously. "But you are not going to use me to do it. If you want to talk, we will do it in private. If not, get out of the hotel."

Beth faced his level gaze and knew that he meant what he said. No doubt he would call security if she refused to go with him, and they would toss her out ignominiously. *That* would give those nasty tabloids a real field day.

In response, she jerked her arm out of his grasp and turned to face the elevator doors in silence. The silence continued between them after the doors opened and they got on. Upstairs, at his luxury suite, Jackson stuck his key card in the door and stepped back for Beth to pass into the room before him. He followed, snapping the door closed.

Beth marched across the spacious sitting room to the windows at the far end. She stood for a moment, staring out at the view of Town Lake. Jackson, who had struggled to bring his fury under control on the ride up, walked halfway across the room and stopped, arms folded across his chest.

"All right," he began tightly. "What are you here for? If you expect me to pay you to stop the stories, you're dead wrong. I don't bow to extortion."

"Extortion!" Beth gaped at him, his words startling her out of her anger momentarily. "You're accusing me of extortion?" The idea was so absurd that she almost laughed. "Are you nuts?"

"No. And you can stop the histrionics, too. They're not going to convince me to pay you, either."

Her fury came flooding back at his words, so much so that she trembled under the force of it. Her hands itched to slap him. "How dare you! How dare you accuse me of asking you for money? After what you've done to me and my family? Do you honestly think you can scare me off with this talk of extortion?''

"I am not trying to scare you, Miss Sutton." Prescott struggled to keep his voice under control. He disliked this woman intensely, all the more so because he had liked her a great deal when he met her. It made him even angrier that seeing her now—her eyes bright and her cheeks flushed with rage, her body fairly vibrating—his body was responding to her in an unmistakable and very masculine way. He wanted to shake her, and at the same time, he wanted to kiss her, and that fact made him boil.

"I'm merely telling you the truth," he said carefully. "The money you got from the tabloids is all you're going to get."

"What are you talking about?" Beth took an involuntary step toward him. It required all her self-control not to rush at him, screaming and scratching. "What money? All I've gotten from the tabloids is grief, and you know it!"

"You mean you were foolish enough to talk to them without getting paid?" Prescott quirked an eyebrow in an infuriating way. "No wonder you're coming to me now."

"I am not here for money!" Beth shrieked. "What is your problem? Don't you understand English? I *do not want* any of your filthy money. I wouldn't take it if you offered it to me. You are a lying, treacherous, backstabbing son of a bitch, and I hope you choke on your money."

"Then why did you come here?" Jackson moved forward, his eyes bright with anger. His brain was filled with pictures of grabbing her by the shoulders and shaking her until she stopped her crazy, circuitous, infuriating talk—and immediately after that, kissing her until she melted against him, weak and repentant. Jackson pushed down the primitive need and asked curtly, "Did you expect me to welcome you with open arms?"

"I don't expect anything of you. Not anymore. I just wanted you to know what I think of you. I wanted to tell you what a snake you are."

Beth hated him. She hated his smug, handsome face, hated his calm control in the face of her own livid anger. She wanted to sink her hand into that thick dark hair and pull. And as she pictured that with great delight, she pictured him jerking her up hard against his body and bending down to kiss her. The rush of pure, unadulterated lust shocked her into silence.

"Dammit!" Jackson slammed his fist down on the long table beside him, making the lamp shake. "What the hell are you talking about? You went to the tabloids and told them that—that *dreck,* and now you're accusing *me* of being a snake? You have a lot of nerve. Or are you just insane?"

For a moment Beth could not speak. She stared at him, dumbfounded, as his words sank in. Finally she croaked, "Are you serious?"

Now it was his turn to stare. "What? Yes, of course I'm serious."

"You think—you honestly think that *I* went to the tabloids?"

"Well, of course. Who else? *I* certainly didn't run to them saying that I was the father of an illegitimate child by a woman I had kept secret in a little town in Texas!"

Beth pressed the palms of her hands against her temples. She wondered if she were in a madhouse. Jackson, watching her, felt his anger draining away. It occurred to him that perhaps she really *was* mentally unstable. Wasn't there some woman who had claimed postpartum insanity as a defense for killing someone?

"I did not tell the tabloids anything," Beth growled. "It had to have been *you*. You did it for the publicity."

Jackson let out a noise of disbelief. "After all the time I've spent avoiding those vultures, you're saying that I voluntarily told them this libelous stuff?"

"Well, *I* didn't!"

"Don't try to pull that on me," Jackson said in disgust. "*Scandal* called my publicist for verification of your story. That's the first I heard of it. My publicist denied it, of course. Then he called me and asked who the hell in Texas would have given *Scandal* a story about my having a baby in some backwater town there. He said they told him they had bought it from a woman in Texas, and that she had backed it up with pictures.''

"It wasn't *me!*'' Beth had a sick feeling in her stomach that she had been terribly wrong.

"That very first story quoted you as saying you met me when I was touring for *Pursuit.*''

"I didn't say that!'' Beth protested. "That Julie Whatever called me and started asking questions. I didn't know who she was. She asked me how I met you, and I said, 'on the road.' She surprised me so much that I just answered automatically. But that's all I said. I didn't even know about your touring for *Pursuit.* Then she offered to pay me $10,000 for my story, and I hung up on her. The next thing I knew, there was this story about my giving birth to your son splashed all over the front page. Quinn said you had probably given them the story for the publicity, but I said, no, you wouldn't do that. Then that Carrigan guy—''

"Who?''

"The man from that other magazine, *The Insider,* the one who's been hounding me for the past three or four days! He told me that he had talked to you and wouldn't I like to give my side of the story? But I still thought they were lying, that you wouldn't do that to me. Then today Cater brought home another one of those tabloids, and it had an article about your fight with my brothers at the hospital. It had a picture of you with the bruise on your cheek, and it made it sound like they all jumped on you and beat you up.

Well, it was pretty clear where they had gotten such a slanted story. But I still didn't want to believe it, so I called you to ask you about it, and I found out you hadn't put me on a list for my calls to be accepted, like you said you would. Naturally you wouldn't want to hear from me after you had done this to me."

Jackson stood for a long moment, looking at her. "I did nothing to you."

"It didn't look that way!" Beth snapped. "It looked like you had casually ruined my life—told the world I had an illegitimate child, held me up to public ridicule, sicced all those newspapers and magazines on me. How you could have believed that I would do that to myself! To my family!" She turned away, then swung back as a new thought hit her. "How could you have thought I would do that to you? After the way you helped me, if I had sold some tabloid that lie, I would have had to be the lowest, most despicable person ever! How could you think that of me?"

"Over the years, I have discovered that people are capable of almost anything, especially where money and fame are involved."

Beth shook her head. "I would hate to see the world the way you do."

She walked past him toward the door. Jackson turned, watching her, and as she opened the door, he said, "No, wait. Don't go."

Beth hesitated, then let the door close and turned back to him. He crossed the room until he stood directly in front of her, gazing down into her eyes. "I'm

sorry. I—I didn't want to think badly of you. When
David told me, my immediate reaction was that it
couldn't have been you. I didn't want it to be you.
But, you see, I knew it wasn't me or my people, and
it made sense that it was you. And when they said
they'd bought it from a woman in Texas…well, it
seemed pretty obvious. I wasn't surprised. Nothing
that anyone could do anymore would surprise me. A
few years ago a woman claimed that I had fathered
her child when I had never met her in my life. She
was trying to get money from me, figuring I would
buy her off rather than go to court. I had a business
partner I trusted—he was a friend, as well—who em-
bezzled money from our business for months. One of
my friends was stalked by some guy for almost two
years. He said that my friend had stolen a movie idea
from him. He also thought that Nazis were hiding out
in his attic. People are crazy. They're greedy. They
seem to be willing to do almost anything just to get
themselves in the news. I'm sorry, but it is easy for
me to believe that someone would sell me out to a
tabloid, even someone I liked.''

He paused, then added, ''And I did like you. But
I've learned that trusting someone just because you
like them is a good way to get burned.''

''I understand. I guess it's easier not to be rich and
famous.'' Still, she could not completely get rid of
the little pang of hurt that came from realizing how
despicable a person he had believed her to be.

He must have seen it in her eyes, for he reached

out and took one of her hands between both of his own and said quietly, "I'm sorry."

"Then do you believe me now?"

"I suppose you could have made this whole thing up." Looking into her eyes, he knew he didn't believe that at all. "But I don't think so. I believe you."

He had not let go of her hand, and he raised it to his lips now and kissed her knuckles softly. Beth felt a quiver dart through her. Her hormones, she thought, were absolutely, utterly out of control. A few minutes earlier she had been consumed by rage; now she was getting all weak in the knees over the merest kiss.

"I apologize for doubting you," he went on. "And I apologize for blocking your call." He smiled.

Beth pulled her hand away from his. This man's smile had entirely too much effect on her.

"How about you?" he asked. "Still think I'm the one who gave the story to the tabloids?"

"No." She paused. "But how did they get the story? I mean, if neither of us told—and I'm positive that no one in my family would have—then who did?"

He shrugged. "Someone who saw me at the hospital and recognized me, I guess."

"But how did they come up with all that other stuff? About Joseph being yours?"

"Maybe the rag just made that up. Or they could have interviewed someone at the hospital...the nurses there thought I was the father. After all, that's where they must have gotten the story about the fight. No

doubt gossip had amplified it, and the tabloid probably sensationalized it, too. Their version was wilder
and more interesting than the truth—which, unfortunately, is why they print things like that instead of
bothering to get the facts.''

Beth stood for a moment. She didn't know what
else to say, and there was really no reason to stay any
longer. Yet she did not want to leave. ''Well...'' She
glanced toward the door. ''I better go now. Cater and
Cory will be waiting to hear whether they have to
bail me out of jail for attacking you.''

Jackson smiled slightly and reached out a hand,
taking her arm. ''Don't go. Why don't you stay and
have dinner with me?''

''I'd like to, but I have to be back to feed Joey in
two hours.'' She smiled ruefully, realizing how very
far away her world was from this man's. ''I'm sorry.
I'm afraid I don't live a very glamorous and exciting
life.''

''You would be surprised at how unglamorous and
unexciting my life is,'' he responded. ''We could eat
now, if it's not too early for you. I didn't have any
lunch, so I'm starving.''

''Me either.'' She had been too consumed with getting to Austin and confronting Jackson to stop and
eat. ''That'd be great, if you want to.'' She hesitated.
''Will there be a picture of us eating in the papers
this week?''

''Surely that wouldn't rate high enough on the excitement scale. But if you want to, we can have it

here in the suite. That's what I usually do." He smiled. "You can see exactly how exciting my life is."

"Mmm. Sounds like you're almost as much of a shut-in as I am. Today is the first time I've been off the ranch since Joey was born."

In the end, they decided to go downstairs and eat. Jackson's earlier companions were eating at another table in the hotel restaurant, and they cast surprised glances at Jackson when he walked in with Beth. He grinned at them and held Beth's chair for her.

"They'll be eaten up with curiosity," he told Beth, a mischievous glint in his eye. "I suspect that by now they've copped to who you are. Now they're wondering whether the story about Joseph is true, after all."

"You going to tell them?"

"I don't know. I may let them stew for a while. It will be interesting to watch them maneuvering to find out."

They spent most of the time talking about Joseph. Jackson wanted to hear the details of his progress in the past three weeks, and Beth was more than happy to supply them. She reflected that she would never have believed that she would be sitting here with a world-famous producer and director, telling him about her baby's smiles and weight gains. But it did not feel odd; Jackson was perhaps the easiest person to talk to that she had ever met—or, at least, easy for her. She felt, in a way, as if she had known him for years. On the other hand, she was also aware of a little sizzle of excitement in her gut that reminded her that she didn't know him at all, that he was drop-dead sexy, and the first man that she had felt the slightest interest in in eight months.

"What about you?" she said after a time, smiling sheepishly. "Here I've been going on and on talking about the baby. You haven't had a chance to get a word in edgewise."

"I like hearing about Joseph. And what about me? I have nothing exciting to relate. Just days of setting things up for filming, of looking at locations and talking to people, hiring people, signing contracts. It's the part I like least about a film. When we actually start shooting is when I begin to enjoy it." He did not add that he had not intended to stay in Austin this long, that he had lingered, overseeing things that his assistants usually handled, just because he had been restless and reluctant to return to L.A. Sitting here now, looking at Beth, he wondered if he hadn't been subconsciously hoping that she would show up.

"And when will that be?"

"I go to L.A. the day after tomorrow. Then we'll be back in Austin in six weeks to begin shooting. After a couple of weeks here, we move out close to you for the barren land scenes. That's to accommodate one of the actor's schedules. After that, we return to Austin for another month or so."

"Close to us? Really?" Beth could not stop the pleased smile that spread across her face.

"Yeah. The location I was scouting the day I met you." Another thing that Jackson had chosen not to examine too closely were his reasons for deciding that the locations thirty and forty miles from Angel Eye were much better than the ones Sam had found two hours away from the town.

"That will be nice. Will you come by and see us? Maybe *The Insider* won't be camped on our doorstep by then."

"Yeah. I'll come see you. I'll even brave *The Insider* to do it."

"Wow. I *am* impressed."

When dinner was over, Jackson walked her out to her car. He found that he did not want to say goodbye to Beth in the full public view of the restaurant or the hotel lobby. She unlocked the door of her car, and they stood for an uncomfortable moment. He felt like a high school kid again, he thought, not wanting to say goodbye to his date and not knowing how to keep her there. He could not deny the sexual feelings that had been stirring in him the whole afternoon with her. Yet he felt odd feeling that way about Joseph's mother, as if he were breaking some sort of taboo. She was, after all, a new *mother;* doubtless the last thing on her mind was sex, and she would probably be appalled if she knew that the whole time they had been arguing this afternoon, he had been thinking about kissing her.

"Well, goodbye," she said, opening the car door.

"Goodbye." He held the door open for her as she stepped into the wedge between the car and door.

They stood for an awkward moment, neither of them willing to take the last step away. He bent, meaning to kiss her on the cheek, but at the last instant, his lips went to her lips instead. Their mouths touched as soft as velvet, and clung. Jackson braced his hands on the car door on one side of her and the roof of the car on the other, holding back from touching her. Beth felt enveloped by his warmth and scent, but she ached for more. She wanted to feel his arms around her, wanted to step into him, to wrap her arms around him and hold on for dear life. Yet she could not let herself do that, as if it would make the moment too real, too scary and fraught with problems. So only their mouths touched, tasting and exploring. Her hands dug into the material of her dress; his clenched upon the metal of the car.

When at last Jackson pulled back, both of them were breathing heavily. He gazed down at her flushed face, her eyes glittering like stars, and he wanted to jerk her against him and kiss her again. Instead he drew a deep breath and stepped back. Beth swallowed and managed a trembling smile, then quickly ducked into the car.

He walked away, not looking back. Beth went limp, crossing her forearms on the steering wheel and leaning against them, waiting for the trembling in her limbs to stop and her breathing to return to normal. *What was going on here?* She had come here breathing fire, furious with him and wanting only to slice him to ribbons. Now all she wanted was to be in his arms again—preferably naked and in a bed.

It was just the aftermath of pregnancy, she told herself—a flood of hormones that pulled her in strange directions. It was something she should have expected. It was no portent of the future. It had nothing to do with Jackson Prescott himself, other than that he was there—and quite handsome, of course—and potently male.

She drew a shaky breath. Who was she kidding? It had everything to do with Jackson Prescott and that sexy smile of his, those luscious blue eyes, the sharp angles of cheekbones and jaw. He was, in fact, devastating to her senses and, she was honest enough to admit, devastating to her emotions, as well. If she was smart, Beth thought, she would stay far away from him. He would not fit into the simple and uncomplicated life she had envisioned for herself and her baby, a life free of things like reporters hounding her and having her name splashed all over the tabloids—or having her heart broken again by another man far more worldly than she.

But then, Beth had never been one for playing it safe. And she knew that if Jackson Prescott did show up in Angel Eye two months from now, she would gladly open the door and let him in.

Chapter 5

The furor in the tabloids gradually died down. After a few more fruitless days, the reporter from *The Insider* disappeared. There was another article or two, but they were mere rehashings of old stories, and after another week, Beth was pleased to find that she had slipped quietly back into anonymity. The reporters stopped calling, as did curious acquaintances. Beth's life returned to normal—or as normal as life could be with a new baby.

But even that was settling into an easier routine. Joseph began to sleep through the night, supplemented with a short nap in the morning and a long one in the afternoon. All the redness and discolorations of birth had faded, and he was turning into a beautiful plump baby with a mop of dark hair.

Cater had returned to his house in Austin, so it was just Beth, Cory and her father at the ranch, and even Cory would be returning to college in Austin soon. But Beth was now able to manage both the baby and the house without feeling as if she had been run over by a truck. Sometimes, when the baby was asleep, she even tried sketching again. She did not yet start to work again in oils, but she was beginning to feel restless and a little eager to get back to her work—something she had wondered about ever happening again when she was in the heavy lassitude of her pregnancy.

She drew pencil and pen-and-ink sketches of her father or Cory or scenes around the house. She even found herself a few times trying to draw a picture of Jackson Prescott from memory, though she never could seem to get it right. She was not, she thought, familiar enough with his face—though it seemed to her that she thought about him so often that she should be.

He called her a few times from L.A.—short unimportant conversations that were mostly about Joseph and his new accomplishments or the business that was keeping Jackson occupied in Los Angeles. But Beth always got a knot of excitement in her stomach whenever she picked up the phone and heard his voice on the other end of the line.

He was returning to Austin soon, and only two weeks after that he would start shooting near Angel Eye. Beth would have been aware of that fact even if

Jackson had not told her, for the entire town of Hammond was gearing up for the coming of the movie crew. They were staying in a motel in Hammond, which had the closest motel to the desolate area where they would be filming. Hammond had not had this much excitement for years. The weekly newspaper kept up a "movie watch," and locals were excited about being extras in the film.

Still, Beth was astonished when the doorbell rang late one afternoon, and she opened the door to find Jackson Prescott standing on her doorstep. "Jackson!" she cried, before she could stop herself.

Her hand flew up to her chest, and she felt suddenly hot, then cold. Her stomach started to dance. "What are you doing here?"

"Filming a movie, hadn't you heard?" He smiled, taking off his sunglasses. "You going to let me in?"

"Of course. I—I'm just so surprised to see you." Beth stepped back to let him enter the foyer, resisting an impulse to check her hair. She was sinkingly aware of the fact that she was wearing much-worn denim shorts and an old tank top, rather too stretched by her larger breasts. "Uh, I, how did you find our house?"

"Everyone in Angel Eye knows where you live. Didn't you know that? I stopped at a convenience store and asked, and they were quite happy to tell me. Guess you don't worry much about security here."

Beth chuckled. "Not really."

"I took the road the kid told me, checked the mailboxes, and voilà! Here I am. I was afraid you might have a gate or something. What *was* that thing I drove across when I turned into your road? It felt like I was driving on a washboard.''

"That's a cattle guard, city boy." Beth smiled. His casual way had allowed her nerves to vanish, and now she led him to the den, where Joseph was lying on his back in his playpen, moving his arms and legs and batting at the activity toys dangling from the webbed strap strung across the top of the playpen. "You want to see Joseph?"

"Of course." Jackson's eyes went to the backs of Beth's legs as she bent over the playpen and picked up the baby. She had certainly gotten her figure back, he noticed. Her legs were shapely and looked a mile long, and she filled out the skimpy top admirably.

Beth turned, baby in arms, and Jackson pulled his gaze back to her face. "Look at that!" he exclaimed, staring at the baby in wonder. "He's so big!"

Beth beamed. "Well, you have to remember, he's almost three months old now. You want to hold him?"

"Sure." He took him with the exaggerated care of one not used to infants and held him, looking down at Joseph long and carefully. "He's beautiful. Or shouldn't one say that about a baby boy?"

"Why not? He is."

Jackson caressed the baby's cheek and traced one eyebrow. The baby stared back at him gravely, pacifier firmly in place, and arms and legs pumping. Suddenly Joseph grinned hugely around his pacifier, as if he and Prescott shared some secret and hilarious joke. Jackson let out a delighted chuckle.

"Did you see that! He smiled at me."

"Uh-huh. Maybe he recognizes you."

"After three months?"

"You were one of the first people who ever held him. That's got to make an impression."

Jackson put his finger against the baby's hand, and Joseph curled his little hand around it firmly. Jackson bent his head closer, staring into his face and talking, trying to win more smiles. He was rewarded with a coo and a frenzy of kicks.

Beth, watching the two of them, felt a lump rising in her throat. She realized that this was the way she would like to draw Jackson, him standing there holding the baby, so large in comparison, bent over in awe and affection, held captive by the little creature.

They spent the evening in the den, playing with the baby and talking. Beth's father came in and joined them, and they wound up watching an old movie on television. Beth was rather amazed. The last thing she would have expected of a hotshot Hollywood director was to spend a family evening playing with a baby and looking at the tube with her dad.

He did not stay late. "Have to get up in the morning early to start filming," he explained as Beth walked with him to the door.

"How early?"

"Five or so."

"Five?" she repeated, stunned.

"Yeah. Glamorous, huh? People always think movie people stay up late partying and then sleep till noon. Well, usually I do stay up late, watching the dailies. But I never sleep late. We have to get everything set up, take advantage of the light. Every day is money gone, so you have to make the most of each one."

They had reached the front door. He laced his fingers through hers and led her outside. They strolled over to his car. "It's hectic. I probably won't be able to get over here much."

"I understand." Her heart began to beat a little faster. His words must mean that he wanted to see her more. *Or was it just the baby that brought him here?*

He turned to face her, leaning against his car. "Would you come visit the set?"

"Really?" Beth smiled. "Would it be okay?"

"Sure. I'll put your name on the list. They'll let you in and tell you where to go."

"When?"

"Tomorrow. Or whenever you'd like. I'll approve you for every day. That way you can come whenever you get the chance."

"That's very nice of you."

He grinned. "Nothing's too good for the mother of my 'secret love child.'"

Beth grimaced. *"Puhleeze."*

"They've stopped, haven't they?"

"Yeah."

"Bigger fish to fry." He took her hand and laid it flat against one of his. With his other hand, he traced each of her fingers, slowly, almost meditatively, watching the movement of his finger. "I'm sorry you were put in that mess because of me."

"It wasn't your fault. All you did was be a Good Samaritan."

"Yeah, but it certainly wasn't your fault, either. I'm even sorrier that I doubted you." He looked back into her face in the dim light cast by the moon and stars. "I'm too cynical."

"It's easy to understand, if you have to deal with that kind of stuff all the time."

"The tabloids usually aren't that bad about me. I'm not a real celebrity, a star. I think they jumped on it because they've never been able to pin any sort of scandal on me before. When they got the chance, they went at it full blast."

"So you've always been a good boy?" Beth could hear the hint of flirtation in her voice, and it surprised her a little.

He grinned. "More like a dull one." There was an undercurrent of seduction in *his* voice, as well, a certain husky quality that did strange things to Beth's insides.

"I doubt that." She swayed forward slightly.

He did the same. "Trust me. I'm Old Reliable."

"And what should I rely on you for?" she asked lightly.

Jackson's only answer was to bring his hands up

to cup her face. He gazed at her for a long moment, and his hands slid down her neck and onto her shoulders. The touch of his skin on her bare flesh sent a shiver through her, and Beth was reminded suddenly of how long it had been since she had been with a man.

She told herself that Jackson was slick and sophisticated, and that in any situation with him she would probably be in over her head. Joseph's father had been like that—wealthy, worldly—and look what had happened with him. She had to be more careful this time.

But then Jackson's mouth was on hers, and Beth stopped thinking at all.

She wrapped her arms around his neck and gave in to the sweet pleasure of his kiss. His arms went around her, and he pulled her in tightly against him. They kissed for a long time, oblivious to the world around them. Finally Jackson raised his head. His eyes glittered, and his face was flushed and slack with desire.

Beth drew a shaky breath. "Well..." she said. "I...uh..."

"Yeah." Reluctantly his arms fell away from her. "This is probably not a very good thing to start."

Beth shook her head. "Yeah." She realized that her verbal and physical signals were confused, which, when she thought about it, pretty much reflected what she felt inside—confusion. This was not what she needed at the moment. All her energies should be concentrated on the baby and on getting back to work. She did not need romantic feelings mixing up her insides.

"I better get back inside," she murmured.

"Okay. Will you come to the set?"

She nodded. "Tomorrow, if I can get someone to baby-sit Joey."

Baby-sitting, of course, was the least of her problems. There was always someone around who was happy to take care of the baby. It had, after all, been sixteen years since there had been a baby in the family. She had said it only to have an excuse for not showing up.

However, after a night of tossing and turning, going over all the reasons why a man was the last thing she needed in her life right now, Beth did not even think of using her ready-made excuse. Instead she called Daniel's son, James, who quickly agreed to come over and take care of Joseph for two or three hours—provided that Beth would introduce him to Jackson Prescott.

"I'm the only one who hasn't met him," he said plaintively. "And I'm the only one who would like to."

Beth chuckled. "Well, he said he would come over again, and when—if—he does, I'll introduce you."

So the next morning, at ten, she drove to the spot where they were filming. A guard stopped Beth long before she reached the trailers and the huddle of people in the distance. He checked his list, talked to someone on a walkie-talkie and a moment later a young woman showed up, looking harried, and escorted Beth along the dirt road to the center of the activity.

The trailers stood to one side. Stretching in front of them was a barren patch of ground, then a battered car in front of the facade of a wooden shack. There was a small truck on a set of tracks leading away from the car, and atop the truck were a seat and a camera. There was various other equipment scattered around, none of which Beth could identify except for banks of lights and a long boom with a dangling microphone. Several people stood or sat under a canopy, protected from the blazing August sun. A number of other people scurried around moving equipment and measuring things, talking into headsets. It looked like utter chaos.

Off to one side, apparently oblivious to the hubbub around him, stood Jackson, dressed in shorts and a T-shirt, with an old ball cap on his head to ward off some of the sun. He was talking to an older man with a long, graying ponytail and a backward-turned hat. Jackson was talking and gesturing, and the older man was nodding. The girl who had escorted Beth edged toward the men and caught Jackson's attention. He asked her a question, and she answered, pointing toward Beth.

Jackson turned and saw Beth, and a smile broke across his face. "Beth!"

He left the other two and came over to her. "Hi. You came. I wasn't sure."

"Yeah. Here I am."

He stopped just short of her and stood a little awkwardly. "I told Jackie to get you a chair in the shade. It's the most comfortable seat in the house. I have to work." He nodded toward where the other man stood waiting for him.

"Sure. I understand."

She didn't talk to him again until they broke for lunch, but she found it interesting to watch the filming. After a long time the chaos died down into stillness. An actress came out of one trailer, and an actor out of another, and two more people came forward from under the canopy. They took up their positions on the porch of the "shack" and beside the car, and then there was another round of waiting while more things were checked and people hurried out to fix the actors' hair and makeup for a final time.

There were a few minutes of filming, then several more takes, involving more checking of hair and makeup, and finally everyone broke away. The actors returned to their trailers and the canopy, and the chaos began all over again. Beth noticed that throughout the morning, which included several apparent crises, including an argument with the head cameraman and a tantrum by one of the actors, Jackson retained his calm. It was no wonder, she thought, that she had instinctively realized that he could handle a race to the hospital and a frantic birth. He was used to handling problems every day of his life.

Lunch was a catered buffet under the canopy, and Beth ate it with Jackson, sitting at a table in one corner of the little pavilion. Everyone left them alone, but Beth could feel the curious glances from the cast and crew.

"Don't you have one of the trailers?" Beth asked curiously.

Jackson grinned. "No. Just the two stars. The other trailer's the makeup and costume rooms. One corner of it is a little office, which my assistant works out of. Directors always seem to be in the middle of the fray. It's the way I like it. I want to keep my eye on everything. The last thing I need is to be shut away from it in a trailer."

"At least you would be out of the heat," Beth commented, sitting back and fanning herself with an empty paper plate.

He looked concerned. "Are you too hot? You want to go into the makeup trailer for a while?"

Beth laughed. "No. I'm fine. You forget, I grew up in this heat."

"I'm glad you came out."

"Me too."

"You want to have dinner tonight?"

"I thought you were going to be too busy."

"I have to eat. We could meet in Hammond. What do you say?"

"Okay." She knew it was foolish. She had given

herself a thorough talking-to last night. There was no future in an affair with a director from L.A. To begin with, they lived thousands of miles apart, or at least they would once he returned to Los Angeles after the filming. With a new baby, there was no room in her life for a man, period, much less for one who would breeze into it for a few weeks and then breeze right back out, leaving her no doubt sadder, but probably not a whit wiser.

Besides, they lived such utterly different lives. Though she lived in a city, she was used to a quiet, serene life. She spent most of her days alone in her studio, painting. She didn't go to glittering parties. She didn't spend her days under the high pressure of deadlines. She worked and lived at her own pace, answering to no one, and that was the way she liked it. She was no more likely to give up her life than Jackson was to dump his career among the movers and shakers of Hollywood.

It was, obviously, a romance that was doomed from the start. Yet Beth could not bring herself to administer the deathblow cleanly and early. She liked being with him too much. So she agreed to have supper with him that evening. And when they found that everyone stared and whispered when they went into a restaurant in Hammond, Beth smiled and suggested that perhaps it would be easier if the next time they had dinner at her house.

She saw him frequently after that, despite his earlier statement that he would have little time on location. Somehow he seemed to make time, coming out almost every day to the ranch for an hour or two before he went back to watch the dailies. Beth noticed her family was getting used to having him around. James, who had been overawed to meet him, soon was chatting away with him about old films as if they had known each other all their lives, and even Daniel and her father allowed that he was "all right."

The baby, it was clear, soon recognized Jackson, who could always make Joey gurgle and coo and smile. Beth began sketching scenes of the two of them together, and when she found the pose that she liked the best, she decided to start an oil portrait, her first since she'd moved back to the ranch. If it turned out well, she thought, she would give it to him. Jackson had admired the large portrait of her mother that she had done a few years ago for her father and which hung over the mantel in the living room.

Jackson spent most of Saturday evening with her at the ranch house, and after she had put Joseph down to bed for the night, with the monitor beside her father's chair as Marshall watched an exhibition game in the den, she took Jackson outside, promising to show him the delights of an evening out in West Texas.

"We going dancing?" he asked in some amusement. "I better go back and put on my boots."

"Nope. Nearest dance hall's an hour away. I was thinking of someplace closer. Here, take this." She shoved a cooler at him and grabbed some quilts, waving him out the door. They put the quilts and cooler in the back of her father's pickup and climbed in the front.

Beth set out from the house, driving a way Jackson had never gone before, following a track that led deeper onto the land instead of out to the road. After a while the track disappeared, and Jackson realized that they were simply driving cross-country, dodging mesquite bushes and sagebrush and cows.

"Where are we going?" he asked as they bounced and rattled along. "By the way, can you bruise a spleen?"

Beth chuckled. "We are going to look at something I'll bet you've never seen, city slicker."

"Coyotes?" he hedged.

She smiled. "This looks like a good spot."

Beth pulled to a stop. Jackson glanced around. He couldn't see anything about this place that was different from any of the rest of the land. It was all dark, with darker lumps of bushes here and there.

"Come on." Beth jumped out and walked around to open the gate of the pickup. Jackson obediently followed.

Beth hopped up into the bed of the truck and laid out the blankets, then gestured for Jackson to join her. She opened the cooler and pulled out two beers, handing one of them to him. Then she lay down on the truck bed, patting the blanket beside her. Jackson lay down where she'd indicated.

"Is this it?" he asked.

Beth chuckled. "Yep. This is it. Lying out looking at the stars." She pointed straight up. "But look at them! You never see anything like that in the city. I know."

He had to agree. The night sky was enormous and velvet black, darker than it ever was in any city, and it was filled with a multitude of coldly glittering stars, the moon a silver-white crescent among them. It was relaxing, soothing, to lie out here in the cooling evening, surrounded by utter quiet and the vast reach of the empty land below and the starry sky above. Jackson could feel the strains of the last few stressful days oozing out of him.

He took another swig of his beer and set it beside him, then crossed his arms behind his head and gave himself up to contemplating the vastness of the universe for a while. Beth, who had seen the same view thousands of times, still gazed at it in admiration. In her career, she dealt with beauty—recreated it, brought it out in rich textures and glowing colors, struggled to add it where it was not. But nothing she could ever do could compare to the beauty of nature, the perfect blend of color, texture and space. It was a fact that she had realized anew time after time, always with a pang that was part ache and part joy.

They started to talk, first about how the filming had been going and when he and the others would be returning to Austin to finish filming there, then drifting to her work and her house in Dallas, and finally to what it had been like growing up in Angel Eye, Texas.

"I always wanted to get out," Beth remembered with a smile. "Now I find it rather peaceful and beautiful in its own stark way. But back then, all I could see was the dullness and the gossip and the never-ending emptiness. I felt like if I stayed here I would smother to death."

"Me too. Where I grew up was a little bigger, different landscape—magnolias instead of mesquite— but stagnant. Choking. I couldn't wait to get out."

"Course it didn't help having three older brothers who were the biggest guys in town. I hardly ever went out the first two years I was in high school because all the boys were so scared of Quinn. Thank God he graduated and went off to college, so at least I managed to have a few dates my junior and senior years."

"You have an interesting family—an artist, a rancher, a novelist, a cop—that's a mixed bag."

"Well, we never believed in being ordinary." Beth smiled. "And the boys aren't as different as it sounds. Quinn's a cop, and Cater writes mysteries. When they were young, all three of the boys had the biggest collection of *Hardy Boys* mysteries you've ever seen. That's what I read, too. I'm probably the only girl in the world who didn't read Nancy Drew. Probably the only reason Daniel didn't do something similar was because he got married right out of high school, and they had Jimmy pretty quickly. So he stayed here and got work in Hammond, and Dad gave them some land. And ranching's in all the boys' blood. Whenever Dad or Daniel needs extra workers, Quinn and Cater come to help.''

''Which way do you suppose Cory is going to go?''

''I'm not sure. He's still at that stage where he's interested in half a dozen things. But I think at heart he's a rancher. Now, Jimmy, Daniel's son—''

Jackson laughed. ''I don't think that boy's interested in working the land.'' Jimmy had bent Jackson's ear about movies and directing every time he had found Jackson at the house, and he had been ecstatic when Jackson had told him he was welcome to watch the filming. Jimmy had been on location every day since and was quite annoyed that school was starting next week, so he wouldn't be able to see the last few days of filming.

''Mama was artistic,'' Beth went on. ''I guess that's where we get it. She drew and painted when she had the time, which wasn't often. And she used to tell the most wonderful stories. I remember she always said that when we kids were older, she wanted to write and illustrate children's books. But then, about the time the rest of us were getting big enough we didn't need so much seeing after, along came Cory. Then she died.''

''That must have been hard for you. How old were you?''

''Thirteen. Yeah, it was hard. She was my friend and ally, as well as my mother. You know, us girls against the guys. And being a teenager, too—there are just some things a father and brothers can't help you with. My friend Sylvie and her mother always went shopping together, and sometimes they fought over what Sylvie could buy, but they had *fun*. Her mom would stay up when Sylvie was on a date, and when Sylvie came in, they would talk about it. Sometimes, when I went on a date, I would go over to Sylvie's to dress and do my makeup and hair so that when I said, 'How do I look?' I'd get a response like, 'Oh, I like that color eye shadow,' or 'Hey, your hair is different,' instead of 'Fine, honey.' Dad wouldn't have noticed my hair unless I dyed it green."

Jackson chuckled. "Your dad's great. We walked around the yard the other night—looked in the barn, looked in the corral, checked out the row of trees he planted. I'll bet he didn't say more than two sentences—and both those times were when I asked him a question. Then, when we came in, he nodded at me and said, 'You're good company, son.'"

"That's Dad. The less you talk, the better company you are. He said he got used to not talking, being out on the land by himself so much, you know. But he was a good father. He tried really hard to make up to Cory and me for Mama dying. He went to all our school plays and parent-teacher conferences. He was in the stands at all the boys' games. He even went to my dance recitals." Beth giggled. "I can still remember looking out in the audience and seeing him sitting there with this look of grim resignation on his face.

Poor man. I think he felt guilty because he never re-married after Mama died. He told me once that he thought he should have given us another mother, but he couldn't bring himself to put some other woman in Mama's place. He loved her so much.''

They were silent for a moment, then Jackson asked softly, ''What about Joseph's father?''

He could feel Beth's body go rigid beside him. ''What about him?''

''Well, he seems conspicuously absent,'' he said cautiously.

''He *is* conspicuously absent. And he is going to remain so.''

''Does he even know that Joseph was born?''

''No. He doesn't even know about the *possibility* of his being born.''

''You didn't tell him you were pregnant?''

''No.''

''Don't you think he at least has the right to know he has a son?''

''He has *no* rights.'' Beth sat up, her jaw clenched. Why did Jackson have to bring *him* up?

''I'm sorry.'' Jackson laid a hand on her back.

She flinched, but when his hand remained, warm and undemanding, she relaxed a little. ''No. *I'm* sorry.'' She let out a long sigh and lay back down. ''I get a little…antagonistic on that subject.''

''So I see. I didn't mean to upset you. I was just thinking about it from the male perspective. I would think he would want to know, to be a father to Joey.''

He turned on his side and lay propped up on his elbow, looking down at her.

"You don't know Robert. I don't think he would give a flip about knowing about Joey. It's my guess that he would tell me that he already has two sons and, besides, how does he know that Joseph is really his? That's the sort of man Robert Waring is."

"I see."

"He's cold, calculating, deceitful—" Beth drew a breath and forced herself to relax. "Oh, I'm not being fair to him. He's also charming—extremely charming *and* handsome, *and* sophisticated, *and* intelligent. I met him at a party at a bank opening. I had painted the portrait of the chairman of the board that hung in the lobby, so I got an invitation to the grand opening. Robert did business with them. He was urbane and witty, and after the opening, he asked if he could take me out to a late supper. Well, it went on from there. I would see him every few weeks. He lived in Chicago, and he came to Dallas often on business. I suppose that's why it took me so long to figure it out. I didn't know that back in Chicago, he lived with his wife and two teenage boys."

"Ah."

"Yeah. Ah." Beth grimaced. "I was hopelessly naive. It never even struck me as odd that the only numbers I had for him were business numbers—his office phone, his pager, his cellular phone. He frequently worked late, and usually if we talked in the evenings, he was at his office. I assumed he was a bachelor who wasn't home much—if I thought at all. Looking back on it, I'm not sure I did.''

"No need to kick yourself about it. People don't expect someone to lie to them at every turn, particularly someone they're close to. If a person sets out to fool you, they will—unless they're really *bad* at it.''

"He wasn't bad at it. Not at all. I found out by accident. I was doing a portrait of the bank president's wife—a very nice and very chatty woman. We talked a lot while she was sitting for me, and sometime in there, I mentioned Robert and having met him at the opening of their new building. She said, 'Oh, yes, Robert, I've met him several times. Such a charming man, and his wife is so elegant.' You can imagine how I reacted.''

"Mmm-hmm.''

"I'm sure I turned completely white, but I hid behind my easel and managed to say, 'Oh? I didn't realize he was married.' She told me that he very much was and had two sons. Then she said that I mustn't get mixed up with him, of course not knowing it was a trifle late for that. He was, she said, a terrible ladies' man. So after she left, I called him up and asked him if it was true, and he told me yes and not to be hysterical. He made it quite clear where I ranked on his list of priorities, which was somewhere down below his golf game, I think.''

"I'm sorry. I know that's terribly inadequate, but…''

"Well, live and learn, Dad always says.''

"Some lessons are harder than others, though."

"Yeah. About a month after that, I figured out that I was pregnant." Beth smiled a little to herself. "It was hard at the time. But I can't really say I regret it. Otherwise I wouldn't have Joey."

"That's true. He is worth a lot of pain."

"Yeah."

Jackson gazed down at her for a long moment. He brushed his knuckles down her cheek. "I am not married," he said. "Never have been."

Beth looked back at him, wondering where this was going. She could not read his expression, for his head was backlit by the light of the stars and moon. "What are you telling me?"

He smiled. "I'm not sure. I guess...that I'm not the same sort of man as Robert Waring."

He paused. It was on the tip of his tongue to blurt out that he loved her, that he wanted to have much more than a few evenings with her. But he stopped himself. *That was crazy.* He barely knew Beth Sutton. He was an adult, not some crazy teenager who fell in love on the basis of an intense meeting and a few hours spent in her company. He had a movie to shoot. In a few more days he would return to Austin to resume filming there, and after that he would go back to Los Angeles.

Jackson wanted to kiss her. He wanted to make love to her out here under the stars. But something held him back. Making love did not necessarily mean making promises for the future. But, somehow, he felt that with this woman, for him, it would be a promise.

He bent down and kissed her lightly on the lips. "We had better be getting back."

"Right now?" Beth asked, her eyebrows rising. She had seen the hesitation on his face, the desire that had flickered in his eyes and been squelched. "But you haven't gotten to the best part of one of these Angel Eye evenings."

"Oh? And what is that?"

"This," she replied, hooking her hand behind his neck and pulling him down for a kiss.

Chapter 6

Her lips were soft and melting, and Jackson could not keep from responding to them. A kiss, after all, was not making love, and he would stop long before they reached that point.

Their lips clung, their tongues twining around one another, seeking, exploring. It seemed to Jackson that the more he tasted her, the more he wanted. They kissed again and again, their desire escalating.

Beth shivered and pressed up against him, her arms wrapping around him. It had been so long since she had felt this kind of passion, this roaring, rushing ocean of desire that swept her along almost mind-lessly. *Had she ever felt it?* She couldn't remember it—not like this. She had meant only to kiss him as she had the other night. She had, she admitted, felt a trifle annoyed at his ability to turn away from her so easily, and she had wanted to prove that she could make him desire her. But now she found herself at the mercy of her own passion, her body, its desires dormant for so many months, reawakening to its own needs.

His mouth was urgent and hungry, every kiss a demand and a delight all in one. His hand moved down her body, setting up a wild tingling wherever it touched. He cupped her breast, his thumb circling her nipple through her blouse. Beth let out a little moan, and she felt a tremor run through Jackson's body in response.

They broke off their kiss, and Jackson rained kisses down her throat and onto her chest. Completely forgotten were his plans for restraint and control. His fingers went to her blouse, unbuttoning it and delving beneath her lacy brassiere to touch the soft orb of her breast. His touch felt so right, so good, that Beth unconsciously moved her hips. She realized that she had been wanting this for days—maybe even weeks. She just had not acknowledged it, had not wanted to accept the fact that she could again be this hungry for a man...if, indeed, she ever had been. She could not remember feeling such a volatile storm of sensations and emotions before. It was, frankly, a little frightening.

"No, wait." Beth edged away, putting her hands up to his chest.

Jackson stopped, his breath rasping in his throat.

For a long moment he struggled for control. Then, with a groan, he rolled away onto his back and flung one arm across his eyes.

"I'm sorry," Beth said, sitting up. "I know I'm the one who started that, but...I don't know, it was all moving too fast. I'm not ready for—" *For what? Commitment? Sex? Loss of control?* "I don't know. I don't want to make another mistake."

He nodded. "You're right. This probably isn't the time or place." He had known that before they kissed—*now if he could just convince his raging libido of that fact.*

"No. You were the one who was right. We should have gone home when you suggested it." Beth began to scoot toward the gate of the truck.

Jackson reached out a hand and grabbed her arm, stopping her. She glanced at him. He smiled. "Maybe so. But I'm glad we didn't."

Heat rose in Beth's cheeks, but she flashed back a grin. "Me too."

The next day, Beth was standing in line at the grocery store in Angel Eye, a basketful of diapers, baby food and food in front of her, when she glanced over at the magazine rack. There, on the front of the tabloid, right next to a picture of a car trunk lid on which an image of Jesus had supposedly formed, was a picture of her and Jackson walking out of some door. They were talking, their heads turned toward each other, and they were holding hands. Across the top of the photograph, the headline blazoned: Prescott's Secret Love Nest!

Beth groaned, then glanced quickly around to see if anyone had heard. She wondered if anyone else had seen it, if they had recognized her. After another furtive look around, she snatched the top issue of *Scandal* off the rack and looked at the picture up close. The door they were exiting, she decided, was the front door of the ranch house. She couldn't stop a little smile at the thought of how her father would react to having his home labeled a "secret love nest."

How had they gotten this shot? She decided that it must have been taken with a telephoto lens, with the photographer sitting somewhere out of sight. She certainly hadn't caught a glimpse of anyone taking their picture at any point. *But how had they known to send a photographer out to take it?* It boggled her mind the way the tabloids were able to jump so quickly on a story. She supposed that someone on the movie crew had tipped them off—or any of the townspeople of Hammond or Angel Eye who had happened to see them together. She and Jackson hadn't been very secretive about their relationship.

Beth read through the story, a mishmash of truth, speculation and downright lies. But it sounded convincing, even to her. They even mentioned in the story that her child was named after Jackson's father. Beth shook her head. She had never thought that *that* decision would come back to haunt her.

For a brief moment, she thought about calling Julie

McCall at *Scandal* and setting the record straight. But even a moment's immediate reflection made her change her mind. For one thing, it would be hard to convince the woman that there had been nothing between her and Jackson, not when they had a picture of the two of them holding hands. For another thing, she rather doubted that the tabloid cared about publishing the truth. They just wanted a good story, and no doubt a ''secret love child'' and ''secret love nest'' were more appealing. What was it about secret love that was so intriguing to people, anyway?

Maybe no one would notice, she thought desperately, but that hope was dashed when the cashier looked up and saw her. ''Why, hi, Beth! How are you? See you got your picture in the papers.''

Beth smiled weakly. ''Yeah. Hi, Maggie Lee.''

''What will your daddy say about all that?'' the checker went on, snapping her gum and dragging Beth's groceries over the scanner.

''He won't like it. I imagine you can guess that.''

Maggie Lee chuckled. ''Sure can. Marshall never was one who liked attention.'' She paused for a moment, then asked, ''So what's going on with you and that movie fella? You-all going to tie the knot or what?''

''We're just friends. You can't believe all that stuff in the tabloids.''

''Aren't they a hoot? I just love those things. But, you know, I figure some of that stuff has got to be true. They couldn't just publish those things if they were bald-faced lies. There has to be some kernel of truth there, that's what I always say.''

Beth suppressed a sigh. She wondered how many people reasoned as Maggie Lee did. Probably a lot, she decided in despair. She endured the rest of Maggie Lee's conversation, paid her bill and got out of the grocery store as fast as she could.

''Don't let it bother you,'' Jackson counseled when he came over that evening and she showed him the copy of *Scandal,* which Peg Richards from up the road had thoughtfully dropped by. ''Just shrug it off.''

''Doesn't it bother you?''

''Some. But there are worse things. At least they aren't accusing us of killing somebody or being unfaithful to our spouses or something. They've done worse than this to people before.''

''I suppose.'' Beth leaned over his chair, looking down at the cover again. ''It's just—oh, I hate having people know stuff about me. Even worse, having them think they know stuff that isn't true. I even thought about calling the magazine and telling them what really happened.''

''Uh-uh,'' Jackson said quickly, shaking his head. ''Trust me. You do *not* want to talk to them. I've known people who have made that mistake. They would turn your words around, and you would come out looking like a fool or someone wicked. Remember how they ran with that one thing you said to them last time?''

"Yeah, I know." Beth sighed and went to pick up the baby, who was beginning to make fussy noises in his playpen. He wriggled his arms and legs, fighting to go to Jackson, and she obligingly plopped him down in Jackson's lap.

"Don't worry," he reassured her. "You get used to it."

"I'm not sure I would." Beth sat down beside him, distracted from her irritation with the article by the sight of Jackson with the baby.

She had been working on the portrait of him with Joey off and on for several days. She had gotten to where she worked on it every day during the baby's nap and often in the evenings after Jackson left and she put Joey to bed. At the moment she was suffering from her usual midwork doubts and was afraid that the finished product would turn out all wrong. Well, she consoled herself, if it did, she didn't have to show it to Jackson.

She continued to look at him, wondering how a man playing with a baby could be so sweet and so sexy all at the same time. She hadn't been able to stop thinking about the other night in the bed of the pickup truck. There were times when she wished that she hadn't stopped. She looked at Jackson's fingers, long and thin, big-knuckled, with a light sprinkling of hair across the backs of his hands. He had beautiful hands, she thought, and remembered them roaming her body through her clothes. She found herself wishing that she could feel them against her bare skin.

"We're going back to Austin in a couple of days," Jackson said and shot her a sideways glance.

Beth's heart dropped. She wondered if he had seen the disappointment in her face. "Oh. Well…"

"It's not that far to Austin," he went on. "I was thinking that I could take a weekend off soon and come to visit…if you'd like."

"Sure."

"Or maybe you could come to see me there." He was still looking at her in that cautious way, and Beth realized that he was feeling his way along, unsure of how she would react.

It made her smile to think that this world-famous director was not entirely confident of her interest in him. "I'd like that," she told him honestly. "But I can't leave the baby."

"Bring him with you. I rented a house for the time we're in Austin. You could both stay there. I could rent a crib. And I can set my assistant to finding a nanny to take care of him for a while if you wanted to go out and do anything. You could stay a few days…if you'd like, of course."

"Yeah," she answered, smiling. "I'd like. Very much."

Beth was excited the whole drive up to Austin. She told herself that it was because it was the first time she had taken off with the baby on her own for any length of time. But she knew that was not the reason for the quivery anticipation in her stomach—or at least not for most of it. She was excited about seeing Jackson again. It had been over a week since he'd left Angel Eye. She wondered if he had missed her, if he had thought about her every day as she had been thinking about him. She wondered if his nerves, too, were jangling with anticipation. *Would he be happy to see her? Or would he think that she wasn't as pretty, as funny—as anything—as he remembered her?*

Many of her questions were answered when she pulled into the driveway of the house to which he had directed her and, before she had even gotten out of her car, the front door of the house opened and Jackson came out, grinning. An answering smile broke across Beth's face, and she quickly opened the door and jumped out. Jackson was down the steps and across to the circular driveway in about three steps, and he pulled her into his arms, lifting her off her feet.

"It feels like it's been forever," he said and kissed her thoroughly. Beth was rosy and laughing by the time they stepped apart. "Has it only been a week?"

She nodded. "And a few days."

"Every day seemed about thirty-six hours long." He pulled her into his arms again for another hug. Behind them, the baby set up a wail.

"Oops. I'd better get Joey out of his car seat." Beth slipped out of Jackson's arms and got into the back seat to unstrap the baby. Jackson was already reaching to take him when she turned around.

"Wow, look at this fella!" Jackson exclaimed. "Hey, slugger, you've grown since I saw you last. Same baby blues, though." He kissed the baby on the forehead, then cuddled him against his shoulder. "Do you think he remembers me?" he asked with a tinge of anxiety.

Beth had to chuckle. "I'm sure he does. He's crazy about you. In fact, I think he missed you. He was a little cranky at the beginning of the week."

He shot her a look. "Oh, right. I'm not *that* gullible about him."

"I'm serious! I really think he was wondering where you were."

Jackson gave the baby another pat and handed him back to Beth so that he could carry their bags into the house. "I thought we would have dinner here tonight," he said. "I guessed that you might be tired from traveling. We can go out tomorrow, if you want."

"You cooked?" Beth asked, surprised, as she followed him into the Mediterranean-style stucco house.

"Do I detect a note of chauvinism in your voice?" he responded tartly, then grinned. "Actually I had it catered. Believe me, you'll like it better."

He carried her bags through a spacious entryway and down a hall. On one side of the hall were rooms. On the other side were rows of windows, looking out at a spectacular view of Town Lake.

"Wow!" Beth stopped and looked down. Right below them was a sparkling aqua swimming pool with a miniature waterfall, and beyond it the bluff dropped straight down to a small inlet. In the distance the lake shimmered in the late-afternoon sun, the sails of boats bright triangles of color against the dark water.

"Yeah. Beautiful, isn't it? The family that lives here is on vacation in Europe. Fortunately they were willing to extend it for an extra month." He turned into the next door. "Here's your room."

It was a modernistic room with stark white furniture, accentuated by a neon bright bedcover and drapes. Beth stepped into the room behind him, relaxing at his words.

Jackson saw her expression. "What? Did you think I was going to plop your things down in the master bedroom? I told you—no strings attached."

"I know." She smiled. "It's just nice to have my opinion of you confirmed."

He opened a door and stepped through into a small sitting room. "I put the crib in here. I thought this would be a nice place for him."

"It's great," Beth answered honestly. "We might just move in with you."

"Is that a promise?" He smiled, then turned serious, pulling her into his arms loosely, the baby between them. "I'll tell you the truth—I've been lonely as hell this week. Every evening when we stopped, for an instant I would feel this anticipation, but then I would remember that I wouldn't be going out to the ranch to see you and Joey. I would have given a lot to have come home and heard just one little gurgle or coo—or that crazy wind-up swing that plays faster the tighter you wind it.''

Beth laughed. ''Maybe I should have brought the swing with me.''

Jackson left to set out their dinner, giving Beth a chance to change and feed the baby. When she came out, Jackson had the table set in the breakfast room, where they could look out over the water as they ate. Beth put Joseph down on a blanket in the middle of the wide, empty floor, accompanied by a few of his toys. Replete and dry, he amused himself while they ate a leisurely dinner and talked.

They stayed up late, long after Beth had put Joseph down in his bed, enjoying being together too much to go to bed. Beth knew she would regret it the next morning, but she did not retire until she was yawning so hugely that Jackson pulled her to her feet and turned her in the direction of her bedroom. She gave in, and he walked her to her door. There he kissed her good-night, and though the kiss turned into several kisses, at last he pulled away and went back down the hall and up the stairs to the aerie of a master bedroom on the floor above.

They spent a lazy Saturday, lounging by the pool or playing with the baby. That evening a smiling gray-haired woman, whom Jackson characterized as ''bonded and certified and thoroughly checked-out,'' came to sit with the baby while Jackson and Beth went out to eat. Beth went a little reluctantly; it was the first time she had left Joseph with anyone but a member of the family. However, with a mental squaring of her shoulders, she walked out the door. And only twice during the evening did she give in to the urge to phone the sitter to see how Joseph was doing.

However, she could not bring herself to stay out after midnight, and the first thing she did when they got back to Jackson's house was to go to the baby's room and peer over the side of the crib at him. Joey was sound asleep, of course, his chubby-cheeked face a study in relaxation. Beth smiled down at him, swallowing the lump in her throat.

She heard a noise and turned her head. Jackson had walked quietly into the room, and he came up now to stand behind her. He encircled her waist with his arms and leaned his head against hers, and for a long moment they simply stood, watching the baby sleep.

Then, softly, they slipped out of the room and back down the hall to the modernistic living room. The large sectional sofa was a buttery soft dark green leather, a lovely contrast to the immaculate white carpet, which Beth shuddered to even think of keeping clean. They sat down together on the sofa and stretched their legs out in front of them. He slid his arm around her shoulders, and Beth leaned against him, letting her head rest on his shoulder. It was a natural and very pleasant feeling, being with him this way, almost as if they were an old married couple relaxing together with the baby asleep down the hall.

They talked desultorily as they sat. After a moment's silence, Jackson said, "I wanted to tell you why I asked you about Joey's father."

"It's all right. You don't need to explain. It was a natural question. I just overreacted."

"I don't know about that. But I don't think it was really an idle question on my part. You see, I found out last year that I have an eighteen-year-old daughter that I never knew about."

"What?" Beth sat up, jolted, and turned to look into his face. "Are you serious?"

"Very," he replied grimly. "When I was sixteen, I was very much in love with a girl. Jessica Walls. She was a year younger than I was. We had all these plans, how we were going to go to college together and get married when we were juniors and—well, you know how kids are. We were serious and intense. The summer before my senior year, right about the time I turned seventeen, she moved away. It took me completely by surprise. She came over one evening and told me she and her mother were going to Atlanta for the summer. The summer turned into my whole senior year. She wrote me the next August, after we'd been exchanging letters all summer, and told me she wouldn't be coming back at all. I was heartbroken and furious. I felt that she had betrayed me. I didn't do well in school. I dropped out of sports. It was a bad year. Anyway, when I graduated, I had no desire to go to college, and I hadn't exactly been a stellar student anyway, so I decided to go far away. The West Coast seemed as far as I could get. I wound up in L.A. and sort of lucked into that first movie. I got interested in directing and, well, after a while, I forgot all about Jessica.''

He sighed and stood up, beginning to pace in front of the couch. ''Until last year, that is. She wrote me a letter, and in it she told me that the reason she had left town all those years ago was because she was pregnant. Her family was very religious, and she said it broke her parents' hearts. She felt guilty and bad, and when her parents insisted that I know nothing about it, she agreed, to please them. She and her mother went to live with her aunt in Atlanta. Her aunt was several years younger than her mother, and she had never been able to have children. So she took the baby and raised it as her own. It was a little girl. The aunt named her Amy.''

''Why did she tell you after all this time?''

''Because Amy needed money. Her aunt has been very sick for the last few years, and they've had big medical bills. They don't have enough money to send Amy to college. So Jessica decided to break her vow to her parents in the hopes that I would give her the money for Amy to go to school. She sent me a picture of her, I guess to convince me that Amy really was mine. It's pretty obvious that she's a Prescott.''

''So what did you do?''

''Gave her the money, of course, and I paid off the medical bills, as well. I would do more, except that it would make Amy wonder. She thinks the college thing is some kind of scholarship that Jessica got for her from her employer, and she doesn't know about the medical bills. But if I gave them more money to live on, she would have to wonder.''

"She still doesn't know that you're her father?"

He shook his head and sat back down beside Beth. "No. I wanted to see her, but Jessica was dead set against it. She says Amy has no reason to believe that she's anything but the aunt's daughter. She doesn't have any of those yearnings that adopted children have to know their real parents, and they don't want her to be disturbed.'' He shrugged. "Hell, I can hardly insist on it, knowing how it would shatter her life. I mean, Jessica has been living there close to her all those years, and she never let on.''

"Oh, Jackson…'' Beth reached out and put her hand on his arm. "I'm so sorry. It must be hard for you.''

"Yeah. It's weird. I mean, I never even knew she existed, and now, even though she's really a stranger to me, I feel a connection, a *longing* to know her. My life would probably have been completely different if Jessica had told me. Hell, Jessie and I might have gotten married, and I'd be back home in Alabama being a roofer or something.''

"A loss for the movie world.''

"I guess. I suspect her parents were right and it would have been a bad decision. Both of us would probably have wound up miserable. Still, it's hard knowing you have a child and you've never even seen her. That you've missed all those special times, that if she saw me, she would look right past me and not have a clue who I was."

"It's her loss, too," Beth told him, putting her arms around him and leaning her head against his shoulder. "You would have been a great dad. I can see it with Joey. You're wonderful with him."

"I love him," he said simply. He smiled sheepishly. "Does that sound silly?"

"No, not at all. I think it's wonderful." Beth could feel her throat swelling with emotion.

He stroked his hand across her hair. "I'm glad you think so." He hooked his forefinger beneath her chin and tilted it so that she was looking into his face. He looked at her for a moment, then said softly, "Because, you know, I think I love the little guy's mother, too."

Chapter 7

Beth stared at him in shock. Jackson chuckled. "Caught you off guard, huh?"

"But—but you couldn't."

"Why not?"

"I mean—well, it's too soon. You're probably mistaking your feelings because of our sharing Joey's birth and—"

"Elizabeth Sutton, are you trying to tell me that I don't know my own mind—or my own heart? I am thirty-six years old, you know, and have been functioning on my own for some time." His eyes twinkled with amusement.

Beth had the grace to blush. "Of course I don't mean that you don't know what you think or feel. It's just—well—" She faltered to a halt as she realized that, of course, that was exactly what she *had* meant.

Jackson was a grown man and obviously not the sort to fall in love every few weeks with a new woman. After all, he had gone this long without getting married even once, which in Hollywood was no mean feat. Warmth spread throughout Beth as she accepted that he *did* know what he meant; he *did* love her.

Jackson smiled. "I'm not asking you to reciprocate. I know it's sudden. But I wanted to tell you how I feel."

"Jackson, I..."

He shook his head, placing his forefinger against her lips. "You don't need to say anything. I don't expect it."

He bent and kissed her lips lightly, tenderly, then raised his head and gazed down into her eyes. Whatever he saw there must have pleased him, for his face softened with feeling, and he bent to kiss her again, this time more deeply. Beth let out a sigh of pleasure, and her arms went around his neck.

Their lips moved against each other with ever-increasing passion, until Beth's blood was racing hotly through her veins. Desire pooled between her legs, setting up a throbbing ache. She moved her legs, unable to keep still, and delighted in the immediate and unmistakable response of his body. They had shifted and moved as they kissed, until now they were lying pressed together full-length on the sofa. Their arms were tight around each other, and their legs intertwined. His hand roamed down Beth's back and onto her hips, cupping and caressing, then finally down onto her legs.

She had taken off her hose and shoes earlier, when she had gone to check on Joseph, so his hand slid over bare flesh. He moved upward, beneath her dress, caressing her thigh. His fingertips reached the lacy edge of her panties, and he hesitated, then edged beneath the lace. Beth shivered at the intimate touch.

She was on fire, aching for him. She didn't want to think about the future or the consequences. She wanted only to feel, to give herself up to the fire roaring through her. His mouth left hers and trailed hot kisses down her throat while his hand roamed over her buttocks, squeezing and caressing. Beth murmured his name, and Jackson groaned in response.

"You're beautiful," he whispered. "So beautiful."

He rose up on his elbow and looked down at her. "I want you."

For answer, Beth merely smiled. It seemed to be enough, for he stood up, reaching down to pull her up, too. They started up the circular stairs to the master bedroom, pausing every few feet along the way to kiss and caress each other again, all the while peeling off various articles of clothing. Their progress was slow, and by the time they reached the bed, they were naked, with a trail of clothes behind them.

They fell on the bed and rolled across it, kissing and touching each other in a frenzy of desire. Finally, when they could stand the teasing no longer, he moved between her legs. She opened to him, arching up to meet his thrust. He went deep inside her, and Beth let out a long sigh of satisfaction as he filled her. He moved slowly, afraid that he might hurt her in this, her first lovemaking since the baby, but after the first brief twinge of pain, Beth felt only pleasure. She wrapped her legs around him, urging him on, and he began to move faster, pounding into her with all the force of his passion.

He let out a hoarse cry as his seed poured into her, and Beth clung to him tightly, her own tidal wave of pleasure rushing through her.

Afterward, lying awake in the darkness, Jackson's arm around Beth, he said softly, "Don't go tomorrow."

"What?" Beth murmured sleepily, floating on a hazy wave of contentment.

"I don't want you to go back to Angel Eye tomorrow. Stay for a few more days. You could do that, couldn't you?"

"Sure." Beth smiled. "I could do that."

She wound up staying for the rest of the week. She hadn't intended to. She was afraid that they would grow tired of each other, that their budding relationship would start to bend under the stresses of togetherness. She worried that Jackson would press her to reveal her feelings for him, now that he had told her that he loved her, and she wasn't prepared for that. She wasn't even sure how she felt about his loving her, let alone how she felt about him.

But, to her amazement, none of her forebodings materialized. He did not mention again that he loved her. She could feel it in his caresses and see it in the way he looked at her sometimes, but those moments only created a feeling a warmth inside her, not anxiety or pressure. Nor did he ask how she felt about him or even try to work the conversation in that direction.

They did not grow tired of each other. Jackson was gone most of every day, working, leaving Beth to putter around the house, taking care of the baby and doing whatever she wished. She visited Cory and Cater a few times. Cater lived in a restored turn-of-the-century house, and he let Cory have the garage apartment out back while he was going to U.T. Cater, who was plotting his newest book, was stuck and was happy to avoid the problem for a few hours of talking or playing with the baby or going to a movie. Of all her brothers, Cater's personality was the most suited to Beth's, and though he was not the closest to her in age, they got along the best. Cory, as always, was thrilled to have an opportunity to see Joseph. It had surprised everyone the way he had fallen for Joey, for Cory had been the most sports-oriented of the boys, the most likely to return to the ranch, not someone interested in children. Now he was talking about changing his major to elementary education.

Beth told herself that this week was not a real indicator of what life with Jackson would be like, that it did not show that he was the perfect man for her. After all, she wasn't working and had nothing to do but take care of the baby in a beautiful home and putter around doing whatever she felt like. When she and Jackson were together, it was special, not something that was going to continue to happen for the rest of their lives. It was fun because it was temporary, and at the end of the week they would return to their lives.

Beth drove home on Sunday. Jackson asked her to stay a few extra days. He had to return to L.A. Thursday, he told her, so they wouldn't be able to see each other on the weekend. But much as Beth did not want to leave, her mind kept telling her that she should. She was with Jackson too much, she thought; it was coloring her thinking. She was drifting into thinking that she was in love with him, that they might have a life together, and she told herself that such thinking was dangerous. They were very different; they led different lives and expected different things. She needed to be by herself, she thought, to see things from another perspective.

The other perspective, she quickly found, was loneliness. She had hardly driven out of Austin before she began to miss Jackson. She told herself that it was silly, that it was only temporary.

Unfortunately the temporary condition went on far too long. Beth found herself wanting to turn and say something to him. She stored up little anecdotes about the baby or Angel Eye or her father to tell him. She missed his laugh. She missed his smile. She missed his warm arms around her. At night in bed, she woke up and reached for him, then realized with a dropping heart that he was not there. Sometimes she cried, even as she told herself that she was being ridiculous.

To occupy herself, she worked on her portrait of Jackson and Joey with renewed zeal. It was coming to life beneath her hands, and there were moments when she was sure it was going to turn out to be one of the best things she had ever done. She thought about Jackson's face when she gave it to him, and the thought made her smile.

Jackson called her every night, even during the time when he was in Los Angeles. He sounded tired, and Beth was aware of an urge to be with him, to make him smile with a quip or a story, to smooth the frown from his brow and massage the knots of tension out of his neck and shoulders. He told her that he missed her, too, and they made plans for her to drive up to Austin again as soon as he returned.

Then Joseph got a cold. It was the first time he had ever been sick, and Beth nearly panicked. His nose started running, and he had the sniffles. His skin was hot to her touch. He got worse as the evening went by, and her father's assertion that it was only a cold did nothing to ease her fears. The doctor's office was closed when she called, but one of the other pediatricians in the practice soon returned her call. He, too, did not seem overly impressed by Joseph's symptoms, and he suggested that she bring him into the office the next morning, meanwhile giving him liquid acetaminophen to reduce the fever. But Joseph was cranky and wouldn't go to sleep. He continued to cry, no matter how much she rocked him or patted him. He would fall asleep for a few minutes, then wake up and cry again.

About nine o'clock she called Jackson. "Joey's sick."

"What's the matter with him?" Jackson sounded alarmed.

"It's a cold. The doctor says it's not an emergency, and so does Dad, but he sounds so awful and chuggy, and he won't sleep." To her surprise, her voice hovered near tears. "I'm sorry to bother you."

"No. Don't be sorry. Listen, I'll drive down there."

That did make tears start in her eyes. "No, that's okay. It's not anything, really. I know I'm being a worrywart. I'm sure the doctor's right."

"But you shouldn't be worrying alone."

He made it to the ranch in less than three hours, setting a speed record for time from Austin, Beth was sure. When he rang the doorbell and Beth opened the door, her heart lifted. Joey was just the same, but suddenly she *felt* better. Jackson enfolded her and the baby in his arms, and Beth leaned her head against his shoulder, feeling comforted.

Insisting that Beth go to bed and get some rest, Jackson stayed up with the baby, rocking and walking with him. Finally he lay down on the bed with Beth, the baby between them, and the three of them slept.

* * *

About five o'clock, the baby woke up, crying, and Beth fed him. Jackson sat up, sleepy-eyed, and rubbed his head, looking around him vaguely. "How's he doing?"

"Okay, I think." Beth grinned sheepishly. "I feel like an idiot for getting you down here. Kids have colds all the time."

"Yeah. But it's a first for this one. And for you," Jackson replied, smiling. "I better get back to Austin. Why don't you and Joey come with me? We could take him to a pediatrician there."

She shook her head. "No. I'm sure he'll be fine. I probably ought to take him to his regular doctor. They have his records."

"Okay. Will you come up when he's feeling better?"

Beth nodded. "This weekend, probably."

"And you'll call me if he gets worse—or you'll come to Austin?"

"I promise."

He reached out and cupped her cheek tenderly. "I love you."

"I love you, too," Beth replied automatically.

Jackson froze, staring at her intently. "Really?"

Beth smiled self-consciously. She hadn't even known she was going to say it until she did, but she knew that it was the truth. "Yes. Really."

He grinned. "Beth..." He reached out and took her hand. "When you come to Austin this time, stay with me. I mean, for longer than a week or even two. I—I want you stay with me forever.''

Beth stared at him, astonished. "What are you saying?''

He paused, considering, looking a little amazed himself. "I think I'm asking you to marry me.''

"What!'' Beth jumped to her feet, fear clutching her stomach. "But, Jackson...this is so—''

"So sudden?'' he ventured, his eyes lighting with amusement. "So unexpected? Isn't that what they say in old novels?''

Beth giggled. "I guess so. But I'm serious. I don't think you've taken the time to think about this.''

"I don't have to think. What matters is how I feel. I know that I love you. I know that I've been miserable for a week without you. I know that I was happier that week when you and the baby were with me than I have been at any other time in my life.''

"But, Jackson...''

"But what? You just said that you loved me.''

"Yes, I do. But that's a big step—from loving someone to marrying them. People do fall out of love.''

"I'm not going to fall out of love with you. And I won't stop loving Joey, either. We're a family, Beth, and we have been since the day Joey was born. I knew it then, but I was too embarrassed and disbelieving to say so. From the day I met you, I haven't been happy apart from you.''

Pleasure flushed Beth's cheeks, but she stepped

back, shaking her head. "I don't know. I—I'd have to think about it. There are things to consider. I mean, you have to live in Los Angeles. And I live in Dallas."

"You could do what you do anywhere in the country. There are just as many—no, I'm sure there are *more* people in L.A. who want to have portraits painted than there are in Dallas. If nothing else, it's bigger—and think of the egos. I have a room in my house that would be perfect for a studio—great sun, a beautiful view. But we don't have to live in Los Angeles, either. We could live wherever we wanted. There are lots of movie people who don't reside there. Between computers and faxes and phones and planes, you can communicate all you want with the studios. Hell, you can't get away from those people anywhere in the world. I know—I've tried."

Beth smiled faintly. "It's not just that. It's the idea of Joey having to grow up the child of a famous person, of his always being thrust into the spotlight. Those tabloids messing in our lives. Having people intrude on me and my family like that—following us and taking pictures of us and popping up everywhere, printing wild stories all the time."

"They *are* a fact of life. But you'll learn to deal with them. I promise. I have. And, really, this is the most exposure I've had in them except for when I dated Melanie Hanson. Even then, it was because they wanted stuff on her, not me. Once this blows over, they'll hardly ever have stories about us. Directors and producers just aren't the fodder that actors and singers and models are. And I promise you that I will put everything I've got into making sure that you and Joseph are shielded from them. It's possible. Other people have kept their kids out of the limelight.''

Looking at him, Beth wanted to say yes. Her love for him welled up in her, but still she held back. She had to be practical, she thought. She had to think for both herself and Joseph. She could not afford to make a wrong decision again just because she was in love with a man. She had to make sure that there was a solid basis for their relationship, that they could make it work.

Seeing her hesitation, Jackson reached out and took her arms reassuringly. ''Hey. You don't have to give me an answer right now. I'm not trying to rush you. I love you, and I'm willing to live with your decision. If you don't want to marry me, I'll accept it. If you want to wait for a while, that's fine, too. This isn't a now or never proposition. I told you—I plan on loving you for the rest of your life.''

Beth smiled gratefully at him. ''Thank you. I do need time to think about it. I just don't...want to make a mistake.''

''Sure.'' He bent and kissed her on the forehead, then stepped back. ''You're coming up this weekend, if Joey's feeling better?''

She nodded, and he left. Beth followed him to the door and stood watching until his car disappeared in a cloud of dust down their road. *What was she going to do?*

Beth spent the rest of the week nursing Joey through his first cold. As her father and the doctor had indicated, it was a rather minor ailment, and he was feeling better by the end of the day, his fever gone. Within two days, his runny nose was drying up, and he could breathe more easily.

Beth found that her own problem, however, was not as easy to deal with. She kept thinking about Jackson and his proposal, in a quandary about what to do. She thought of how much she loved him and how happy they had been together. But she reminded herself that she had to be logical, that one week of getting along beautifully did not mean that their whole lifetime would follow the same pattern. *What would their life be like when they had to deal with problems? How would they get along when things were rocky instead of smooth?* And no matter how much she loved him, she just was not sure that she could handle the fame. She had hated the way the tabloids had intruded on her life. *Wouldn't it be much worse once they were married?*

When she wasn't worrying over her decision to marry or not marry Jackson, she thought about Robert Waring. Ever since Jackson had told Beth about his daughter, she had been wondering if she had been wrong not to tell her former lover that she was pregnant. Maybe his reaction wouldn't have been what she expected. Even if he was a creep, maybe he would have been interested in Joseph; maybe Joseph would benefit from having a father.

Wouldn't Joey wonder about his father when he grew up? And what was Beth to say about the man? That she had decided without even asking Robert that he would not be interested in knowing whether he had a son? That she had decided for both of them that Joseph should have no father? Perhaps things *had* turned out better because Jackson's girlfriend had not told him that she was pregnant. But perhaps they hadn't. At least Jessica had had the excuse of being a teenage girl who had listened to her parents' advice. Beth had made the decision all on her own, as a grown woman. *What if she had just been punitive toward the man because he had hurt her?*

That thought cut Beth like a knife. She couldn't bear to think that she might have made a decision that was unfair or even harmful to her child simply because she wanted to get back at the man who had deceived her. And how could she ever really be free of the man if she knew that she had deceived him in turn?

Finally, on the morning when she was to drive to Austin again, still debating what she was going to tell Jackson, Beth decided to end one of her worries. She picked up the phone and dialed a Chicago number, a little surprised to find that it took her a moment to recall it. Once it had been indelibly etched on her brain. It was Robert's private line, and his secretary did not pick it up.

After three rings, Robert's familiar low voice answered, crisp and efficient. For an instant, Beth's throat closed and she could not answer.

She cleared her throat. "Hello, Robert."

There was a stunned silence on the other end of the line.

"This is Beth Sutton," she went on.

"Yes. I recognized your voice," he replied coolly. "I just could not believe that you had had the nerve to call."

"What?" Anger bubbled inside Beth. *He* was upset with *her?*

"After that righteous indignation of yours, now I find out that you were seeing that Hollywood director all the time. My secretary showed me a copy of that tabloid and said, 'Elizabeth Sutton? Isn't that the name of the woman in Texas who used to call you?' Of course, she just thought it was a curiosity. She didn't realize you had been telling me you were in love with me all the while you were having an affair with him."

"I can't believe this. *You* are accusing *me* of infidelity? After what you did? To begin with, those stories are untrue, and even if they were, at least I wasn't married with two children. I wasn't cheating on my spouse!"

"You were lying," he retorted evenly. "I find it

hypocritical of you to berate me because I lied to you."

"I didn't lie to you. Honestly, Robert, I wouldn't have thought you naive enough to believe the tabloids. Or is it just a convenient excuse for you? Makes you feel less in the wrong?"

"My God, Beth, I saw the picture of you with him on the front of one of them." For the first time there was the faintest thread of emotion in his cool voice.

Beth had to smother a giggle at the thought of Robert, handsome and dignified in his Italian suit, picking up a tabloid and devouring it. "Well, believe what you want, Robert. I called you because over the months I have realized that I—acted unfairly."

"Stop right there." There was an irritating smugness in his voice. "Please don't humiliate yourself, Beth. I can assure you that there is no chance of our resuming our affair."

Beth let out an inelegant snort. "That is *not* why I called. What I *am* trying to tell you is that when I found out that I was pregnant, I made a unilateral decision to keep the baby and raise it as a single parent. I decided not to even tell you. I've thought about it a lot recently, and I realize that I may have been unfair. You probably had the right to know that I was pregnant with your child. I shouldn't have kept it from you."

There was another long silence. Then Robert's glacial voice said, "If you think that you are going to get a dime out of me for that baby, you are dead wrong. The whole world knows that it's Prescott's.''

"It is *not* Jackson's child,'' Beth snapped back, fury rising in her. "How dare you accuse me of something like that!''

"Don't be absurd. It's obvious that you're hoping to get money out of me in return for not bringing a paternity suit. And I'm telling you right now that you won't win. That child is not mine, and I will not let you extort me into paying child support.''

For the first time in her life, Beth was so furious that she literally saw red. It took her a moment before she was in control of herself enough to speak evenly. She thought of this man, who would not even acknowledge Joseph, and she thought of Jackson, driving three hours to see Joey when he caught a cold. "You are absolutely right, Robert. You are not his father and you never could be. Jackson Prescott is his father.''

She hung up the phone with a sharp click. Then she threw her things into the car, wrapped up the portrait of Jackson and the baby and stuck it in, too. At last, after strapping the baby in his car seat, she set out for Austin.

Her confrontation with Robert Waring had left her feeling free, not only of him, but of the fears that her relationship with him had engendered in her. She wanted to race to Jackson, to tell him that suddenly, from an unexpected source, she had been shown the path she should take. Maybe her heart had played her false with Robert. She had fallen impetuously in love with him without really knowing him. But her affair with Robert Waring was a far different thing from the love that had developed between her and Jackson, just as Jackson was a far different man than Robert.

Even though she had spent only a brief time with Jackson, as she had with Robert, she knew Jackson as she had never known Robert. She had seen him in a crisis; she had felt his support and strength. They had weathered some bad times; she had just been fooled by the fact that they had done so with laughter and warmth. The race to the hospital, childbirth, even the ridiculous confrontation between Jackson and her brothers, had all been problems, as had the stories splashed all over the tabloids. It was simply because they had gotten through them so well that she had thought they had never faced anything but happy times.

She had seen Robert for only brief stretches of time, moments that had been consumed with the physical fire between them. But she and Jackson had been together day and night. They had been together making love and changing Joey's diaper. She knew him—knew how he acted, what he thought, how he handled things. Perhaps she did not know every detail about him, but she knew the essentials, the things that really mattered, as she had never known with Robert Waring. It didn't take a lifetime to figure out that she loved Jackson or that he was the right man for her. It only took letting go of her fears and listening to her heart.

She zipped along the roads leading to Austin, listening to music and singing along. She hoped Jackson would be home when she got there, as he had been the last time.

He was. But this time when he came out to greet her, there was an oddly wary look in his eyes. Beth hopped out of the car, smiling, and ran to leap into his arms and hug him fiercely. She began to rain kisses all over his face, and he laughed with delight, finally seizing her face between his hands and holding her still long enough for a thorough welcome kiss.

They got the baby out of the car and carried the bags inside. Jackson carried the baby, talking to him and checking him out for any lingering signs of his illness. Beth walked into the open living area and whirled around to face him. She beamed across the room at Jackson.

"I've got something to tell you."

"Wait." Jackson sighed. "You'd probably better see this first. You're going to come across it sooner or later. We might as well get it over with."

Beth frowned, his grim expression sending tendrils of fear creeping through her. "See what?" She had the awful feeling that all her plans and hopes had just come to naught.

He crossed to the coffee table in front of the sofa and picked up a thin magazine. Beth let out a groan, recognizing a tabloid even at that distance. "Not another article."

Jackson nodded. "It's a beaut."

He handed it to her. Across the top, above the name *Scandal*, ran a headline about the mummy of an alien baby, thousands of years old, that had been found in Egypt. The rest of the paper was filled with a picture of Jackson with his arm around a beautiful blond woman. Both of them were smiling broadly and obviously happy. The caption read: Prescott Dumps Texas Cutie, Returns to His First Love. The woman was Melanie Hanson, one of the most beautiful and popular actresses in Hollywood.

Beth's heart felt as if it had dropped to her toes. For a moment she couldn't speak. She simply stared at the picture as though, if she looked long enough, it would somehow change into something more acceptable. She looked up bleakly. "Jackson?"

"God, Beth, don't look at me like that. It's not true. I swear to you that it isn't."

"But that's you. That's her. It doesn't look spliced."

"It's not. That is us. We had dinner together when I was in Los Angeles last weekend. And we were happy to see each other. But it isn't what they say. Melanie and I are friends. That's it. We are very good friends. It doesn't mean any more than a picture of you and one of your brothers with your arms around each other."

"But you said the other day that you and she were once an item. Didn't you?"

"Yes. And we were. We dated some when she first starred in one of my movies. But we quickly realized that we weren't interested in each other romantically. We liked each other, but as friends. We've been good friends ever since. She and I have gone out like this a hundred times, and they've never made a big deal of it before. It's just because of the stories about you and Joseph. They're trying to keep the story going. To sell papers."

"Oh." Beth had been watching his face, and now she looked back down at the paper in her hand. It seemed bizarre that any man would not be madly in love with a woman as beautiful as this one.

"It's you I love, Beth. You are the only one." He looked at her anxiously, his muscles so taut with tension that the baby picked up on it and began to whimper in his arms.

"Okay. I believe you."

Jackson let out an enormous sigh of relief. "Thank God." He started toward her. "I was afraid that I was going to lose you."

"No. I've learned to have faith in you. Not the tabloids." She grinned. "Besides, I'm making a vow. I am going to learn to deal with them."

"I promise you, I will put a stop to these stories somehow. I won't let it happen again."

"That's going to be a pretty tall order. You know how the tabloids are about Hollywood weddings."

He stopped again, staring. "What? Are you saying that—"

"I mean, when we get married, they'll be flying over with helicopters and trying to sneak into the church and all that, won't they?"

Jackson's face lit up. "Yes, they will. And you know what, at this moment I don't really care."

He crossed the remaining stretch of floor in two long steps and pulled her against him with his free arm. The baby, in his other arm, cooed, watching them intently, as Jackson bent and kissed Beth.

Jackson raised his head, grinning. "Hell, we just might invite them to the wedding."

* * * * *

THE NINE-MONTH KNIGHT

Cait London

For Mommies and Daddies who crochet baby booties,
or would like to.

Chapter 1

"Am I being sent off to kindergarten?" Ethan Saber, president and CEO of Saber Baby Foods and heir to the Saber fortunes, flicked the yellow sticky paper square his secretary had just slapped on his suit lapel.

After tagging him, his efficient secretary, Mrs. Daisy Hewson, had just rushed out of his office. Ethan frowned; he had glimpsed tears in the usually placid green eyes of Daisy.

The breeze from his open office window gently toyed with an array of other yellow sticky papers pasted across his desk, stirring them like little square flower petals. Perhaps the flower image had come to him because of Daisy's sweet, delicate scent. At thirty-seven, Ethan had had little softness in his life—his parents had died in a plane crash when he was eighteen. An only child, he'd teethed on Saber's business interests, and labeled a "boy-genius," he'd taken over the reins of the company while getting his college degree.

He'd had no time for softness, or indulging in whimsy. For the past five years, Daisy had given him a taste of feminine softness that had only sharpened his awareness of his sterile, cold life away from the office.

Ethan smoothed the yellow paper square with a caress of his fingertips and settled down with his thoughts about Daisy Hewson—newly flustered and disorganized widow. Daisy had served him efficiently for years and now it was his time to understand her needs.

Midmorning noises of Denver, the settling into a workday, purred through the window. Ethan glanced out at the huge, modern Saber Baby Foods sign, glistening in polished copper. Everything was as it should be as March moved into April—snow upon the mountains west of Denver, the scent of spring tantalizing, but not yet arrived…everything was as expected, except Daisy.

Widowship had befallen Daisy just three weeks before, and though a little pale, she had worked through the first day of her husband's death—

A low, protective, primitive snarl vibrated near him, and Ethan realized it had come from him. Howie Hewson, Daisy's husband of ten years, was no more responsible than the children who dined on Saber

Baby Foods. Yet Daisy had clung to her marriage, shoring it up with her paycheck from Saber, until Howie had plowed his race car into a sheer mountain cliff.

Ethan shifted in the executive chair, shaken by the arousal hardening his six-foot-two-inch muscular body.

At eight-thirty on an everyday Monday morning, sweet, quiet, efficient Daisy Hewson, dressed in her neat, pink shirtwaist dress, had just sent him a hot steamy look from beneath her lashes. Wisps of her naturally sun-lightened hair had escaped her smooth chignon, and her eyes had darkened to meadow green. She looked as if she wanted to paste herself to him, and the bodice of her pristine blouse had heaved several times as if she couldn't catch her breath. Ethan had not been able to pry his gaze from her breasts and when their eyes met, something live and hot crackled between them. He could feel traces of the powerful jolt running through him now, lingering over his skin and lodged in his bones.

He'd wanted to sweep sweet, newly widowed Daisy Hewson over his shoulder and bear her off to his lair—

Then with shocked, wide green eyes and a horrified gasp, Daisy had slapped him with the sticky paper note. She had hurried out of his executive office with a tiny, muffled and horrified cry.

Ethan sat up quickly, disgusted with himself. He'd lived a life of control and he had compassion for his employees' lives as they revolved around his own sterile existence—come to work, put in a hard, hard day, go home and work more.

He patted the yellow paper square on his lapel, keeping it on him. As a new widow, Daisy needed to be understood and cherished. Instead Ethan had wanted to—he glanced guiltily at his desk and blinked away the image of Daisy lying hot and rosy beneath him.

His hand trembled as he removed the sticky paper and brought it to his nose for Daisy's light fragrance. He forced himself to relax. Having the dynamic, surprising hots for a new widow, and a woman he respected and liked, disturbed him.

Women hadn't been his favorite jar of pureed carrots. In his limited experience, women were more like—he foraged for the right comparison, thinking of Saber's lines of baby food, beginner to intermediate to toddler finger foods. Women were like Saber's toddler chicken and noodles, finger food version. Once off the predictable spoon-to-lips path, women were slippery, elusive and didn't always run with the pack. Daisy, however, had always been there for him—like his handy pocket recorder.

Ethan read the note Daisy had slapped on him, caressing it with his thumb. *I am so sorry. I forgot your dry cleaning and I have lost Norman's Carrot and Pea file. I believe I shredded it on Friday. I'll understand if you fire me.*

"Not a chance. I'm not letting you go," Ethan

muttered, because as much as he liked and respected Daisy, she wasn't getting away from him. Not after *that look.*

Ethan inhaled abruptly as he replaced the note to his lapel. He liked the idea of Daisy tagging him as if she'd just bagged him, and he was her property. He wanted to protect Daisy and soon everything would return to normal. In a year or so, after the pain of Howie's death had eased, Ethan might ask her out to a quiet dinner and proceed with a quiet, firm courtship to secure her.

Daisy huddled in Saber's dark paper-supply room, her stomach playing an uncertain yo-yo. She shivered, wiping away the slight perspiration on her upper lip that nausea always brought.

Ethan Saber was the most respected man she knew. He was a perfect employer, even when he was wrestling with a business problem, and he was always courteous and thoughtful to her, never taking her for granted...and she had almost jumped him.

At thirty-one, Daisy had experienced her first gripping need to pounce on a man, drag him upon any flat surface and have him.

In that moment, Ethan's expression had swung from surprise and curiosity, into a darker emotion. His black brows had jammed together in an instant frown. His jaw had locked as a dark and primitive emotion had flickered in his brown eyes—just for an instant, because Ethan was always a gentleman.

Daisy shook with that desire now, trying to shove it away.

She placed her trembling, damp fingers over her face and tried to dislodge the image of Ethan rubbing his hand across his expensive business shirt. The gesture was his everyday, thoughtful one, and it had never affected her. Yet today, that whorl of hair beneath the taut fabric had fascinated her and she wanted that roughness pasted and sweaty against her aching breasts.

She looked down at her breasts. They were fuller, and more sensitive than she could believe. The slightest brush caused them to peak and ache. "I know I am pregnant. Howie's hit-and-run to the finish line on the night before he died—"

She groaned, mourning the debts of Howie's funeral and the payments she could not meet. She heard her wail echo off the filled shelves of the neat room, just as the door jerked open and Ethan's tall, powerful body blocked the hallway light.

"Daisy?" he asked softly, finding her in the shadows.

"Please don't turn on the light," she whispered, wanting to fling herself into Ethan's strong arms and huddle against him. Unlike Howie, Ethan was a man to depend on, a gentle, thoughtful man. "You'll be late for your meeting, and you don't have your dry cleaning—I forgot to pick up that power suit you like to wear in negotiation."

Her unsettled stomach began to churn and as Ethan

came toward her, Daisy threw out her hands. "I won't blame you, if you fire me. I'll do my best to find you the most efficient, experienced replacement possible—"

"You shouldn't have insisted on coming back to work so soon—on working the morning of the funeral. You need time off to deal with your loss—" Ethan began in his deep, soothing voice.

He was so kind, Daisy thought hazily, just before she spewed her breakfast on the gleaming Italian shoes of Saber Baby Foods' heir, president of the board and CEO.

Without a pause, Ethan grasped her arm in one hand and stuffed paper towels into her other hand. "I see we have a problem," he noted briskly.

"We?" she panted, her stomach still churning, as she wiped her mouth. Anger crackled through her; "we" hadn't just thrown up on the boss's expensive shoes. "We" weren't facing unpaid bills and a baby. "We" weren't a woman with aching breasts and a sudden, shocking, palpitating desire to rip off the boss's shirt. Daisy groaned, shaken by her unfamiliar anger.

Ethan quickly stepped out of the unsavory breakfast pond, wiped his shoes and tugged her gently to one side. He pushed the door shut, blotted her lips with an elegant monogrammed handkerchief and then enfolded her briefly in his arms. "You're shaking. You're ill. I knew you shouldn't have come back to work so soon, but you insisted. Every day, your haunted look has worsened. You haven't taken time to deal with your tragedy. This is my fault for asking too much of you, too soon. I want you to go home right now and take the rest of the week off.''

She wilted against him, drained by sleepless nights and hours of trying to juggle bills. Against hers, his body seemed too safe— ''I can't go home. I have to work. You don't understand. Mr. Saber, you're going to fire me and I have to hunt for another job.''

Ethan snorted eloquently—an arrogant, in-charge, powerful male snort. He picked her up and carried her back to his office as if it were a task he performed every day. As he passed Miss Morefield, the wide-eyed office gossip, he ordered, ''I don't want to be bothered. See to it. Daisy is ill. Send the janitor to the supply room.''

Miss Morefield pounced on anyone's poor fortune, happily empowering herself. ''Daisy has been making mistakes, expensive ones all week. I saw her climbing into the outside trash bin on Friday, sobbing like a maniac over shredded files—''

Miss Morefield shrunk from the whip of Ethan's grim stare.

''Stop squirming, Daisy. You're not going anywhere until we resolve your health, and this nonsense about me firing you. I have no plans to do that, and don't tell me I do,'' he ordered as he entered his office and kicked the door shut. Then he paused, and as in an afterthought, pushed off his besmirched shoes before carrying her to his large desk chair. He sat, cra-

dling her in his lap as he poured ice water from the
carafe on his desk and lifted the glass to her lips.

"Drink. Rest here a few moments before you use
my private washroom to refresh. You're shaking. I
don't want to fill out an accident report because I let
you get back on those shaking legs too soon."

Daisy drank, then pressed the cold glass to her hot
cheek. She'd just thrown up on Saber's no-nonsense,
CEO's shoes! Ethan's big hand urged her head to his
shoulder, then settled lightly, impersonally across her
thigh. "There now. Take it easy. Something is wrong,
Daisy. I'd like to help."

She shuddered delicately, sitting very stiffly upon
him. "I am sorry about the Norman's Carrot and Pea
files. Our shredder is very effective."

He smoothed her dress lightly, his hand skimming
her thigh. "Saber is known for acquiring high quality
products. I'm certain that the files can be duplicated
easily by Norman's."

Ethan sniffed the air close to her hair. "I've been
meaning to ask you— Are you wearing a new fragrance? It seems…tangier…zestier…muskier, than
your usual fresh scent."

"Soap," Daisy explained, listening to the solid
beat of his heart. She didn't want to tell him that to
save money, she had been pilfering the hand soap in
Saber's ladies room and washing her clothing with it.
Guilt wrapped around her as if it were a shroud. Everything about Ethan was solid and dependable…if
only— "Ah…I can stand now. The gossip—"

Ethan's snort was eloquent, as he helped her to stand. He took the glass from her. "Take your time in the washroom, and don't lock the door. I wouldn't want to break it down, if you collapse. When you come out, be prepared to tell me what is bothering you. I have no plans to release you, and I can understand your grief and temporary disorientation. I lost my parents at a young age and had to take over the Saber helm immediately. I had no one to lean on, as I want to do for you now. I don't want to lose a good employee because I did not take time to help." After a quick, hard searching glance at her, Ethan turned his attention to the stacks of paper on his desk.

Daisy blinked at those stacks. They weren't her usual neat style, preparing Saber's CEO to meet his challenges. She hadn't sorted incoming from outgoing and hadn't placed the appropriate files on his desk— it was a mess. She hadn't collected outgoing mail since the middle of last week. She noticed the new roll of stamps on Ethan's desk—he'd been mailing his own— Horrified that she wasn't performing to top standards and that Saber's CEO had not complained, Daisy glanced guiltily at his damaged shoes. Ethan's neatly pressed shirt was wrinkled from her lying against him, and *he had carried her through the gray, posh, dignified halls of Saber Baby Foods!*

She escaped into the executive washroom, to splash cold water over her burning cheeks. She gripped the sink and stared into the shadowed eyes of a condemned woman, because once Ethan wanted to solve a puzzle, he did, and he had no patience with employees who performed badly. Daisy pulled away the combs tethering her ruined chignon, ran her fingers through her smooth dark blond hair and prepared herself for the worst—unemployment.

"You've taken off your jacket! Your sleeves are rolled up and *you are not wearing a tie!*" Daisy exclaimed as she came back into the room. Her gaze locked to the unfamiliar vase of flowers on her employer's usually neat and sterile desk.

"Shoot me," Ethan returned evenly, and realized that in all their five years together, he had always been careful about his office attire. When taking over the reins of Saber, he had been a youth, and needed the protective shield of a business suit; he hadn't changed the concept of image and business. Since he had no friends, other than business acquaintances, there was no reason to change the standard he had set early in life.

He sensed now that he faced a real challenge to make Daisy understand how dear—he corrected the term—how much he needed her effective, pleasant self near him. Removing his jacket, tie and rolling up his sleeves was a move toward an informal, friendly relationship with a woman he respected, and whom he wanted to trust him. The bouquet of flowers that he had quickly snatched from Martha Bush's desk added a touch of intimate softness. He hoped the one-hundred-dollar bill would sufficiently compensate

Martha. He stood and guided Daisy to a chair near his desk. "I want to know what all this is about, Daisy. You can trust me."

She wilted tiredly into the chair and for a moment, his hand hovered over the freed skeins of her dark blond hair. She looked so worn, filled with sleepless nights as she looked up at him. "I know."

Ethan tumbled into that shadowy soft green gaze, the air crushed from his body. He leaned back against the desk, gripping the edge hard to keep his hands from touching her flushed cheek. "Upset tummy?" he asked gently as she twisted her hands—such soft capable hands, taking dictation at the speed of light, neatening his desk...

Startled, Daisy stared up at him. "Tummy?"

Ethan realized that his conversations with Daisy were usually set in business language. He smiled briefly. "A word I picked up from Saber's Happy Tummy ads. Are you feeling better?"

"Yes...no."

"You look a little pale." Ethan reached behind him for a small jar of Saber's best Apple Pie. He popped it open and stuck a sampling spoon into it. "Here. The stuff is actually good. I have some when I'm running fast or my stomach is acting up. The meats make a good paté or sandwich spread. I've got crackers in my desk—would you rather have Saber's chicken?"

Daisy shook her head and took the small jar, examining it as her hands trembled. "Baby food," she whispered in a haunted, hollow tone that echoed uneasily in Ethan's keen mind.

When Ethan tapped the bottom of the jar with his finger, Daisy dutifully took a few bites. Then she looked at him, her green eyes shimmering in tears. Her helpless expression snared Ethan's scarred heart and he found himself plucking her into his arms. He settled down into his chair, with her on his lap. Daisy began to cry—at first just a whimper, and then as Ethan murmured, "There, there," she released a mournful wail that terrified him.

His terror settled into an awareness of how soft Daisy's body was, lying against his. How an elusive musk circled and enticed him. Her packaging was perfectly feminine, round and firm, and needed no explanatory labeling of ingredients.

Ethan swallowed slowly. He was a man without honor, one who craved the woman he should have been comforting. He realized that his open hand was lying on her thigh, his fingers slightly possessive. Ethan moved his hand upward gently, only to discover his fingers locked to her soft thigh. He swallowed again, imagining those thighs locked around him. "I am a cad," he muttered.

"I'm pregnant!" she returned in another frustrated wail, shaking in his arms, her expression desperate.

"That's...nice," Ethan managed to say after he caught his breath. His mind raced at warp speed, darting back to Daisy's insistence that she work, barely taking time off for the funeral. His business mind kicked in—Daisy was alone, defenseless and perfect for takeover.

His honor slapped him, cold and hard, and he gathered Daisy protectively to him. For years he'd watched her struggle with her lazy, spoiled husband. Howie's calls sometimes caused her to pale, and she was forever cubbyholed with her checkbook and a calculator during her lunch break. Or patching socks. Howie never took Daisy to lunch, and always dressed spiffy to her plain, cheaper clothing. Just once, Ethan wished, the dead would rise, and he could punch Howie in his soft, spoiled, woman-chasing gut.

"There's no insurance. Howie cashed it in," Daisy was saying. "This week the telephone company cut off the service. Not that anyone calls. My parents died four years ago. I couldn't pay the electricity bill— Howie had just added more power gadgets to his sports car."

Daisy's dam of secrets had cracked and broken; Ethan understood why his usually efficient, calm secretary had been unnerved. He gathered her tighter. He remembered a telling scenario: When Daisy's parents died within a month of each other, Howie couldn't be bothered to come home from a fishing trip with his buddies.

Ethan nuzzled Daisy's silky, fragrant hair. It caught, webbed along his jaw and Ethan wallowed in the caress. He gave himself to developing a plan to keep Daisy near him at all times. He gathered himself for a long shot, sliding it out to Daisy in a calm that veiled his excitement. "You need to trust someone, Daisy. Someone to share your dark moments—you are just recovering from your—"

The word stuck in Ethan's throat; he did not like to think of Howie touching Daisy. Ethan used all his concentration to focus back on acquiring Daisy in a more personal mode. "You're facing too many difficulties now, Daisy, and perhaps it's wrong of me to offer this now, but I've had an idea brewing for a time. If you are pregnant—"

"Oh, I am. Those baby-test things—twice—said so. I don't have money—I had to drop my health insurance from Saber's. We couldn't afford it and the race car Howie wanted." Her fingers gripped his shoulders and Ethan tensed, fighting the desire to crush her to him. He'd been alone for most of his life and now, deep inside him, he knew that he needed Daisy.

Daisy. The image of a slender stalk, topped by a lovely swaying, fragrant bloom and softening a bleak, rock-filled desert landscape, slid through his mind. Winds buffeted and bent the flower, tore at it, yet the sweet daisy remained—sweet. His arms tightened. Sweet and curved, packaging that needed no labeling.

She raised up suddenly, her face on a level with his. Anger vibrated through her, her green eyes narrowed at him.

Ethan watched, fascinated as this new Daisy emerged.

She slashed her hair back from her flushed cheek. "Howie made a habit of hurrying to the finish line."

"What?" Ethan blinked. Howie was an average race car driver, never quite breaking out of the pack.

"Don't you understand? *He hurried to the finish line,*" she stated indignantly. "You'd think that when creating a child, a man would have the decency to make more than momentary contact. That he would cradle and caress, and—"

Ethan's body hardened immediately. He'd been celibate, except for a short-term affair, in which he discovered that his wealth was more appealing than he. He'd tried desperately to find emotion, a relationship, and had failed. He'd decided along the way that he was no bargain as a companion, a man who would be desired for himself, other than his fortunes.

Now his desire to have Daisy, to be her friend, shook him. "I understand 'the finish line.'"

"He always hurried to the finish line. Here I am, pregnant and without the—without the…nice memories of conceiving the child I've always wanted. Not that Howie wanted children. He was meticulous about that. Except he was really excited about the next day's race, and he— Ohhhh!" Daisy wailed in a frustrated tone as she stared at the ceiling and tightened her fists.

A man who did not enter into others' lives and had little experience with emotional women, Ethan felt as if he were tiptoeing through a spongy, snake-filled bog. He patted her tightly curled fists. "A woman should have moments to cherish," he managed to say masterfully, swamped with images of how he wanted to make long, slow love to Daisy.

She gripped him by the shoulders, leaning closer, her nose almost brushing his. A soft, fragrant skein of hair clung to his cheek. Ethan, fascinated by this new Daisy, leaned back.

"Men," she said finally, her tone condemning the sex as pond scum.

"Not all men are so...hurry to the finish line," Ethan argued, pleased with himself for coming up with a soothing, yet protective statement for his sex.

"Would you?" she demanded hotly, as she released his shoulders to cross her arms over her chest. "Would you just flop over and do it, talking about how fast to take an inside curve in the next day's race? Would you?"

Ethan breathed lightly. The insight into the Hewsons's sex life shook him. He had supposed all married couples complied to the national average. He struggled for control, then gently placed a hand on her back. He followed his takeover instincts and urged her closer. "I think that creating a child should take time and consideration. Like a good marketing plan, building momentum to the correct moment of—ah...presentation. Then later, there should be an amount of, ah, goodwill, like a symphony that ends gently."

Daisy slumped, her blast of anger gone, and Ethan waited for a heartbeat before settling her head gently against his shoulder. He rocked her gently, wanting to soothe her, and silently cursed Hewson's lovemaking techniques.

"I'm too emotional," she muttered.

"It's good to get these things out." Ethan smiled confidently into the softness of her hair.

"I haven't had time for friends. There was no one to talk to—you can't just burst upon people and…and I can't sleep."

"I know. The shadows beneath your eyes are becoming." He nuzzled her hair, closing his eyes as he slid into an image of Daisy's creamy body spooned against his as they slept in his bed.

"I've kept you long enough. You're a busy man. I'm sorry—"

Ethan tensed, sensing that she was preparing to leave him. "You're not going anywhere," he stated firmly, and in an afterthought not to frighten her, he added, "Not just yet. I need you."

Daisy eased to her feet and smoothed her slightly wrinkled, pink shirtwaist dress. She ran her fingers through her hair, smoothing it, and Ethan's breath caught as the sunlight lingered, glistening in the silky strands. "I am mortified. I shouldn't have told you all this. I've never told anyone about Howie's—" She flushed, her trembling hands going to her cheeks. "I'll just clean out my desk and—"

Ethan's hand shot out to capture her wrist. "You're not going anywhere. I said I need you and I do— Saber Baby Foods needs you. Now sit down."

Daisy responded well to the employer order, and

Ethan pressed his point. "You've never had a sick day—except those to nurse Howie."

The bastard hadn't cared if his wife were ill, but a slight cold turned Hewson into an invalid.

Ethan waited until Daisy settled into the chair by his desk. His arms felt empty; his whole body felt empty, and he felt alone without her. When had she become so much a part of his life?

Desire for her was a new element, only an hour old, and Ethan struggled to adapt, and woo Daisy into his plan.

Ethan focused on the plan he needed to make himself appealing to Daisy; he would make no mistakes. He turned his chair from her, staring out into the Denver skyline to the mountains, just as he did when he dictated to her.

"You'll be late for your meeting, Mr. Saber," Daisy reminded him quietly. "The advertising company is ready to demonstrate their new campaign for Saber Baby Desserts."

"They can wait." Ethan punched an intercom button to Daisy's outer office. "Cancel my ten o'clock, Miss Morefield. And stop listening at the door. Daisy is helping me to develop a brand-new product and we don't want to be disturbed. She has the essential research I need."

Miss Morefield sputtered a moment, then issued a crisp, "Yes, sir."

Ethan continued to look out the window; he didn't want Daisy to see his eagerness to move into her life.

Ethan allowed himself a brief smile. He had expected to take slow, firm steps to gather her to him, but now— Ethan smiled grimly. He would raise the child as his own. The bottom line of solving the crisis was that Daisy needed a home and a family and he would give her ease.

Daisy would be a perfect mother. A perfect warm wife, a companion, and together they would share life. And sex...when the time was right. He almost felt guilty; taking advantage of a woman in Daisy's position wasn't honorable, but he would do his best to make her happy. "Daisy, Saber Baby Foods needs you. I need you," he added for a touch of honesty. "My new product line idea has been brewing for some time and you're the only one I will have approached with the idea. We need good solid research before presenting the new line, and Saber Baby Foods has always maintained top quality, and testing...research, has been our standard."

He listened, trying to pick through the quiet sniff behind him. "Feeling better?"

Her hesitation was enough to make him pivot the chair toward her. He wanted to see her face when he presented his idea to woo Daisy into his private life. Ethan braced his palms straight on his cluttered desk—he noted Daisy's guilty wince, and decided to deal with it later. He plucked the sticky note from his palm and steepled his fingers, looking over her.

Her gaze dropped to another sticky note pasted to his forearm; Ethan removed it gently. "I've always been involved in the testing and research phases of our product. If this idea is solidly based, Saber Baby Foods could run right over our competitors. Without firsthand experience, I would have no basis to judge whether we should make this substantial investment or not. Product lines should always be thoroughly researched. Do you agree, Daisy?''

"You're always quite thorough, Mr. Saber."

"Ethan. It's time you called me 'Ethan.' I want to be your friend, Daisy, and friends call each other by their first names, don't they?'' he asked gently.

"I guess so." She slumped as if doomed, the sunlight glistening on her hair, catching in the various golden shades. She needed a flower garden to care for, a flower among flowers, Ethan thought whimsically before turning back to the step-by-step process of getting Daisy to see him as a man.

"I need a pregnant woman," Ethan announced boldly.

Chapter 2

"I want you to feel at home," Ethan said two days later, as he opened the door to Daisy's new bedroom. She moved past him into a room larger than her entire tiny apartment. Her entire apartment building could be fitted into Ethan's home.

He glanced at her keenly, then carried her clothing boxes to a cushioned window seat. The shabby, string-wrapped boxes contrasted the elegant, contemporary-styled room. Except for mementos of her family, Daisy had sold everything but her mother's old electric sewing machine to the tenants of her building. She was starting a new life, and carried a new life within her, and Ethan had said he would provide for the baby's needs, even establishing a college fund upon the baby's birth. She couldn't turn down Saber's experimental research offer, with a hefty, monthly retainer to serve her personal needs. She intended to save every penny during her stay with Ethan.

He turned to her with that slow, steady, firm, square-shouldered posture as when he faced the board on difficult matters. "This research project—understanding the cravings of a pregnant woman and the cravings of her male companion, their needs—is absolutely useless without the test individual—you, Daisy—feeling absolutely comfortable in your environment. I want you to devote time to making yourself comfortable, here...in my home...with me. I want genuine reactions from you...at all times of the night...there is a monitor between our bedrooms, which you can turn off for privacy."

Daisy took in the wide, French doors veiled by sheer panels, the expensive contemporary furniture and the bold solid colors of dark brown and gray. The room was starkly masculine as was the rest of the elegant, cold house. Ethan had explained that he had changed little since his parents' deaths, and Daisy mourned the little boy who was not allowed pets or ball games. His palatial home looked like an expensive, cold shell. She shivered, realizing that the room reflected the lack of warmth in Ethan's life. She wrapped her arms around herself, suddenly terrified of the offer she couldn't afford to refuse.

Ethan had no ulterior motives, of course. Their relationship was strictly business and he needed her for intensive research. Saber's investment would run into millions, Ethan had explained, and the continuing craving-needs research of the pregnant woman and the male close to her, had to be rock solid—all the way through the baby's adjustment to Saber's Baby Foods.

Daisy shivered again. In the past two days, her craving-needs had run to kissing Ethan's mouth and tearing his shirt away. That wild desire still quivered within her, leaping like digital lights at one whiff of his masculine lime aftershave and his other, more subtle scents. Ethan Saber was so elegant, so prime, so unaware and innocent of her lurking, unexpected desire for him. She bit her lip. "Are you certain you need me?"

Ethan slowly took off his suit jacket, ripped off his tie and briskly rolled up his sleeves. He opened the drapes, letting in the afternoon sunlight. His eyes, a wonderful shade of melted chocolate, locked with hers. Daisy thought of how much she liked chocolate, in fact craved it now, when Ethan stated, "I need you desperately…ah…the project needs you. Are you uncomfortable living here…with me? It's the only way, you know, to be right on hand when you get those midnight cravings. Good research isn't developed on a hit-and-miss method. It's a note by note, building process, right until the final moment."

"Of course."

"Good. We're agreed," Ethan said, a happy note threading his deep voice. "We'll take the rest of the week, settling you in, getting you comfortable…you know, shopping for furniture that suits a woman like yourself...decorating things—like pots and plants, and those things I see in other homes...and in catalogs. I understand that women like personalized kitchens and bathrooms, so let's not forget those things. You know, familiar gadgets, if you have a cooking urge. I'm rather looking forward to shopping with you. Your apartment seemed homey—like you—and if that is what makes you comfortable, that's how this house should look."

He flipped open the top few buttons of his shirt, exposing a tanned chest lightly sprinkled with hair. Daisy's fingers flexed at her side, aching to prowl through that triangular patch of black hair. Since Ethan had held her on his lap, she craved the press of his body against hers, his arms safe and strong around her. She shouldn't want him, couldn't want him so desperately, yet like a magnet or a sonar system, her body knew exactly where his was at all times. His intentions were strictly business, while she had basically true, but ulterior motives—to be near him...to feel safe in whichever nest Ethan chose to protect.

Daisy tensed, realizing that in the past, she had always protected the nest, paid the bills and made financial decisions; Howie could not tolerate the stress. Now, she had put herself and her baby in Ethan's capable hands.

Ethan's capable hands. A sensual thrill scurried up

Daisy's back. His hands were very large and strong and warm. They were gentle hands—

He nodded to a door. "My room is through that door and to the other side is a smaller room I thought would make an excellent nursery."

A nursery. Where babies were held and loved, and parents stood holding each other when the house settled into night. Howie never cuddled her, or held her more than a few, quick, necessary moments and now Daisy ached to be held. He was her first young love and when she tried to talk to Howie about intimacy, she got a barrage of information on souped-up carburetors. She felt like crying. She'd grabbed Ethan's offer with both fists, unable to resist, even for pride's sake. The lure of financial security, Ethan's new tenderness, and…the immediate closeness of his body had been just as intoxicating as his clean scent.

He bent to place a light, quick kiss on her cheek. "I understand that pregnant women need affection," he explained. "It should be good for the baby, too, a friendly kiss to comfort. I wouldn't want to fall short of helping proper research. A happy, healthy, comfortable environment for the new mother, that's what we are going to create."

Daisy tried to keep focused, her nipples peaking and aching beneath her peach cotton shirtdress. "Ethan, are you certain the research budget for this project includes redecorating your home? After all, you're paying me a tremendous salary, in addition to picking up the medical tabs and putting stock away for my baby.''

"Our baby. I'm playing the expectant father's part, remember? The expectant male is an unexplored market and it isn't wise to overlook possible spin-off lines. I'll be with you every step of the way, Daisy. From the time you go to sleep, until you wake up in the morning—make certain you call me if you have morning sickness. We can work here—" The corner of his mouth tugged, smothering what appeared to be a pleased smile. "I have an office in the other wing. I want you to tell me everything, all of your feelings, those little urges women get. Emotion swings, food cravings...everything."

She had to make a gesture at honesty. "Ethan, you are a respected businessman. Your reputation is meticulous. People will gossip."

Ethan's expression hardened, revealing the determined businessman beneath the surface, the man who always got his way. "There will be no gossip about you. Got it?"

Daisy's tears welled over her lids and down her cheeks. "I'm going to be sick," she whispered, praying desperately that she wouldn't ruin the lush carpeting. She glanced at an empty oriental vase—one that belonged in a museum's Ming dynasty room.

Ethan's big hand shot out to gently claim her arm; he eased her onto the brown bedspread. "You're going to lie down, right now, and I'll have Cook bring you up some toast or crackers to settle your stomach.

I've already read volumes on morning sickness remedies. You should have a bit of something before you rise in the mornings. We'll start that tomorrow. I'll bring a tray to you.''

His grin was sudden, unexpected and quickly gone as he swallowed heavily. He seemed to sway and those marvelous chocolate brown eyes dimmed slightly. ''I'll just get a cold washcloth for your forehead.''

She glanced up at him as he swung her legs onto the bed. ''You're pale.''

''I don't like to see you cry. I think of all the times you cried and no one was there for you...how much pain you must have shielded as you came to work each day.''

He swallowed unevenly. ''And yes, I am feeling a bit queasy. Where is a jar of Saber Baby Food when you need it?'' he asked, his tone threaded with frustration. Tiny beads of perspiration glistened on his upper lip. His usually neat hair stood out in peaks and for just a moment, Saber's impeccable, tough president and CEO looked vulnerable.

No stranger to the vulnerable or upset-stomach game, Daisy tugged his hand. Taking care of Howie's demands had left no time for friend-making, and she desperately needed a friend now. ''Come on. Lie down beside me. We'll both rest for a moment, okay?''

He looked shaken, his free hand running through his hair, rumpling the peaks again. He stared at the space beside her as if it might turn into a deathly swamp at any minute, filled with alligators.

Daisy noted the dark circles beneath his eyes. He'd worked night and day to get the research project going, to get her into his home, and seeing that she ate properly—after discovering there were no groceries in her refrigerator. He'd taken time to take her to breakfast, lunch and dinner, canceling all his important projects—just for her. And the research project. She decided that it was time to start the sharing process with Ethan, telling him the little needs as they occurred to her. "I would like you to lie down with me, Ethan. You seem so imposing standing over me, and I can't decide if I'm sleepy, or if I need a good cry."

"I'll go. I think you need sleep," he stated firmly, quickly, as if her crying terrified him.

"We could talk." Daisy remembered her frustrated wail while he held her. The sound would frighten any man and she gripped his hand when he would have pulled away.

She eyed him, the frightened male in her new lair. On the other hand, this situation wasn't her doing. He'd moved like a freight train, changing her life, and preparing for a new one to suit him. She no longer felt like crying, or felt sympathy for Ethan. She wanted to have him lie down beside her, darn it.

She wanted all six feet two inches of Ethan Saber, lying at her side, within reaching distance. He'd wanted her; he'd gotten her. She glared at him. "This is my first whim,'' she stated too quietly. ''You wanted whims, didn't you?'' she snapped at him.

Her anger surprised her. But Ethan had wanted honesty, saying that without her sharing her thoughts, whims, cravings and needs, the research was invalid. Daisy was alone, frightened of the future and needing Ethan beside her. ''This isn't going to be a convenience thing, is it? Where you respond to my needs when it suits you?''

''I'll always be here when you need me,'' Ethan answered with a touch of anger in his voice. Good, Daisy thought, he's not having everything his way. This guinea pig situation was supposed to include him.

Howie had never responded to her needs. Someone had to pay. The previously sweet gentle Daisy shivered inside the new strong one as Ethan smiled tightly, kicked off his shoes and lay down gingerly on the bed beside her. He sat up quickly, reached to remove her shoes, let them drop and the mattress sagged slightly with his weight as he lay down again. He turned his head slightly on the pillow sham until their gazes met and locked. A heat Daisy didn't understand simmered in the sunlit afternoon. Without looking away, Ethan reached to push a bedside intercom button. ''We're taking our naps now,'' he said in a tone that laid a warm flush over Daisy's skin.

A pan clattered in the background, as if dropped, then a woman asked slowly, ''You, Mr. Saber? You're home in the afternoon and taking a nap? Ah, this call seems to be coming from the west wing, the, ah, unused room next to yours.''

"Yes. I'm sleepy and Mrs. Daisy Hewson, my... my friend will be living with us. She is to have anything she likes. Please accommodate her every whim," he said lightly, as if his naps were an everyday occurrence, as if he intended to sleep where he wanted.

She breathed quietly, shaken that she had demanded such intimacy from Ethan, Saber's tough CEO and heir, and that he had complied. His warmth curled out to her, seduced her, comforted her. Mortified by this new emotional Daisy, she stared at him.

"How are you feeling now, Daisy?" Ethan asked softly, as if their heads had been lying on pillows side by side for years. He folded his hands over his flat stomach.

"Everything is moving so fast."

"I meant what I said about your every whim. We can't know what you want, if you don't tell us. Make that a point, will you?"

The thought nagging her shot out into the shadows between them. "I want you to rehire John Bellington."

Ethan's expression hardened. "I can't do that."

"John has a family. Two small children. I know he was fired for gossiping about me. I can't have that on my conscience."

Ethan turned slowly on his side facing her. "You

care about everyone else, don't you? What about you?''

They lay too close, the shadows playing on the planes and angles of Ethan's face, his hair feathering the pillow. Daisy sneaked a glance down at him. He was even larger at this close horizontal range—there was so much of him. Desire whipped around her once more. What kind of a woman was she? Newly widowed, pregnant and wanting Ethan desperately, while he had been a perfect gentleman simply being kind during a research project.

"Who cares about you?" he repeated softly, smoothing a strand of hair back from her cheek.

"I haven't…haven't had time to make friends. Howie's racing demanded time and—"

"Let's not talk about Howie, shall we? Not now? I'll have a chat with Bellington and he's got his job back, thanks to you." Ethan's deep voice held a sharp, firm note. He took her hand and placed it over his chest, where his heart beat strong and safe beneath her palm, as if she could hold what he was, all of his power with her light grasp. She yawned, suddenly relaxed and exhausted after a barrage of uncertain and unfamiliar emotions, and Ethan murmured softly, "I'd like to be your friend, Daisy. If you'll let me. We've known each other for five years and we've always respected, and I hope, liked each other. We've always worked well together, and we'll go on that way—as friends. Now go to sleep and I'll be here for you when you awake."

* * *

Friends. Ethan mocked himself with the word as Daisy moved restlessly beside him in the late-afternoon shadows, arching and moaning sensually as if— Ethan closed his lids and shuddered. He clamped his hands together behind his head, to keep from reaching for her. Okay, so he was a one hundred percent predatory male, scheming to have Daisy within his grasp.

Daisy gave a little gasp, undulated her hips and ran her open hands from her hips up to her hair, winnowing it with her fingers. She licked her lips as if preparing for a kiss.

Ethan wanted that kiss more than air. He wanted to dive into it, give himself to her, tell her with his body how much he adored her.

Hewson may have hurried to the finish line, but in her sleep, Daisy was taking her time. Her bare foot reached his calf and began rubbing it. Ethan heard himself groan, his body hardening immediately as Daisy rolled on her side, her hand reaching out to skim his chest. The feminine purring began again, and Daisy eased her leg over his.

Ethan shuddered; Daisy's purr shifted into a needing, pleading tone as she gently lifted over him and settled lightly upon him. Her scent curled around him, that musky heady scent underlying her usual fresh, flowery ones.

"Daisy? Daisy, who am I?" Ethan asked softly, not to awaken her. The question hovered in the sunlit air, the scent of newly mowed grass coming from the manicured lawns. Ethan's heartbeat stopped as he waited; she must have loved Hewson so desperately—

The hair on Ethan's nape lifted as Daisy nuzzled his throat, then nibbled it. "Mr. Saber. Boy genius. Brilliant president of the board and CEO of Saber Baby Foods, and my Ethan," she whispered possessively after her tongue flicked his ear. She panted delicately as if she couldn't catch her breath. "I need you, Ethan. Oh, how I need you."

Ethan blinked, his thrusting body warring with his need to protect Daisy—from men taking advantage of her. He realized he had just lifted his hips to hers— He heard his husky, uneven question, "How, Daisy? How do you need me?"

As head of Saber, people always needed him. Ethan had to know about Daisy's needs—

"Desperately. Naked. Long. Slow. Sweaty and sweat...*ohhh!*" Her hips pressed down upon his hardened body and her arms slid around his neck.

Ethan eased his hands from beneath his head and slowly, stiffly placed them at his side—the effort costing him another pain-filled groan.

"I ache," Daisy whispered sensually, softly against his ear. She slowly straddled him, her full skirt bunched between them. "All over. Do something, Ethan. Help me."

Over him, her body heated and Ethan realized he was shaking. Every male instinct told him to take

Daisy. But wrapped in this soft, curvy package was the sweet Daisy he wanted to protect, to gently ease into his life. Making love to a sleeping woman, one deeply tired, and forced into taking his business offer, reeked of villainy.

Okay, so he was predatory, desiring Daisy. But not on these terms. He cursed Hewson for dismissing foreplay, any kind of play, and— Ethan's hand reached to cradle Daisy's head, his fingers soothing her scalp. He didn't have experience soothing women, but for Daisy, he would try. "Shh," he whispered.

Her head moved slowly in his hand, nudging it like a kitten needing petting. Ethan remembered a lullaby that his nurse had sung to him in troubled times—he gently rocked his body side to side, caressed Daisy's scalp and sang softly in her ear until she slept heavily. He eased her to his side, and lightly smoothed her skirt down, saving her embarrassment. Daisy nestled quietly into a deep sleep. It was a good feeling, having Daisy sleeping beside him.

Ethan realized he had dozed, his hand holding Daisy's. He awoke to cooler air, a shadowy room and Daisy staring at him. "Why did you hold me on your lap?" she whispered.

"It seemed right," he whispered back. "I haven't had much experience with women, but I didn't want you to be alone. I still don't. I'm glad you're here."

"It's an unusual feeling, being held like a child. Especially by you. You're so..." Her gaze skimmed down his body and after a gulp, Daisy whispered, "So big."

"My parents were tall." And cold, Ethan added. He didn't want Daisy inside his shadows. "Do you like—ah...me holding you?"

"I'll think about it. I'll write a memo, if you like."

"That isn't necessary." For once, Ethan did not want a dissection of the whys. "Are you hungry?"

Daisy lay quietly that night, the large unfamiliar room circling her. In the next room, Ethan had been pacing. She thought she noted muttering sounds. How she wanted to be held by him. How she needed— Daisy gasped slightly. She'd never been a sensual woman and now her entire body ached, her flesh too tight and her nerve endings at attention. A carefully shielded question to May, a receptionist in Saber Developments and the mother of five children, gave Daisy the answer. In pregnancy, women had different cravings and now Daisy shockingly craved Ethan's hard body next to hers, in hers. She needed to hear his deep, rich voice curl around her, those arms surround her, holding her as though she were precious to him, a part of him.

Daisy ran her hand over her flushed face. Only weeks ago, Howie had made insufficient love to her and now she craved Ethan. What kind of a woman was she?

One that needed and never had, the answer came back. The tightly reined emotions of her entire life hovered too close. She felt primitive, earthy and—Ethan suddenly reminded her of a huge, luscious, perfectly sculpted banana split, topped with whipped cream, maraschino cherries and chopped walnuts. She gripped the sheet, pulling it up to her chin. Her gaze traced the leaf shadow patterns on the ceiling. She didn't understand herself now, the baby already making a difference in her body.

The quiet knock at her door startled her. "Yes?"

"May I come in?" Ethan asked.

"Yes, of course." Darn. Ethan was wearing a long silk robe over his pajamas. She craved just one glimpse of his chest, that wide expanse of muscle, tanned skin and those adorable little whorls of black hair—not too much, but oh, so sexy—

Daisy inhaled. Sex had never been on her menu. Ethan approached her bed, his face in the shadows.

For just a moment, she wanted to nab him, and pull him into her bed. Daisy braced herself against the shocking need, glad for the night, shielding her guilty blush.

"I've been thinking," Ethan stated, in his CEO business voice. "I forgot. You don't like me standing over you. We'll talk about this in the morning."

Why, he's shy, she thought. He's uncomfortable. "Are you having second thoughts about the research project, Ethan? If you are, I understand." She feared that in the morning, he would tell her that she wasn't needed. She needed Ethan to need her.

He ran his hand through his hair, the frustrated gesture new and endearing to her. He was sweet. Considerate. Intelligent.

He sat slowly on the bed, braced his forearms on his knees and looked at the floor. Was it so hard for Saber's CEO to tell her that he did not want her? That he had acted out of sympathy, rather than the clinical marketing research project he'd proposed?

"I called Bellington tonight. He has you to thank for getting his job back, and we understand each other now."

"I'm glad."

Ethan looked down at her, his broad cheekbones gleaming in the dim light. "You're very soft, Daisy. You'll be a wonderful mother and I think we should get married," he added in a brisk, businesslike tone. "To stop any further gossip. There is no reason we can't get married. The baby will be mine in name— if that suits you—and that should stop all gossip. If you want, we'll have an attorney lay out papers, protecting you. Yes, above all, I want you protected and provided for. Ah...you and the baby."

The scent of his shower, his damp hair clung erotically to the air. Daisy ached to touch the gleaming newly combed strands. She was dreaming and hoped she wouldn't wake up. "Marriage? To you?"

"Just a formality. An arrangement between friends. I know I'm pushing, Daisy, but logic tells me that this is the best way. I've come to depend on my instincts and basic logic, Daisy. They've served me well when I had to take over Saber's at eighteen. Instinct told me to fight for my right against the board, and I did. Our marriage could all be explained very smoothly—that Hewson had asked me privately to take care of you, if anything happened to him—'' He glanced at her. ''What is your first take on this concept? Your initial response?''

Daisy's unsteady emotions rose, and boiled over. She began to cry, the tears sliding from her lashes down her cheeks. She dashed them away. ''Howie would never do that. He never kissed me good-night, either. He never patted my bottom in one of those fond little gestures, and—'' She realized with horror that a wail of truth exploded into the room as she demanded fiercely, ''Do you know how I feel? Do you, Mr. On Top of It, Controlled, Mr. Saber Baby Foods?''

Daisy groaned and flopped to her stomach. Apparently pregnancy also brought out an evil temper, one she hadn't known existed.

Her eyes widened at the tentative, yet fond pat on her bottom.

''Is that what you wanted, Daisy?'' Ethan asked huskily as his large hand spread over her bottom, warming it.

She burrowed into the pillow, groaning. Why did she have to tell him *everything?* She squirmed under the light pressure on her backside and realized Ethan's big hand was caressing her, shaping her bottom slowly, firmly.

"I, uh, better go," he muttered, yet his hand continued to caress her.

"Don't." Daisy feared the gentle caress, the first of her adult life, would stop. She studied his technique—an open hand, big, warm, comforting, firm, yet light. Perfect.

He sighed heavily and took away his hand. "I shouldn't have touched you. Women have never been my strength. You and I have had a good relationship at the office, working together, but I've never understood exactly how they think. You'll have to tell me what you want from me, what makes you happy. I want that, more than anything. For you to feel happy and secure. For the baby. For you. You deserve to be happy."

Daisy breathed quietly, hit by an avalanche of needs and wild, sexy thoughts. She took Ethan's wrist and replaced his hand to her bottom. "I meant, don't go. We seem to be having an intimate discussion. I need that now, I think. Talk and, ah, something gooey and rich and—"

"Daisy? Are we having a craving?" Excitement tremored through Ethan's deep voice, then panic. "You haven't made up a potential list of midnight cravings. Cook hasn't prepared— Are you certain you should be lying on your stomach?"

Daisy turned slowly to watch Ethan. His hand slid around her hip to rest on her stomach. She caught his wrist in both her hands. He stared back at her. She'd never seen him so intense, so focused as he asked, "What is it, Daisy? What do you want?"

She wanted to devour him. Stake him out on the wide bed and have him, and find relief for her body, and then sleep as she had never slept before, twined around Ethan's big, hard, naked, warm body. She licked her lips, and stared at him, unable to think of anything but how he would feel against her, in her. Her breasts ached, needing the cup of his hand. Poor Ethan. He didn't know how appealing he was to her now, the tiny life within her upsetting her usual restraints.

"I get hot just looking at my man," May had said, describing her pregnancies with a wicked, knowing laugh.

Ethan frowned. "Daisy? What's wrong? You're getting all flushed and hot looking."

"I think I have a hormonal imbalance. Yes, I'll marry you. That would be wise."

"We'll see the doctor about that first thing in the morning. I have a list of established obstetricians." Ethan blinked and shook his head. "You will? You will marry me? Now, I know it's too late and you're tired, so we'll talk about this in the morning."

"I won't change my mind." She sat up, deliberately allowing the sheet to fall from her chin.

Oh, yes! Yes! Everything she wanted to see in a lover's eyes, in a husband's eyes was there—the heat, the hunger, the storms—as he found her breasts.

"We'll take care of you, Daisy," Ethan stated

firmly, delight running through his voice. He dragged his gaze upward, touched her mouth with it and began to smile as if he had everything he wanted. His boyish grin fascinated her. "Now what are you craving? We're just minutes from the store. What do you suppose the time is from the moment of the first craving until the moment of satisfaction?"

Long, she thought. Very long, and thorough. Topped by heat and discovery, and kissing—yes, lots of kissing. The hungry, tongue, nibbling kind, blended with tender, seeking ones—

"You're blushing, Daisy," Ethan murmured tenderly. "Don't be afraid to tell me your every desire. I'll see that you are well served."

Chapter 3

The next week, while April played in the sunshine, Ethan traced the movements of his bride around the conference table, placing the information folders in front of the board members.

After the brief ceremony, Daisy's lips had lingered in their kiss, her fingertips digging into his shoulders. The look she had sent him caused a startling heat, his body hardening unexpectedly and he'd swept her deeper into his arms, claiming her as his own.

When the kiss was finished, Daisy had stepped back, her lips swollen, her face flushed and her eyes sultry. Ethan could not stop inventorying her body, which seemed to quiver beneath his gaze. Her nipples thrust out at him, the simple cotton shirtwaist dress taut across her chest. Ethan wanted to dive into Daisy, bond and mate with her. He ached, rock hard from his knees to his chest. A savage, unfamiliar headache began at the base of his skull as he forced himself under control. For the first time in his life, as he returned to the office with Daisy, Ethan had been forced to drape his coat over his arm, shielding his lower body.

His desire had shaken him. It wouldn't happen again. Not with sweet Daisy. He intended to win her into his life gently, not by ripping the clothes from her and placing his lips upon her magnificent, round, soft— Ethan tightened his muscles, forcing control. He had to be very careful with Daisy, not to let her know his desire. It frightened him and he was certain it would terrify her.

When Daisy completed circling the conference table, she returned to his side, preparing to sit in her secretarial chair, slightly behind him. Ethan stretched out a hand to capture her slender wrist. He caressed her soft skin with his thumb and held her when she would have moved away. He treasured the matching rings that bound them together, running his thumb across Daisy's. Ethan drew her down onto his lap while the board members stared, mouths opened. Daisy squirmed in his arms and Ethan bounced her lightly, "Stop fidgeting, Daisy."

"This is improper office behavior," she whispered furiously at him. "I'll get you."

Ethan breathed quietly. While the board watched this new development intently, Ethan reveled in the challenge Daisy had just sent him. He leaned closer to whisper to her, "Maybe I'd like to be got. We're going out tonight. Don't bother about arrangements, I'm making them."

"I always make your social arrangements. I keep your schedule."

"Not this time. You've been shoving me into business dinners for years, sending my friends flowers—"

Daisy crossed her arms and glared at him. "They were women," she muttered. "You've had involvements, Ethan. Affairs."

"Let's keep this between us, hmm? I've never—" Ethan skipped all the nevers he hadn't done with women and promised himself that Daisy was his first in every way. The order was to test this new twist in their relationship, because Ethan had no plans to be alone on his wedding night. He felt delicate, needing intimacy and reassurance.

The air heated, sizzled and steamed between them. Ethan gathered her closer, enjoying the little exciting game that had sprung between them. In his expertise, power testing was important to crafting a true and balanced relationship.

"I have an announcement to make," he stated quietly to the board without unlocking his eyes from Daisy's furious ones. He loved studying Daisy—her softness and her power. Venus, he decided, whimsically. His goddess. All those little textures, just below the surface, immediate responses to his kisses on her cheek, those fond little pats he loved to give her

curved backside. His body grew hard beneath that luscious skirt-covered backside now and Daisy's eyes
widened, shocked. She squirmed uncomfortably and
Ethan stifled a groan before he spoke, "Daisy and I
were married at seven-thirty this morning, just before
coming to work. Daisy didn't want to interrupt our
usual workday, but from now on, we're taking after-
noons off…redecorating, gardening and participating
in newly married activities—" He glanced at Daisy,
who had just gasped.

Ethan shifted her in his arms, trying to make her
more comfortable. "We're getting in shape for a long
haul. I want no emergency calls to my home from
now on. Newly married activities take time—"

He winced. Daisy's pinch hurt. He'd seen wives
nudge and glare at their husbands before, when the
male party stepped into a verbal cowpile. Ethan lifted
his eyebrows, attempting innocence.

Martin Grover's iced water glass toppled from his
hands. Lemuel Jones's lime sucker, a substitute cigar,
slipped from his lips to stick to his watercolor silk
tie.

"You know what they're thinking," his bride finally whispered desperately. "They'll think we're—"

"Yes?" Ethan invited, treasuring, anticipating how
Daisy would express lovemaking with him. He did
not want to hear "hurrying to the finish line." He
intended to make thorough, sweet love to his bride,
all in good time. He'd bank his hungers and see to
her needs. Ethan shivered. He wasn't certain about

banking and making love deposits; he lacked experience in lovemaking. He made a mental note to prowl through bookstores, researching the upcoming project. More than anything, he wanted his bride to be satisfied with their physical union.

Daisy's blush pleased Ethan. Beneath the conference table, he patted her backside comfortingly. "You're all invited to the house...tomorrow night. Dinner," he decided instantly, because he wanted his wedding night alone with Daisy.

"How could you?" Daisy demanded after rushing into his bedroom.

Ethan kicked off his shoes, sat on his bed, tore off his tie and flipped open the buttons of his dress shirt. After hours of her silent accusation and furious looks, he was certain he had crossed some unknown groom and bridal taboo. "How are you feeling, Daisy?" he asked cautiously.

She swept from his room back into hers; the door slammed behind her. The early-afternoon sunlight quaked with tension.

She rushed back into the room, threw up her hands and stated, "Dinner! Dinner for the board. Here. To-morrow night."

Ethan didn't understand the accusation. "Yes. I've found that it's best to present a new project by laying all the details on the table at once. We need to give this new change in our relationship some sort of picture to keep gossip down."

Daisy sailed out of the room, only to return. "I'm pregnant, Ethan. There was nothing in the research agreement about dinners for the board."

"Why don't you lie down and take a nap?" he asked in an attempt at logic and tried to catch more of her delightful scent.

"I'm feeling shaky," she whispered suddenly. "Dinner for the board. Here," she added unevenly as if the thought had tumbled her into a bottomless ravine.

"My staff has had other dinners on short notice. In the past, you've issued the invitations."

"Why did you kiss me like that?" she asked suddenly, then placed her hand over her lips and rushed back into her room.

Heartbeats later, Ethan knocked quietly at her bathroom door. He listened for sounds of retching, and could already feel his stomach lurch in response. "Daisy? Do you need help?"

Daisy stopped kissing the mirror as if it were Ethan. Her lips had left an impression in the steamy surface. She shivered, wrapped her arms around herself and struggled for control. It was her second wedding night; the first one with Howie had been horrifying, devastating, mechanical. This time, she knew what she wanted—Ethan's hard body. Though Ethan's attempts to prevent gossip were kind—an evening out, the gentle byplay at the office, there was only so far he should have to go in the name of research.

"Daisy?" Ethan asked again, his tone concerned.

"I'm sorry," she whispered against the door and brushed the mirror with her lips, just as she wanted to do to Ethan's firm mouth.

Firm. He was firm all over. Power packed. When he had drawn her into his arms, she could feel his biceps nudging her breasts, his thighs pressing against hers, his—

Daisy blinked at the wide-eyed woman in the mirror. Ethan had been aroused. "I thought that only happened before hurrying to the finish line," she whispered to her trembling image.

"Why?" he whispered back.

"Why what?" She couldn't invite him into her intimate thoughts, talk about his arousal and why it had occurred and who he was thinking of and— "Would you go away, please?"

"No." His answer was firm. "You may need me."

Oh, she needed him all right. She needed to finish the hungry kiss he'd begun after their marriage ceremony. She needed his arms tight around her, his body pressed to hers. She needed his eyes burning with it, his nostrils flaring with desire, his body locked to hers, as it had been during their kiss. She needed to feel his temperature rise, his heart pound as though Morse-coding a message into hers.

There was just that moment when his hand had inched lower and briefly cupped her bottom, pressing her to his hardness— Daisy sucked air into her lungs, remembering the caress, as if Ethan wanted to devour all of her, claim her.

She frowned, confused with why Ethan would want her.

"Daisy?" he persisted. "What is this basket of my clothing doing here?"

"It's mending. I've been mending at night. It soothes me."

"There's no need to patch—" Ethan sounded irritated. "I want you to rest. I frightened you today, didn't I? When I kissed you, and later when I held you on my lap. The male body responds to stimuli, unfortunately, and today…today I was regretfully emotional and stimulated. It won't happen again."

Daisy jerked open the door and Ethan jumped back, a towering, powerful male in the newly decorated, feminine bedroom. He'd tossed his shirt on her bed and his chest gleamed, waiting for her fingers to explore him. He ran his hand through his hair, rumpling the black strands, and then locked his hands to his waist, his legs wide spread as if bracing for a blow. She noted his belt buckle was undone, the button above his zipper opened. The desperate need rose to see Ethan, undressed, as beautiful as a Roman statue—without his fig leaf. She glanced at his lower body and squeezed her lids closed. She doubted that a fig leaf would cover what she felt against her earlier in the day.

"'It won't happen again'? You won't kiss me

again?'' she demanded desperately, fearing that he would never kiss her again. Like that—hard, commanding, possessive...hot and hungry. The tender little, reluctant-to-leave nibble at the end was a perfect cherry on the kissing sundae.

He stared at her, tension humming between them. Ethan spoke slowly as though giving his words as a gift. ''I got carried away. You are...soft, warm and curvy. I know I wasn't a gentleman, that my honor shot out the window. But you were in my arms, so fragrant and curvy and feminine, and I found myself—''

''Found yourself?'' She walked slowly to him. He was frightened of her, wary. She saw she must be gentle, if she was to get to her own personal finish line. ''In our five years together, I have never heard you speak of...of desire for a woman, or act anything but a gentleman. I've never heard you say, 'you found yourself' anywhere, because you always knew where you were going. You've never cared enough to make dinner arrangements for another woman.''

''You're different. You are my bride. Brides require hands-on care.'' Ethan inhaled abruptly and Daisy stared at his chest. ''Do you want to touch me?'' he asked unevenly. ''You look as if you do, and I do not want you to spare any cravings.'' He spaced the words, underlying the need for proper research.

''My...my breasts ache.'' Daisy's whisper quivered between them.

"They do?" Ethan's brown eyes darkened as he looked down at her chest, studying each curve with interest.

They *were* married, Daisy reminded herself. She stared at him, unable to move, and licked her lips, remembering his hard, hungry, devastating kiss. Heat rose in his dark cheeks and Daisy realized that she was crushing her skirt, her fingers needing an anchor.

Ethan shuddered, his fists showing white knuckles at his thighs. "We'll ask the doctor what to do about that...to make you more comfortable."

"I feel...incomplete, Ethan," she stated, opening her feelings to him...in the name of research. "Here I am, pregnant and on my wedding night, and—"

Ethan's gaze fused to her face. "What?" he demanded flatly. "You can tell me anything—what?"

Could she tell him? Would she frighten him?

"I don't want you to feel incomplete in any way. You've always been...very complete and sweet," Ethan noted gently.

"I need you," Daisy whispered, her face heating. She'd always needed him, this safe, steady powerful Ethan, and the vulnerable, sensitive man she had just come to know. And at the moment, she did not feel sweet.

"How?" His question was raw, primitive, trembling on the air between them.

She couldn't say what she needed to complete her: that darn finish line with Ethan. He stared at her, then stalked to the intercom and jabbed a button. She noted his big hand trembled as he said, "I want the staff to take the afternoon off. Yes, I know we're having a dinner tomorrow night. I'm certain anything you whip up tomorrow will be delicious. I'll cook breakfast in the morning, no need to arrive too early—" Ethan's face darkened. "Of course, I can cook breakfast. What is there to cracking a few eggs? No, I will not just pop open a jar of Saber's Oatmeal and Apples for Toddlers."

After a pause, he said slowly, too patiently, "Yes, I know you've been cooking my breakfasts for thirty years, but I'm married now and we'll have to make some concessions for that, won't we? I have a bride to care for, and I'm not delegating that duty."

Ethan faced Daisy. The sunlight gleamed on his shoulders, muscles and cords tensing, his jaw locked with the determination she had seen at the office. "Now, about those breasts...yours, specifically," he said. "What do you think might help?"

Ethan nuzzled the softness beneath his cheek; it rippled and heated and he sighed, luxuriating in the scents enfolding him. He tightened his arms around the soft, curved body flowing against him and floated in gentle harmony to the delicate, slow beat of the warmth beneath his lips. Just over there, an inch away, a tiny, delicious pebble needed his attention, and he cupped the soft mound, drawing the sweet smooth pebble into his lips, sucking it gently, while caressing his fingertips over the silky texture. The warmth along his side, Daisy's long leg between his thighs, curled around him, flowing rhythmically to the gentle suction of his lips.

Daisy. Ethan gathered her closer, smiling against her breasts, nuzzling them gently.

She arched slowly, sensuously, stroking his hair, easing closer to him.

Daisy. Ethan lifted his lips to her throat, nibbling on the delicate pulse he found there. He wallowed in her fragrance, the purrs inviting him—

Ethan ran his open hand slowly, firmly down his bride's body, possessively claiming her lush hips in his fingertips. His schedule had unexpectedly accelerated when Daisy had opened herself to his kisses and he'd fed upon her, dined upon her mouth, fusing his lips to hers. She'd whispered about her body, the changes in it, how she needed to be held—by him. The wild tempest of touching and feeding and reveling in textures had shot to a feverish need the moment his hands reached to cup her breasts. Ethan caressed her softness gently and her body surged up to his touch, her incredible hungry sounds curling around him. Her nails dug slightly into his skin and Ethan smiled lazily, happily, woozily and smoothed her plain white cotton panties with his fingertips.

Ethan ached to make love to his bride. To ease into her gently, filling her, to complete what they had begun.

The bedside alarm rang and Ethan tensed, waiting for Daisy to realize that she had slept the night, safely in his arms…wearing only her panties. He held her gently, firmly, because he wasn't certain of how she would react—in the daylight, to him, lying next to her.

Daisy arched and stretched and the whole Daisy-awakening process fascinated Ethan. Her lids fluttered open, and drowsy, dark green eyes stared at him. Ethan wondered if this was how magical wood nymphs awoke upon their petals—

Ethan moved over her, before she could escape. He held her wrists while she trembled beneath him. "Now, Daisy. Don't be frightened."

Her eyes widened and Ethan tumbled into her gaze; he fought for reason because Daisy was definitely panicked. "You touched me, intimately," she whispered unevenly, "and I…"

"Yes, you did. It was glorious, Daisy. Beautiful. You simply went into yourself and found what you needed—"

"I shattered into pieces…." She shook her head trying to clear it, and Ethan wanted to wallow in the golden shades of her hair, webbing the rosebud pillowcase.

"And then you fell asleep. Deeply asleep, as if all the tension you'd held for years had drained from you. You needed sleep, Daisy. You needed that release."

"Release. Yes, that's what it was, as if everything I'd lacked had simmered inside me and came pouring out in one quivering, heated, pounding explosion, until I saw red and spun higher and at the very height, found what I needed. There were tiny contractions inside me that I didn't know existed—ever," she explained with delighted surprise.

Ethan fought trembling, remembering how hot and moist she was to his touch, how responsive she was, as if made for his hand alone. He forced a brief smile to demonstrate his appreciation of her sharing her thoughts with him.

Right now, his body wanted to share more physical delights and less thoughts.

"Oh, how I needed that, Ethan. Thank you." She squirmed beneath him and Ethan groaned heavily, aware of every soft silky curve brushing him. Daisy turned her head to one side, her blush rising delicately up from her throat. "It was a craving, you know. I'm certain it's part of my hormonal imbalance," she explained worriedly.

"Sweet Daisy," Ethan murmured, pressing his cheek next to hers lightly, so as not to frighten her with his morning stubble.

She turned slowly back to him. "But you didn't...you didn't, did you?"

"No." And how he ached to fill her now....

"Ethan. I am shocked. I have vamped you, and you are such a nice man. You were my...my victim. I fed upon you. You've been a perfect gentleman—supportive, tender, never once complaining."

"Any time, Daisy. But I've never been a victim. I liked participating."

She stared at him. "What if I told you that I needed more, Ethan? What would you say to that? I'm horrible, aren't I? There you were, with that magnificent chest and all I could think about was getting skin to skin with you."

The alarm rang again as they stared at each other. Ethan felt himself swell, nudging her gently. Daisy's hips raised and she licked her lips. "Kiss me."

"I'm afraid my control is lacking this morning, dear heart."

Daisy's lashes fluttered shyly, entrancing him. "That's an endearment, Ethan. I like endearments and the way you hold me and whisper roughly, desperately against my ear, nibbling on it. Your hunger was very stimulating...stimulated...yes, I think I am that and there is no explanation. I don't understand it— I've never been a...a sensual person."

She slipped her wrists from his fingers and smoothed his hair. A tidbit of his tension eased as he turned his head into the keeping of her hand. She stroked his cheek, tracing the angle of his jaw down to his chin, then inching up slightly to touch his bottom lip.

"You're heavy, Ethan. Yet comfortable. All bulky and rough skin—" While running an inventory of Ethan's body, she ran her hand across his shoulders, smoothing them. Her nails flexed gently and her hips lifted against his, her eyes darkening. "Ethan, do you suppose you could take care of one little craving for me this morning? Before we go to work?"

"Breakfast?" he asked.

"In a way..."

Ethan slid a glance at his wife-secretary as she moved around the conference room table. Like an invisible antenna his body now told him where she was, tracking that incredible scent that only he seemed to notice.

He narrowed his eyes, taking a quick inventory of the board members. Apparently they hadn't noticed. They'd better not notice. Ethan folded himself within the thoughtful executive's expression and thought about Daisy, his pregnant bride.

After two weeks with his newly passionate wife, Ethan found himself in heaven and in hell.

He realized that Daisy was exploring her new world, adjusting to the nest and being very genuine about her needs and cravings...to help his research. He glanced down at the yellow sticky note she had just placed on the leather folder in front of him. "I need."

He shuddered unwillingly, his body lurching to the thought of Daisy's needs. They vibrated down the length of the conference table to him now. Daisy looked cool in her chignon, her new white blouse and navy suit, yet something escaped her lashes and curled out to nab him.

Ethan felt his nostrils flare, trying to catch her scent. His research told him that it was her pheromones—a deadly little passion-perfume the "needy" female exudes. He tapped his pen on the "I need" note, folded it carefully and tucked it into his pocket; he studied his bride. Tension hummed through his body. Research told him about women's needs—long, slow satisfying lovemaking and the need to be cherished later. Ethan had hidden his women-research books in his executive washroom, which his bride avoided meticulously, apparently respecting his privacy. A stealthy call to an old friend—a doctor—told him that sometimes a woman was more sexually aroused during pregnancy.

Ethan fought a brief, unsteady encounter with his usual morning-queasy stomach. From the other end of the table, Daisy glanced at him, looked again and then hurried to him, filling his glass with ice water and slipping him a cracker. Ethan nibbled on it and glanced at her. He needed comfort—namely her curvy body close to his. He tugged her into his lap and noted the pleased, fond expressions lining the conference table. They were happy for him, Ethan realized, genuinely fond of him and of Daisy. He smiled back, warmed by Daisy in his lap and by people he had suddenly discovered genuinely liked him.

"They like me," he whispered to Daisy, who had gotten used to sitting on his lap, because he liked cuddling her. Ethan's tone was filled with discovery, as if he had never thought about people liking him.

"Of course, they like you. I like you, too. You're a very nice man." She straightened his tie—the one she had mended for him in her brisk waste-not, want-not attitude. He treasured every dainty stitch.

"Sometimes I don't feel nice," he muttered, guilty about his desire for a woman pressed into marriage by her desperate situation.

"That's when I like you best," Daisy purred sweetly.

Ethan stared at her, his body hardening against the zipper she had mended—lately zippers had become a problem for him. He and Daisy were entering some sort of game phrase, tossing a hot simmering challenge between them with increasing delight and skill.

"We've got all weekend to explore my wicked side, sweetheart," he murmured and flung her his first leer. Her blush fascinated him, and only an "ahem" caused him to turn back to the business at hand.

Daisy slowly placed one foot on the bed and began applying cream to her leg, slowly, as provocatively as her limited experience allowed. Her short black nightgown concealed little and Ethan had responded perfectly, hungrily upon first seeing it. He'd taken two steps toward her before stopping. Then he had locked himself in that familiar steel control and turned away to study her embroidery basket, inspecting the baby's tiny folded garments.

For a solid month, she'd taken advantage of him, unable to handle her new desires and logic at the same time. Yet Ethan hadn't delivered a complete package. She needed everything from him, and while he heated and trembled and quivered, Ethan seemed reluctant to complete their sensuality.

Soon, the tiny life inside her would remind him that their relationship was based on business...on research.

Daisy applied more cream to her thighs. Ethan's response to home-cooked meals, friendly intimate little dinners cooked and planned together, fascinated her. His first venture into a grocery store equaled a safari, though he was all business when they came to the baby products and rearranged Saber products to suit him. When stopped by the stock boy, Ethan had bristled and knowing how much trouble he could be when displeased, Daisy had distracted him by a quick kiss on his cheek.

Ethan had stared blankly down at her. Though he often cuddled and kissed her, she had not openly returned the favors. From there, she had moved him into the vegetable section, explaining the necessities of squeezing cabbage and lettuce. In the middle of the melon and grapes section, Ethan had bent over and kissed her fully, hungrily upon her lips. "I like you," he had said evenly, as if testing her response to a new product.

"I like you, too," she had returned just as unsteadily, melting beneath those warm chocolate colored eyes.

Now, still a basically unclaimed, unused groom, Ethan looked so delectable, standing there in her feminine room, fresh from his shower. His bare back gleamed in the lamplight, his pajama bottoms concealing his beautiful, strong, narrow hips and muscular thighs. He had explained that they should sleep together now, so that he could respond to her instant cravings and note how many times she tossed and turned in the night.

Ethan turned to her and Daisy's heart leaped into double-time. "Daisy. I'm guilty of desiring you," Ethan stated abruptly. "It's important that I be absolutely honest with you. I've been a cad. I crafted this research plan to get you into my life...to take care of you and our baby—I think of the baby that way, as ours, if you don't mind."

"I don't mind, Ethan. In my heart, I've begun thinking of him that way, too."

Delight curled around Ethan's face. Why, he's blooming, Daisy thought woozily, happily. He's really beaming an expectant-father grin.

"A boy. You just said, 'him,' and that means a boy. Baseball, football, tricycles—a boy...how much better can it get? Well, there is the possibility of a girl and that might be even better. Two! Sometimes people have two at one time. They're called twins, a double delivery." Excitement ran through Ethan's voice until suddenly, he seemed to sag and he sank onto the bed, holding his face in his hands. "I think I need a jar of Apple Delight...ah...Daisy, I don't think I can make it down to the refrigerator for the olives this time."

Because Ethan's queasy stomach was acting up, Daisy did not push him for the delivery she wanted.

Ethan pulled out his "Romancing the Pregnant Bride" list and scanned his bedroom. According to the reference books on pregnancy, women needed sex—Ethan shuddered, his body leaping into its usual constant hard state at the thought of Daisy and sex. Together. With him. All the way.

So much for protecting Daisy from himself. He glanced at her bathroom, a delightful fiesta of feminine color and scents and listened to the sound of her shower.

He wanted her feminine articles beside his, in the larger bathroom, one they could share. Sharing a bathroom with Daisy—Ethan floated off whimsically into a dream in which Daisy and he soaked in the huge tub, loving each other. The lacy underwear she'd begun wearing had made him drool. The heat coming from Daisy as she looked at him and licked her lips slammed into Ethan almost every quarter hour at work and constantly away from the office as they worked together, building the perfect nest for Daisy's—for their baby. Ethan surveyed the room, filled with new warm country-modern furniture that a married couple would share, and little feminine touches he adored.

He fused his gaze on the oversize maple sleigh bed and instantly tumbled into an erotic journey.

Ethan wanted to make this intended change in their

relationship to be soft, tender, flowing into a marriage bed, where he did not feel a visitor. Daisy's move into his bedroom and bed was significant, marking her trust in him, a commitment that he had no right to ask.

Would she enter this new phase with him? Fear jolted Ethan as he lit the candles around the room, and adjusted the glasses beside the chilling bottle of fine nonalcoholic wine. Cook had grinned when Ethan had requested a picnic hamper, placed near the bed.

The gift! Ethan fought his terror, trying to remember where he had placed the small ribbon-wrapped box. He released his breath; it stood next to the bedside table, waiting its cue. He glanced at the door separating their rooms; it was opened exactly two feet, a distance Ethan had calculated with care to invite and yet not intimidate the wood nymph he hoped to claim—Daisy.

Chapter 4

"Ethan?" Daisy eased the door open slightly. Her short, sleek charmeuse nightie with tiny straps clung to her curves. She couldn't wait to see Ethan's expressive eyes widen and narrow, couldn't wait to see that cute little perky-dangerous-hunter look enfold him as his chest rose and fell unsteadily as though he were forcing himself to suck air.

For five years, she had thought of him as "The Mechanical Man." Insights into his cold childhood and the pressures put upon him at an age when most boys were exploring their manhood, had changed Daisy's opinion. All those barriers to the real Ethan were stripped away now that she'd leaped into his life; now she understood why his reactions at times were so distant—when deeply emotional, Ethan

wrapped a protective shield around him. There was
no mistaking his emotions now. He was so devastat-
ingly appealing when his shoulders and arms bunched
as though forcing himself not to grab her. When she
wore ultrafeminine, sexy underwear, the aura circling
him bristled, peaked, heated—

In the time she had known Ethan Saber, he had
never looked at another woman as he looked at her.
Daisy smiled smugly. She liked "smug," and
wrapped that good, wicked, delicious confidence
around her. She needed confidence on her first safari
into vamping Ethan.

She smoothed the satin down her body, lingered as
the cloth tightened, and Ethan responded magnifi-
cently, his stark hunger reaching out to curl around
her, to crackle like lightning between them, and skid-
ding heat over her skin, and kicking her heart into
flip-flops. She wanted to snag his control, peel it away
and to be grabbed by Ethan, her groom.

Nabbed.

Completed.

She stepped into the candlelit room and Ethan
turned slowly to her, the flickering light playing over
his tall, strong body, the bed turned back and inviting
behind him. "Oh, hello," Ethan murmured coolly, as
though mildly surprised that she would come into his
sanctuary.

Ethan couldn't escape her, not tonight. He'd been
gentle and sweet and unpleasantly controlled in his
attempts to be romantic—picnics, dinner at the the-

ater, snuggling in front of the television, rubbing her feet, massaging her swelling breasts—yet he had always stopped just before the finish line. She wouldn't stand for that, not tonight. Daisy almost felt sorry for Ethan, because she intended to be gentle, firm, and bag him.

He breathed unsteadily now, just as she expected. His eyes glowed, pinned her in the flickering light, tracing her hair, her face and down her body.

Daisy arched sensuously, luxuriating in her new-found femininity that Ethan had brought to life. He swallowed roughly as he stared at her bare legs. "That's a lovely design," Ethan remarked after he cleared his throat. "Red is definitely your color."

She noted the picnic hamper on the floor next to the bed. Ethan followed her look and shrugged. "Midnight cravings...saves the trip to the kitchen. You look—"

Daisy advanced upon him, locked her gaze to his burning one. He smelled wonderful, all shower-soapy and male and inviting. He had focused on her with that wonderful hawk-about-to-pounce look. Even in business crises, Ethan's expressions were not so focused, so heated and desperate.

Daisy placed her hands on his chest; his heart raced beneath her fingertips. She'd intended to give Ethan a sporting chance; he was shy after all. But there was that need driving her— She pushed hard, and Ethan fell back onto the bed. Daisy pinned him instantly, straddling him and holding his wrists so that he couldn't stop her. She kissed him hard, rubbing her mouth against his, flicking her tongue over his lips, and diving into that mysterious, dangerous, tantalizing opening. She opened herself to the heady excitement pouring through her, and bit his bottom lip.

"Daisy!" The word held delight, pleasure and excitement of a male about to pounce—not that Daisy was experienced in that sound.

All in one smooth motion, Ethan hauled her up higher on him as he edged back on the bed, full-length, kissing her as if he needed to suck her into him. That was exactly what Daisy wanted to do to him. She tossed herself over him, the battle exciting her, and Ethan reversed their positions, lodged firmly between her thighs. She clamped her legs tightly around him, and tugged his hair, urging his mouth to fuse with hers.

A flurry of hot, hungry kisses trailed down to her breasts, and Daisy cried out urgently, needing him. Ethan, gentleman as always, responded, matching her needs. She could always depend on Ethan, Daisy thought hazily, her hands wandering over her muscular, obliging, hungry prey. In seconds, the tiny straps of her shift tore away, her bikini briefs met the same fate, and Daisy panted, heated and ached with Ethan's caresses. She tangled her arms and legs around him and they rolled gently to the floor, Ethan protecting her.

The words "victory" and "spoils" flashed through her mind. Ethan belonged to her; she devoured his mouth, slanting, changing, testing and angling for a better grip on him. He trembled while she stripped away his pajama bottoms and then, finally the waiting was over. Ethan eased over her.

With hearts beating against each other, bodies tangled and Daisy undulating, aching beneath Ethan, who thrust deeply into her, reared and thrust again, they became slowly, firmly one.

Eons after Ethan had poured into her, and she had claimed ecstasy to the fullest, Daisy flopped her hands from his back onto the sheets. She stared at her fingers, the pale trembling tips, the vanquished palm and remembered birds mating in midflight, tumbling apart, sated. She'd flown and mated, united finally with Ethan. He nuzzled the side of her throat, kissing her leisurely. "This part is important," he whispered. "Hold still and let me complete my checklist."

He tenderly drank the sigh from her lips, his mouth circling hers, evading her exhausted pursuit. She was too tired to resist, to ask what list, and wondered distantly how Ethan managed to get them on the bed. He continued caressing and kissing her. "You're my goddess," he whispered in that dark dangerous tone she loved. "I'm sorry I hurried. I wasn't expecting to—"

She quivered, reacting to the surprising tight clench of her body. Ethan inhaled, tensing at once. Heat flashed between them, the urgency just heartbeats past and another wave slamming into them with each panting breath.

"I've got you," she whispered back, feeling another craving cruising out of the one that had just passed.

His lazy smile moved along her throat as he filled her again. "Darn. I forgot to inquire about the frequency of..." he muttered amid the driving tropical storm that had just kicked into a hurricane.

In the night pushed away by the gray of a rainy dawn, Daisy slipped her arm around Ethan's waist as he lay on his side away from her. She rubbed her cheek against his shoulder and petted the hair on his chest. The big house settled around them, the rain gently spattered on the windows, making trails in the dim light. "I'm finally safe, Ethan. I'm home."

"We're home, darling Daisy." Ethan corrected her as he turned to hold her, bringing her closer to his heart. In their perfect new world, he knew the rhythms of her heart, her awed emotions. Together, they had created a symphony and now settled back to cherish their rewards, reveling in them. "Here." He reached to the bedside table to give her the small box. "This is for you."

Ethan settled comfortably on the pillows, cradling her against him as she opened the box. Daisy eased the ring from the velvet. It wasn't a wedding ring; she already wore a gold band that matched Ethan's. On the new delicate ring, daisies were joined by two tiny hearts, delighting her. "Why, Ethan. A friendship ring."

"You are my best friend. You've given me more

than I ever hoped,'' Ethan whispered against her lips
as he slipped the ring onto her right hand and kissed
her finger. His dark, steamy look held hers as he
stayed to suck her fingers one, by one. ''Are you going to vamp me again?''

''You can't get away with that,'' Daisy replied unevenly before she nabbed him again.

As Daisy left his office, Ethan watched his wife's
hips sway gently. He tilted his head, angling around
the new vase of flowers on his desk, to get a better
view. In the middle of June and four and a half
months into their pregnancy, Daisy was blooming,
confident and plain old-fashioned sexy. Her skirt
flirted around her slender calves, the motion accen-
tuating her lush hips, decorated by a mocking sticky
note, and gently thickening waist. In her suit, Daisy's
new aura instantly aroused Ethan, even as she sent
him a steamy look over her shoulder and unlocked
his office door, passing through it and gently closing
it behind her.

Alone, he placed his elbows on the desk and rubbed
his temples with his fingertips, trying to concentrate
on getting back to Saber's business pressures—at
least until the afternoon when his wife and he made
love before they napped. His personal pressures had
been drained just minutes ago, shattering them both.

His bride was a hungry, desirable woman and
Ethan fretted about their active newlywed status. He'd
just joined the ranks of the grooms he'd observed,

goony smiles pasted on their faces, shadows beneath their eyes and an unexplained weight drop.

Ethan released a goony smile and caressed his desktop. Happiness poured over him like melted butter. Never in his entire life had he felt so…alive, warm, safe and a part of a family. Daisy had created their tiny family, nudging it into homemade meals, daily sharing of the small things that everyone else took for granted. Ethan didn't. He wallowed in his new life and chucked down two prenatal vitamins, followed by ice water. In a moment, when he was certain that Daisy was dispatching his memos to various offices, Ethan would slink into his executive washroom, pull out the hidden collapsible cot and pour himself into it for a power nap. Lately Daisy's energy level had perked up.

Daisy and her obstetrician had constantly reassured Ethan that repeated lovemaking would not hurt the baby. The obstetrician had refused to take any more calls from Ethan; he had to be accompanied by his wife during visits. At least Ethan was over the queasy part; Daisy had sailed right through it, a much stronger will than Ethan's.

Ethan's fingertips trembled against his hot skin and he struggled to catch his breath. Just one innocent look between them, a huh?-connect, and desire leaped into them both. His desk's papers had been wrinkled, some falling to the floor, and a sticky note—Daddy—clung to the hair on his chest.

Ethan breathed unevenly, trying to catch his breath

and his slowing heartbeat as he inventoried his body: Sitting behind his desk, he still wore a suit jacket, his tie slightly awry over the top button of his shirt, but after that, the buttons were open. His shorts and slacks were somewhere around his ankles. Daisy's scent clung to him.

He sniffed at the closest sticky note on his shoulder. Daisy had changed his life, delighting him.

Slowly, because he insisted she conserve her energy, their home was becoming a warm, comfortable retreat—especially the kitchen, where Ethan sat, entranced by his wife's pie making. When Ethan's arms were around her and Daisy snuggled back against him, Ethan found more peace than he'd thought was possible.

There was more to the Daisy-connection than the physical. Ethan frowned; he wasn't certain that he could give Daisy the warmth she needed. His experience in family matters was nonexistent, and he was feeling his way along a very slippery edge. His goal was to make Daisy his lifetime partner, and Ethan had always been a loner. He shuddered; he could never go back to being a loner without Daisy. There had to be classes in being a long-term contract, highly appraised husband.

Ethan tapped his finger on a yellow note and it stuck. That's what he intended his relationship to Daisy to do—stick.

Daisy opened his office door, locked it and hurried to him. "Ethan, honey, sweetheart—look!"

He went light-headed at the endearments, then Daisy frowned worriedly at him. "You're not feeling woozy again, are you, honey?"

She reached into a drawer, retrieved a jar of Saber's Baby Food, popped open the jar and fed him amid bits of kisses. "There. You're feeling better. Not quite so shaken. Ethan, why are you grinning?"

Saber's tough CEO struggled for an appropriate answer. His wife gave him so much. Sheer, unqualified happiness to a man such as himself, was overwhelming. He leaped over the obvious, "You've just had me," to the one hovering beyond his reach. Elusive and necessary, this new answer was one he needed to form well and slide to Daisy on a romantic platter. Then Daisy lifted her suit jacket and turned to show him her waistband. "Look," she whispered.

One inch spread between the button and the hole. "I think he moved," she whispered reverently. "This morning it was tight, but—"

"Call the doctor. Call 911," Ethan ordered, shaken by the life within Daisy actually moving. He forced himself to breathe. He could not fail Daisy now.

This new emotion—panic—was not good.

"Feel…" Daisy placed his palm firmly on her stomach; a delicate flutter leaped to his touch.

Ethan tugged his hand away, startled. "It's a baby," he pronounced firmly in his best CEO voice.

"Yep. Are you thinking about marketing an oil or lotion product to keep expanding tummies and…you know from getting stretch marks?'' Daisy asked worriedly, peering at him.

Ethan slid both hands beneath her skirt, spanning the slight mound, delighting in it. He looked up at her. She needed something from him and he would give her what she needed. "You'll always be my lovely bride."

That wasn't the elusive thought he needed to give Daisy, but it served to make her smile softly, tenderly. Her fingers smoothed his hair as Ethan angled his head for more of her touch. "You don't regret my maneuvering you into marriage?"

Daisy smoothed his lips with her fingertips, her eyes shimmering with tears. "How could I? You're such a nice man, Ethan Saber."

"I am basically a nice man." Ethan leaned back in his chair, scowling at his board members. He felt as stormy as August's dark swirling clouds outside the conference room. He glanced at Daisy, seated at his side. The dressy tunic top she wore barely showed her six months pregnancy status. Below her straight skirt, her long sleek legs were elegantly crossed at the ankles.

Ethan smoothed the custom-made vest worn over his dress shirt. A male version simulating pregnancy, weight would be added as the pregnancy moved along.

He glared at Daisy; she glared back.

Ethan turned slowly to the board, fixing his palms

flat to the conference table's wood surface. He didn't want Daisy sitting on his lap as he brought up the next matter on his personal agenda. "Then we're agreed...the merger with Foils' is going forward. Now on to another matter— We're pregnant, as you know. According to the planning board in my office, project 'Baby' is right on schedule."

He nodded, acknowledging the approving, genuinely happy expressions lining the conference table. At his side, Daisy stiffened. Ethan plunged ahead, determined to resolve this slight snag in their relationship by stacking facts on his side. "In my research, I've found that there are two problems in which a pregnant couple are certain to disagree—"

"Ethan!" Daisy uncrossed her legs and put her feet flat on the floor. "Don't you dare."

For the past two days, Ethan had his first experiences with a wife's cold, firm back. However, Daisy did not move from his bed; he would have followed her. When she was asleep, he cuddled her gently, delighted with the shifting restless baby within her. Their standoff had to be resolved, before complications. "I've always believed in equal opportunity and it serves me well now with both sexes on the board. That way, I can have Saber's best expertise."

Daisy crossed her arms. "Ethan!"

He crossed his arms over the twin padding on his chest and plowed straight to the heart of the problem. "Damn that Lamaze bunk."

They glared at each other, until Daisy slowly rose

with dignity, smoothed her tunic top and reached for the carafe of ice water. She removed the top, lifted the carafe and poured water slowly over Ethan's head. Then, because she was a professional, Daisy sat, her notebook in hand, ready to take notes. Saber's dignified board snickered until pinned by Ethan's scowl; they straightened uncomfortably in their chairs.

Ethan swiped away the water pouring down his forehead and fought shivering. He brushed droplets away from his simulated female breasts and rounded tummy. "As I was saying...natural childbirth is for the birds and I want my wife's dainty feet—"

"Size eight ain't dainty," Daisy muttered. "Ethan tried to ramrod the Lamaze teacher last night and got us tossed out. He won't say he's scared, but he is."

"Am not!" Ethan regretted the childish retort and crossed his arms over his damp, padded vest.

"He passed out when they showed the first films of childbirth. The first time they showed it, when we started the class, Ethan managed to keep his lids closed. But this time, there he was, all six foot two of Saber's top CEO, sprawled on the floor, pregnant women of all stages crooning over him as he moaned, 'I can't believe that's what happens. Isn't there an automated process? What's the status of the research and development? Isn't there someway to avoid...?' Then he fainted again."

Ethan glared at her. "Are you done reading the minutes, Mrs. Saber?"

"Not yet, Mr. Saber." Daisy briskly checked off

an item on her notebook, as though she had prepared a list and nothing could stop her. "He hovers. I do not appreciate his advice on my embroidery. He's a disaster in the nursery-decorating business, and he has no idea about shopping for toy bargains. He just takes one of each. It's obscene."

"Are you finished, Mrs. Saber?" Ethan emphasized Daisy's name to better gain control. He'd loved every one of those toys, winding up the walking ones, cuddling the teddy bears and the crib mobiles were the best—ingeniously balanced.

She regarded him coolly and checked off another item. "Not quite. I am not permitted to watch anything with live births, including guppies."

"Ethan, sounds like you'd better give the Mrs. some breathing room," George Fenley, father of five daughters, and grandfather to a fleet of granddaughters murmured with a wry smile.

"Breathing" took Ethan to the huff-huff breaths he'd been practicing. "I will not apologize to that Lamaze woman."

Daisy smiled coldly, tightly. "Oh, won't you?"

The withholding of sex was a new experience in the married life of Ethan Saber. For a man who had never bowed to others, had no need to bow to the wishes of others, Ethan now had to face the power of a woman. He now understood why his male employees were occasionally grouchy and snappy and used Saber's employee gym as if they were working to row a steamboat across an ocean. The male partner when in the pregnant stage, was unstable, volatile and sleepless, roaming into the kitchen for midnight cravings and settling amid empty chip sacks, bean dip and jellied candy fish to watch taped soap operas where wives were available and warm and snugly and—hungry. Ethan really missed Daisy's hunger. When his passage through the out-of-favor male stage was finished, Ethan almost understood the mystery of life.

Sulking helped after he reluctantly apologized to the Lamaze teacher.

"You're adorable when you sulk, Ethan-honey," Daisy whispered into his ear, the night of his defeat.

"I'm glad I do it well. I've never had the experience," he muttered, still nettled by the evil Lamaze teacher who now had the upper hand in his life.

"Shall we watch the birth scene again, Mr. Saber? Or are you ready to admit that I might know just a little bit more than you do, despite your impressive library."

"I lack hands-on, but I'm learning," he had returned in an attempt to recover a smidgeon of his honor.

"So long as you understand this is my ship, Mr. Saber. You are not in command."

Now, Daisy ran her fingers soothingly over the fallen warrior and cuddled him in their bed. "You're just feeling delicate. It will pass, my big, strong, sexy man. I want you to be friends with our teacher, Ethan. If everything goes along as it should, I wouldn't want our baby to be an only child and we could be facing our teacher again.''

Ethan snorted savagely.

Daisy kissed his cheek. ''You're going to be a marvelous father, if a little overprotective. There won't be any nannies for our baby, Ethan.''

''No.'' Ethan tossed away his underling status in the birthing business with his memories of his cold childhood, his nonavailable parents.

Ethan smoothed Daisy's expanding tummy. He tried to breathe. They hadn't talked about life after the baby and now it loomed in front of him. After just seeing a home film on the birthing process and talking about the lactating mother, Ethan didn't know if he could manage a logical conversation, crafted to invite and keep Daisy in his life. ''Do you suppose…are you thinking…are we going into production with this new line? Perhaps manufacture another model? Not too soon, though,'' he added, even as excitement rose in his voice.

''Oh, I'm certain you'll work out a schedule, dear.''

''I could have a low sperm count. It's a family trait,'' Ethan admitted uneasily.

''We'll see. You're adorable and sweet and considerate, that's what's important. I know how much your apology cost you, but you did it for me. For the baby.'' Daisy rubbed her cheek against his, soothing him. ''My hero.''

''Our baby. That witch said I was important, like

a second in command. Me, a second in command. I was a boy-genius, Daisy. You understand, don't you?''

"Perfectly. You're my hero. You're always in command." Daisy, with even more lush curves, settled lightly over him. She enfolded him gently into her care and Ethan held his breath as Daisy adjusted to her comfort level. He smoothed her lacy cotton nightgown higher to caress her bottom—and discovered naked, delicious curves. Ethan began to smile, for he recognized Daisy's sultry look. It was going to be a long night.

He snagged one clear thought and reached to shut off the bedside alarm. There was no need to rise too early.

She rubbed her nose against his. "Feeling better?"

Ethan cradled the back of her head in his hand, caressing her scalp, which always caused her to purr and undulate upon him. He had begun to know her very well and liked the comfort of the expected—and surprises. He brought her lips down to his. "Where were you all my life?" he asked, hovering between the mysteries of life and the heat of Daisy's body.

"Waiting for you. You're perfect."

"A perfect employer?" Ethan prodded, wanting to hear Daisy's husky, uneven tone curl around her.

"Am I up for appraisal now?" she asked, sighing as Ethan gently kissed her breasts.

The lush burgeoning softness absolutely fascinated him. "Am I?"

She laughed knowingly. "Aren't you always?"

Later, Daisy sprawled upon Ethan and he brushed her lips with his. "You've made me so happy, Daisy. Not just like this, but you fill my life in all ways. Every day, I'm afraid I'm going to stop dreaming."

She turned to kiss his throat. "You're the nicest man I've ever known, the gentlest."

Ethan's fears, which he had never told anyone, leaped upon him, terrified him. "Do you think I'll be all right, Daisy? As a father? You know I haven't had the wonderful family life you had, and you're a natural mother, but I could fail. Daisy, what if I fail you when you need me? What if I don't do something right and you're depending on me?"

She stroked his cheek, the gesture soothing him as always. "Dear Ethan. You'll be wonderful. Don't be afraid. You're warm and kind and generous. You already know how to cuddle, and frankly you weren't that familiar with cuddling when we got married. It was as if you were afraid you'd break or frighten me. You've got a much smoother approach now—masterful, exciting, enticing with a touch of comfort."

"I am good at cuddling, aren't I? Would you rate me as excellent?" he asked with a grin.

Daisy smiled mysteriously. "Excellent."

She nuzzled his chest and foraged for his left nipple. Her mouth closed over it and she suckled gently. Ethan's body shot into all the softness of a board, after he nearly arced off the bed. "What are you doing, Daisy-dear?" he asked between his teeth.

"You wear that silly padded thing all day long, and the thought of these tasty tidbits, hidden away is erotic, fascinating."

"I want to understand the changes in your body—" She nibbled slightly and Ethan groaned. He groaned louder when the heated rhythm of her lips took him. "Daisy!"

Much later, Ethan realized that he had just completed his first making-up event and there were benefits to infrequent, light marital arguments.

Chapter 5

Daisy settled into her chair slowly, heavily, the tiny bouquets on her cream-colored maternity dress settling gently over the mound of her baby. She smoothed the comfortable cotton fabric, sewn on her mother's sewing machine. She picked up the embroidery hoop, the baby's gown stretched over it. The blue lines of the pattern waited for her needle, while her thoughts needed sorting. She began the outline of a leaf.

Without asking her advice, Ethan had jumped into researching a high-tech sewing machine, loaded with gizmos she'd never use or understand. The familiar gold decoration on her mother's plain stitch, black iron machine gleamed in the evening lamplight. Ethan's background did not involve cherishing gifts from father to son—except the Saber Baby Food Company—or a mother's beloved sewing machine passed down to her daughter.

Daisy looped the embroidery thread and fastened it to the cloth, forming a tiny petal. It was now November and the baby was near. Her time with Ethan had been so short; an uneasiness ran between them and she wanted it settled. She gave him the warmth of a home that he had lacked, and he was easing her through what could have been a troubled passage. They were friends. Sliding into a living arrangement with Ethan was easy because they had worked together for years.

Her needle and thread formed another delicate petal. They respected each other and Ethan's delight in her was genuine. Yet plain Daisy, who came from blue-collar working people, did not fit the Saber House with its grand dining hall, the book-lined study and the fleet of hired people necessary to maintain the huge estate and house. Ethan had had parties—cold little affairs—and as his secretary, Daisy had sent out invitations and had taken care of the usual protocol in a business dinner.

She expertly formed another petal, the petals forming a daisy as she ordered her thoughts. The bottom line was that she did not fit the image of a powerful man's wife, his counterbusiness part, holding socials and executive wives' teas. Ethan seemed unaware of her inability to chat about Versace, Gucci purses or shopping trips to France and Italy. This problem would surely arise. Ethan would see her for what she was—unsuitable. It was best that they both prepared themselves for a gentle ending.

"How is the new line coming? The single-bag idea with all the test samples of stretch mark ointment, a chart booklet and samples of prenatal Saber Baby-Crave foods?" she began gently.

"If you had one of those new sewing machines, you could embroider with it," Ethan murmured, intent upon his sewing machine database, comparing the features in columns.

"My mother loved her plain machine. I love it. When I embroider by hand, it's like stitching a little love into the garment, to protect the wearer and remind them that I care. No, I'd never embroider with a new machine. Instead of buying a new machine, why don't you putter with it? It needs oiling and—"

"What's wrong, Daisy?" Ethan folded the sewing machine file away. "I've sensed an uneasiness in you. Is it something I've done, or not done?"

"Why are you wandering through the house, like some dark laser lord, inspecting it?"

Ethan rubbed the back of his neck tiredly. "You don't like the house. You never go too far out of our living quarters and you don't explore the other wings. You've created a tiny home within this huge house for us, and yet you've never seemed to fit into Saber House as if you wanted to stay. 'That's very nice,' you said, when I gave you that first tour."

"But, Ethan, it is nice." Since they had worked

together for years, she might have known that Ethan's same keen mind was aware of the differences between what he needed, and plain old Daisy.

Ethan ran his hand over the shirt pocket she had neatly repaired for him, the movement a caress. "What if something happened to you in one of the wings while I was away at the office and no one could find you?"

"You're wearing a beeper, Ethan. You're making me carry one," she reminded him gently. "There are maids and butlers and—"

"This house was made for entertainment…for business soirees and hosting potential business alliances. We're not utilizing the facilities for which they were intended."

Daisy stopped fashioning the tiny French loop petals. "I know. I am totally unqualified to be a Saber wife, unfamiliar with ordering people to serve me, and—"

"That is just it," Ethan snapped and sprawled back in his chair, his lids lowered as he considered her.

Daisy shivered, placing her hand protectively over her child. Now Ethan would point out to her how unsuitable she was as a corporate wife. She'd been living a dream—

"Daisy?" Ethan moved out of his chair and scooped her gently into his arms, carrying her toward their bedroom. "You just went pale. What's wrong?"

She couldn't stop the tears streaming down her

cheeks. "I knew you would come to your senses one day. I was hoping that I could give you—"

"Have patience with me, Daisy. I'm trying to learn new skills. Personnel management courses did not cover our relationship." Ethan gently lowered her onto the bed and eased away her slippers. He glanced around the warmth Daisy had created. "Thank you for replacing the buttons on my blue striped jacket and for tightening all the other buttons in my closet. To me, each dainty stitch seemed to be a gift. They also remind me that I grew up very differently from you."

Ethan took her hands, holding them between his larger ones. "Daisy, you are so unique. I wouldn't have you any other way, but adorable and sweet. But we can build a new home."

A separate home for her and the baby. Ethan was moving her out of his life. The baby wasn't his and—

"You know what I was searching for in those hours I prowled the hallways? Memories. Happy ones that would have come from my childhood. I couldn't find them. There were no echoes of laughter." He frowned and reached behind him to rub the small of his back. "Funny, I've never had backaches before."

"It's because you carry me constantly. I've put on weight." Daisy slid her hand around him and rubbed gently. She ached for Ethan-the-boy, remembering her own beautiful childhood with loving parents.

Ethan arched and sighed with pleasure. He lay

down beside her, and folded his hands behind his head. "I want a nest," he stated, turning his head to look at her. "Rather, I want to build a nest. I don't want you worrying about tricycle skid marks on the marble floors. I want the entire composite to be a real home. I love those intimate, economy dinners you serve, made better by the cozy little table. Cozy is new to me, and I like it."

Daisy's heart flip-flopped as he said firmly, "I want to be involved in the planning and upkeep. I'll need a workroom for tending that sewing machine you treasure, and an office. I do not want cold, unused rooms where a child cannot play. The Mortons have something called a 'family room' filled with children's toys and activities, and comfy furniture where the whole family can relax at one time. Sometimes they all sit on the floor. This room has a big rocking chair in it and in my entire childhood, I was not rocked, not even when I was ill as a baby. I want a rocking chair for our child, Daisy. I have unexpected needs and the paternal nesting urge has surprised me."

Ethan lifted on one arm and leaned over her. He placed his hand on her stomach. A tiny kick answered his touch and Ethan held his breath until the baby quieted. "I realize that I am not the baby's biological father, but I will do my best and I apologize for being limited in family experience. I should have long ago seen that you needed a comfortable home, and I don't want to endanger you by stressing you now. Would you mind terribly helping to design a new home for us? Something functional, and most of all warm for a family."

"I'm unqualified to design a home that would suit Saber's top executive, Ethan," she stated gently. "You need servant quarters. You need housekeepers and butlers and maids. You need to preserve your status image. You need what this house has."

"Bird poop." Ethan's flat comment and scowl caused Daisy to smile. "Whatever you do fits my status. I like wearing patched clothes—do you know why? Because you took the time to care about me."

Behind his lashes, something flickered that frightened Daisy. She'd seen that closed, wary look before, but it slid into another expression, one vulnerable and aching. If it hadn't been Ethan Saber, fearless heir and brilliant boy-genius, lying at her side, she might have labeled his next fleeting expression as fear. "Ethan? What is wrong?"

"Did you love him so much that you can't forget him, Daisy? Are you thinking how much better at being a father that Hewson would be, rather than me? He was an attractive man after all, and charmed the office ladies easily...I'm not good at charming...and I've put on a little weight these past few months. I know I've had some moods that weren't exactly level and I don't understand that, either. Am I dull old Ethan and will you lose interest in me and turn to another man? Now that all my mysteries are gone— I didn't have many—will you look for someone more exciting? Daisy, I found a gray hair this morning and my back has been hurting for days."

"If you'd stop wearing that silly paternity vest, you wouldn't have that problem," she said, trying to find her balance with this emerging Ethan. "You've always charmed me. You are a man of integrity, Ethan Saber. Never doubt your charms."

Ethan roughly scrubbed his hands over his face. "I don't understand this placid feeling. I'm always so...so out there, charged up, meeting business challenges, keeping to a schedule and lately, all I've had is an urge to snuggle and neaten. It's as if I'm preparing for a major event and I don't know what—"

"Hold me, Ethan." She needed him in her arms, this sweet man, when she told him about Howie.

She cuddled him close to her, his arms gently enfolding her. "You're feeling uncertain, Ethan, and no wonder. We've both gone through so many changes in the last few months. You've been perfect, except for that Lamaze incident—"

She stroked his hair and waited for him to stop muttering. "I don't know what waits for us, Ethan. But I do know what is real, and that is you're the perfect father for my baby. I know that you excite me today just the way you did when you first kissed me. I know that those few extra pounds just make a little more to cuddle, and you're definitely not dull. You're a beauty of a man, a prize. My hero, and very, very sexy...a rose among men and I'd pick you any day over a man like Howie. That one gray hair can't be seen, but it should be worn with pride. It means you're a man with experience.''

She treasured the curve of his mouth as he smiled. "You're also my warrior, my fierce delight and a pretty darn good masculine bonbon. You'll take off those few pounds when the time is right—if they worry you, but I like them. We could exercise together.''

"So it's all right with you that I consider this baby mine in every way and that I plan to be involved with him?''

"I'd love that, but the baby could be a her, Ethan. We decided we'd like the surprise, remember?''

"Even better. What do you think about the new house idea? Would you want to develop the project with me?''

"You plan to live in it, right?'' she asked, still bothered by her previous uncertainty.

Ethan glared at her. "Where else would I live? Here? Someplace with rotten childhood memories that I do not want our child to have? I don't think so,'' he stated in his firm CEO voice. "We're a team.''

Daisy adored this man she'd come to know and love. In the past months, love had settled upon her gently, in the quiet hours when she turned on her side in the night to watch Ethan. To wonder how she could be so fortunate to have him in her life, caring about her. She winnowed her fingers through his hair and cradled his strong jaw between her palms. "You're not so bad."

"Stick with me, Daisy. I'll get the hang of this family business."

"You already have."

Ethan frowned. "How so?"

Daisy prowled her fingertip across his lips and smiled softly when he kissed it. "Ethan, before we married, I was never totally satisfied in a sexual way...in fact, in any way. That final moment always hovered outside my grasp. But my first time with you...rather from the first time you kissed me, I sizzled."

Ethan sat upright, shocked. "Are you saying that you'd never climaxed before? You've been doing it on a pretty regular basis since we married. Often," he added, amazed. "Daisy, when we first—those first few months, we couldn't get enough— Good Lord, when I think of how often and how and when we— You mean your sex life with Hewson lacked that much?"

"Immensely. I'd rather not discuss details, but I'll give you this insight. I grew up with Howie. Our families knew each other and we slid into marriage. I had grand dreams of changing Howie into a family man, just as my mother had changed my father. But Howie never grew into the marriage and like a fool, I kept hoping. We coasted like that for years and I came to know in my heart that Howie would never love me more than the motors he revved. He would never love me more than himself.''

Daisy inhaled and threw a fact at Ethan that she'd tucked away in an "unpleasant drawer." "The night the baby was conceived was the first instance in months. He hurt me and then he fell asleep. He wasn't a frequent or considerate flyer and this is the last time we're going to discuss him in relation to our sex life, which is very…very intense, beautiful and fulfilling.''

"Do you mean that our sex life is uncommonly good?'' Ethan asked shakily. "That our percentages and averages are higher than norm?''

"Uncommonly and not at all average. You would never hurt me or be so inconsiderate. You've always taken care, even in the rush of our desire. And I've always desired you, dear Ethan. It has to do with how attractive you are to me.'' She smirked and patted his flat, hard stomach.

Ethan grinned, delighting her. His blush fascinated her. "We'll have to slow down. The baby, you know.''

She grinned back and flung her arms wide-open as she fell back upon the pillows. "Kiss me, Ethan. Make me palpitate. Make me throb.''

He laughed outright, one of those quick new bursts of masculine delight that pleased her more every day. Daisy stared at him, enjoying every line crinkling around his sparkling eyes, the warmth framing his lips.

She fluttered her lashes at him, enjoying the new

flirtation tactic. "Don't wear that silly vest anymore, Ethan. I want your studly body next to me, not all that padding."

"Daisy, what are you doing?" Ethan struggled from the depths of sleep, past the sounds of November winds howling outside, to see his wife standing on a chair, flipping a towel over the top of a puffed drape. The mound of their baby pressed against her light cotton shift.

"Mmm? Go back to sleep, Ethan."

"It's three o'clock in the morning, and you've cleaned for days." Ethan whipped out of bed, stalked to the chair and eased her into his arms. "Daisy, you'd polish and scrub this entire mausoleum if I'd let you."

"You were kind to help me wash and dry all those crystals on the dining-room chandelier. I appreciated you helping with polishing the family silver. If you want that new house, what will happen to the servants who love you?"

Ethan blinked, thinking of the staff who had been with him for years. "Max, the butler? Cicily, the maid? Maggie, the housekeeper? John, the gardener? They love me?"

"They adore you and you know it. Haven't you always seen that extra help was hired when needed, and haven't you helped with college tuitions for their children, and what about last year when Maggie had a bout with the flu? You hired a nurse, Ethan. Not many employers would do that."

"They were mine to take care of and so I did. That is not unusual." Ethan floated a bit, high on this new knowledge, at how his staff beamed at him now and coddled his wife's every whim. "But I see what you mean. They are a bit old for the job market, aren't they?"

She patted his cheek. "You love them, Ethan. You know you do."

Ethan shifted restlessly. He was uncomfortable with love. He wasn't certain how it was defined, or how it related to him. "We'll need them, of course, in our new house. But I'll set up a semiretirement plan for them and hours they can help. They need to feel needed, Daisy."

Love. It terrified Ethan. He didn't understand the components or the nuances. "I need you next to me…in bed," Ethan stated shakily, frightened by this new tireless Daisy. He wanted his arms around his wife, anchoring her safely to him.

Three days later, November winds hurled leaves against the house as Ethan hovered in the doorway of Saber House, his briefcase and sack lunch in one hand, Daisy curled in his other arm. "I don't want to leave you. The doctor said the baby was in position and traffic could be bad when you need me."

Daisy rested her cheek against Ethan's chest, listening to his strong, safe heartbeat.

"No more cleaning the bathrooms. Good Lord, I

almost passed out when I saw you on your hands and knees scrubbing."

"That bumpy texture needs a brush, darling."

"Yuck. The things one discovers when helping one's wife," Ethan muttered. "I want to stay home."

"You can't. You're reviewing the packaging for Saber's Mom's and Dad's Prenatal Line." Daisy had to get rid of Ethan. She felt like a watched pot that never boiled. She needed time alone. "Get out."

Ethan leaned down to study her. "If you're going to do more brooding about that foolish notion you have—unsuitable as a Saber wife—I won't. If you're going to take it easy, rummage though the clipping ideas for a new house and take a nap like a good girl, then I'll work this morning and come home this afternoon."

A little twinge sang low in Daisy's body. She couldn't concentrate on her body, if Ethan was hounding her every minute. "Put your feet up...did you take your vitamins?" he was asking.

"I have work to do—" She caught his scowl and smiled innocently. "Nothing much, just thinking, running over a checklist of the baby names, maybe embroidering, and I want to patch that silk tie of yours, the watercolor one that matches your eyes."

"Mmm." Ethan's tone said he wasn't buying the whole package.

Daisy smiled as he gathered her to him, gently, firmly, cherishing her. Ethan placed his chin over her head, enfolding her in his scent, his strength. At times he looked at her as if he wanted to say something, but it eluded him. It was an emotion; Ethan had difficulty expressing his emotions, though his body and his gestures told her that she was dear to him.

She traced his brows, smoothing the worry line between them. Were they playacting? Were they merely helping each other at a time when they each needed what the other could provide?

Experienced with her emotions, Daisy knew she loved Ethan. She also knew she would frighten him, if she told him so.

Ethan could slog his way through vicious board meetings, and she'd seen him step into an alley fight to protect an elderly man from thieves—an eye-opener for Daisy. Ethan had been lethal, his body almost performing a ballet in the oriental defense. Later, his aura bristled with a hard masculine edginess and she had delighted in his…swagger, his commandeering of her, and holding him close as he described his hatred of bullies and how the boy-heir to Saber fortunes often found himself without school lunches.

Physically, mentally, Ethan was on top of his ability to meet challenges. But when emotions were involved, Ethan circled them warily.

"Go." Daisy patted his well-formed bottom, then caressed it.

The kiss tasted of Ethan's hunger and whatever ran through the depths of his warm chocolate brown eyes. "I'll call you."

"I thought I'd take a nap this morning," she returned, feeling much lighter than she had a week earlier.

Ethan frowned. "Daisy, the baby is awfully big, isn't he?"

She patted his chest. "Now, Ethan. You know all about the mother's body preparing for that, don't you? You called enough doctors to double-check."

"Second opinions never hurt."

"I think five should be sufficient."

Ethan scanned her face intently. "Is your bag packed? Are you certain you don't need me?"

"I'll call you immediately—you'll have to trust me, Ethan."

"I've never trusted anyone like I trust you, Daisy," Ethan stated firmly.

Daisy eased down onto the old rocker she'd discovered in a shop. Ethan wasn't trained to repair wood or refinish it, but he wanted to give her and the baby something of himself. His intensity, his desperation to properly restore the chair had frightened her.

She smoothed the curled wood at the end of the arms and went inside herself to the small life that had suddenly settled. Daisy rocked slowly and focused on the new changes in her body.

"We love him, don't we, baby?" she whispered. "He's afraid of us, you know. He's afraid that we give him more than he gives us. He's afraid he won't give us what we need. I think Daddy is afraid of love right now. He likes defined roles, and with love, he isn't certain how he should feel, or what he should do.''

Daisy folded her hands over the baby, tensing as that odd twinge shot through her again. She glanced at the clock—Ethan would just now be surging into his office, tossing out orders to a terrified new secretary. He'd be striding back and forth, tapping his finger on his lip and studying Saber's new Mom's and Dad's Prenatal Line.

Daisy drew her mind back from Ethan to the task before her. She glanced at the bed they shared, the packed suitcase waiting—Ethan hovered in her mind; what was it that bothered him? What haunted him as he hid his study of her? What would ease him?

The baby curled softly within her. Daisy gave herself to the peace of rocking and knowing that soon she would hold their baby in her arms. She needed her rest, because she knew exactly how Ethan would react.

The fender dent in Ethan's gray, custom BMW and the dragging muffler confirmed her suspicions. She unlatched his hand from the car telephone and laced her fingers with his. "Do not call the hospital again, Ethan. Twice is enough.''

"I wish it were me, instead of you, going through this.'' Ethan glanced at her just as a pain soared through her and their eyes locked, Daisy squeezed his hand.

"No more babies.'' Ethan's uneven tone mocked

his attempt to play in-control CEO of baby production.

"You'll be fine."

"It's blasted traumatic." His gaze swung from the streets to hers. "You won't leave me, will you, Daisy? These past few months have been the happiest of my life. You're the sweetest person I've ever known."

"I wouldn't think of leaving you, sweetheart."

"Don't leave me, Daisy...sweetheart," Ethan repeated as he entered the birthing room. He stopped in midstride, locked to the sight of the band crossing Daisy's stomach, which monitored the baby.

"The pains are coming quickly now, Mr. Saber," the nurse said. "You remember your Lamaze training?"

"Lamaze," Ethan whispered unevenly, making it sound like hand-walking to the moon.

"Ethan!" Daisy cried, needing him desperately. He turned pale and another pain hit Daisy.

"I..."

"Mr. Saber, the baby is coming quickly now." The nurse shook him gently.

Daisy had no time to be gentle. "Ethan," she said in a voice that projected roughly through the room as if coming from the depths of a monster-terror movie.

She raised her head and glared at him. All six foot two of strong, macho, capable Ethan Saber seemed to quiver.

"This is it, big guy," Daisy stated harshly. "I'm not going to die, I'm just having a baby. Get your butt over here. This is not game-time and no one is going to rescue you. I want you."

"You want me. You are not going to die," he repeated hollowly and then life seemed to move into him.

Ethan moved quickly to her side and Daisy reached out to grab his tie, drawing her down to him. "Now, you're going to help me and you're not going to pass out, because I can't handle you and the baby. Got it? You remember those *huff-huff, hee-hee* exercises?"

Ethan swallowed and Daisy released his tie. He quickly stripped it away, tossed aside his suit jacket and rolled up his sleeves. His expression was pure focus, intent upon what he must do and Daisy relaxed slightly. She could trust Ethan; he would be there when she needed him.

"Jeez, you're sexy," Daisy whispered after Ethan coached her through the next pain.

Ethan smoothed the damp hair back from her face, his expression haunting her. There was more than fear nagging Ethan Saber. He looked helplessly at the nurse. "Do something for her," he asked humbly.

"I think you're all that she needs, Dad."

He winced as Daisy clutched his shirt in both fists, catching the whorls of hair beneath the fabric. "She's so special—"

"I'm right here, Ethan. You can tell me." But Daisy had an admission of her own. "He's so sexy that I've spent practically our entire marriage making love to him."

"He is a good-looking man," the nurse agreed.

"Without his clothes, he's even better."

Daisy searched Ethan's worried, desperate expression. She had to tell him, careless of the return of his love for her. "I love him. He's the most wonderful man I know. He's my prince, my hero."

"He's blushing, honey," the nurse murmured with a grin. "I think it's time to call the doctor."

Daisy gave herself to the pain, locking, focusing on Ethan's coaching. "What?" she demanded, hearing a wisp of something she needed desperately.

"What?"

"What was that about adoring me?" she demanded, clutching the safety of his hand.

"He is a sweet man. He's shy, though, even with his wife," the nurse whispered to the doctor.

"Tell that to my receptionist. He's been bullying her for months," the doctor muttered, putting his hands on the unborn baby, testing the position.

"I am sweet. Daisy said so," Ethan snapped.

"You adore me?" Daisy prompted amid her pain.

"Of course I do. You know, I do."

"Oh, no, I don't. You're a miser, withholding what you know I want to hear most." Daisy raised up to look down at the doctor who was adjusting the sheet between her spread knees.

"Tell her, man," the doctor ordered. "You adore her and you...what her?" he coached.

After the next pain, Daisy lifted up again to glare at the doctor. "Don't pick on him. He's new to the emotion business."

She fell back on the pillow and stared at Ethan. She had no time to be sweet and understanding. He was on his own. She narrowed her eyes, menacingly at Ethan. "Are you going to tell me you love me, or not?"

"You know I do," Ethan shot back roughly. He glanced uneasily at the doctor who was getting in position for the baby.

"Yes, he has to be *that* close, Ethan, lover of mine, my friend, my tender—"

"Push," the doctor ordered. "Tell her you love her, Saber."

"You stay out of this," Ethan growled, glaring at him.

The doctor snickered. "We're in this together, Saber, and this time, you do as you're told."

"We should push now, Daisy. The doctor says it's time."

She glared at him. *"We?"*

She lifted to look down at the doctor between her raised knees. "*We*, he says. You know we made love so much during *our* pregnancy, that *we* sometimes had to take naps on the sly? At the office, in Ethan's executive washroom? He actually took naps on Saber company time to rest up for our lovemaking."

Daisy could feel herself warming up. "*We* had midnight cravings. *We* had queasy stomachs. *We* had backaches."

The doctor shrugged. "Happens all the time with men who care, really care."

Daisy fell back to the pillow and looked up at Ethan with soft, teary eyes. "I know and that's why I love the big sap."

The big sap had the grace to look uneasy. "You won't want other children after this, and I want you to know I understand. I won't hold you to the baby production idea."

"Fathead. We'll talk about this later."

Relieved that the baby-production matter had been postponed, Ethan cuddled Daisy, placing his cheek along her damp one. "I love you, sweetheart. I was just trying to think of a new way to tell you—"

Her eyebrows went up. She was incensed, raging, pain consuming her. "All this time and you were thinking of a new way?" she demanded, then screamed with pain and frustration.

"I love you, Daisy. You're more than I've ever wanted, or expected. I made a checklist, an appraisal of what you've given me and it was stunning. You've given me delight and laughter and peace. I've never known any of these things before, or the home you've made for us. You complete me. At times, it seems like I've loved you forever, and I know I'm not an easy man to know, but whatever else happens—Lord, Daisy, you think that was all sex between us?"

Another pain hit her, shattered her.

When she could speak, she had to tell Ethan. "I love intimacy with you. It's a part of loving you, sweetheart."

Ethan turned pale. "Intimacy. I could never think of a word like that. It's not in my vocabulary."

"Develop a new one," Daisy ordered in her new CEO voice. "You're inventive, talented and my love. I have confidence in your skills. You can do it."

"Baby coming," the doctor noted. "One more push should do it."

"I love you," Ethan stated firmly. "Be my love, Daisy-waisy, and—are you listening, Daisy?"

"I'll want to hear more later, honey. Really, I do. Right now—" Daisy saw tears shimmer in his eyes, took Ethan's love into her, giving her strength and then she pushed. She screamed as the baby slid into the doctor's hands.

Ethan, holding a baby feeding spoon and wearing a fresh layer of baby oatmeal and peaches, grinned up at Daisy. In the high chair opposite Ethan, little eight-month-old Tristan Saber gurgled at his father.

"How much better can it get?" Ethan asked with delight as he opened his mouth, miming the eating process to Tristan, who obediently opened his little mouth. Ethan spoke quietly to the baby as he fed him. "You've got the best, prettiest, lovingest mommy, a cozy home and Daddy loves you."

Ethan turned suddenly to Daisy, standing at his

side. Ethan was very careful to express his love for Daisy, watching her intently as though he desperately needed her to believe him. "I love you, too. I never thought I could be so happy. Thank you for my life, Daisy," he said formally, still vulnerable from his shadowed, severe past.

"I love you, too, honey." Daisy bent to kiss Ethan's oatmeal dappled cheek, and tasted the tiny globs sticking to his morning stubble. "By the way, on your way home from the office, could you pick up a Saber's Mom's and Dad's Prenatal Pack?"

"No need to. The promotion was a success," Ethan replied as he continued to feed Tristan.

When Daisy remained silent overlong, Ethan turned to her, his expression concerned. Daisy sent him a sizzling look and licked her lips. She placed a sticky paper square that said Daddy on Ethan's chest. "You'll be needing those prenatal vitamins, Pop, because I am feeling very, very sexy," she murmured seductively and bent to whisper into his ear.

He turned to kiss her tenderly, with just that whang of hunger to please her. He served his brand-new, developing product intimacy at her. "You're always very sexy. You'll be exciting to me when we're in our nineties and beyond."

"Nice appraisals are always appreciated, Ethan. By the way, do you still have that comfortable cot in the executive washroom?"

When he frowned at her, Daisy explained with a grin. "A second promotion is on the way."

Ethan stared at her as he placed the tiny oatmeal and peach laden spoon into his mouth. While he studied her, in his thoughtful, business professional look, he took a second spoonful. Slowly delight spread over his expression. "I do love you, Mrs. Saber."

* * * * *

THE PATERNITY TEST
Sherryl Woods

Prologue

Next Saturday's baby shower would be the fifth Jane Dawson had been invited to in the past three months. Every time she turned around, it seemed, another friend or another co-worker was having a baby. She was being overwhelmed by the sight of rounded tummies, radiant faces and silver rattles.

She'd become such a regular at Annie's Baby Boutique that Annie routinely called when something special came in. They'd become fast friends, and the boutique had become Jane's favorite after-school haunt for a cup of tea and some girl-talk.

As a result, Jane's biological clock was ticking so loudly, she was sure it could be heard throughout her hometown. She would be thirty in July, not so old for having babies these days, but definitely getting up there, especially with no prospective father in sight.

Once again back at Annie's, this time specifically to buy a present for Daisy Markham's shower on Saturday, Jane rubbed her fingers over the cheerful yellow gingham liner in an antique carved oak crib that was Annie's latest treasure and sighed heavily. She'd been sighing a lot lately. Wishing, too, and dreaming.

It was getting more and more difficult to hide her envy, as well. *Oohing* and *ahhing* over one more hand-knitted pair of booties, one more tiny outfit, might send her over the edge. Today, she thought looking at the crib, could very well be the day.

"What do you think?" Annie asked, glowing with pride over the refinished piece. She still had streaks of wood stain and polish on her hands. Her no-nonsense short hair was mussed and she hadn't gotten around to so much as a dusting of powder across her face, much less any lipstick.

"Is that not the most beautiful crib you've ever seen?" she demanded.

Jane tried to hide her own yearning to possess that crib—to have a reason to possess that crib—and nodded. "It's lovely."

"Can you imagine?" Annie asked indignantly, buffing the already gleaming surface. "I found it stuck way back in a dim corner of an antique place out on Route 3. You should have seen it. It had been painted half a dozen times at least. Stripping it, I went through layers of white, blue, pink and several more of white paint. It was caked on so thick, it wasn't until I got almost down to the wood that I saw the carving.''

The shop's owner rubbed her fingers lovingly over the intricate design. "A little angel. Have you ever seen anything so precious?''

"Never," Jane said, her yearning to claim it deepening.

Annie grinned. "Well, I know it's too extravagant for a shower present, but I just knew of everyone who comes in here, you'd appreciate it the most. I had to call the minute I put it in the store. Sometimes the urge to share my finds overwhelms me. I hope you don't mind that I left a message at the school. It's not like I'm trying to make a sale. I know perfectly well you don't need a crib.''

Something inside Jane snapped at Annie's offhand remark. "I'll take it," she said as if to prove her wrong. "Just the way it is with the yellow gingham liner and all. Put it on my account and send me the bill.''

Almost immediately she regretted the impulsive words as Annie gaped.

"But—''

Jane cut off the shocked protest. "You can have it delivered to my place, right? John will bring it by Saturday morning, won't he?" she said, referring to Annie's husband, who frequently helped out with deliveries on weekends.

"Of course, but—''

"Thanks," she said, cutting off her friend's ques-

tions, logical questions for which she obviously had
no rational answers. ''I've got to run. I have a PTA
meeting tonight. All the teachers have to be there
early to greet the parents. We're trying to butter them
up so they'll help us raise the money to upgrade the
cafeteria. Don't forget to wrap up that little pink
sweater and bonnet for Daisy's shower. It's Saturday
afternoon. You can send the package along with the
crib.''

''Of course.''

Jane felt Annie's puzzled, worried gaze follow her
as she left the store and walked up the hill toward the
old brick school.

Not until much later, after the PTA meeting, after
she was back home and sipping a cup of tea, did she
concede that Annie might have cause to wonder what
an unmarried, uninvolved woman was going to do
with a baby crib. Hopefully she could come up with
a plausible explanation before everyone in town concluded that she'd turned into an eccentric old spinster
whose hormones required serious adjustment.

Annie's devoted husband, still handsome and fit at
fifty, delivered the crib at 9:00 a.m. on Saturday. He
set it up in Jane's spare bedroom and never once
asked why in the world she'd bought it. Jane swore
her undying gratitude to the man for that.

After he was gone, she made herself a cup of raspberry tea and sat down in the tiny bedroom to admire
the crib. She dreamed of the day when she'd have a

baby of her own sleeping on the pretty yellow sheets, when she could decorate the walls of the room with bright paper and a border of ducks and rabbits and put a rocker in the corner. The image was so clear, she felt an incredible pang of longing to make it real.

"But it's not real," she told herself sternly, forcing herself to leave the room and close the door firmly behind her. The purchase of that crib suddenly seemed foolish. She was months, if not years, ahead of herself.

This time it was her friend Daisy who was having the baby, her third. She already had two boys and had discovered that this one would be a girl. She and her husband were over the moon about it, even though the boys were teenagers already and this baby had been a huge surprise.

Jane told herself that the sharp stab of envy she felt was normal, the alarm going off on her biological clock, so to speak. Buying a crib, however, was a bit of an overreaction. Maybe she should call Annie, admit she'd made a ridiculous mistake and have John pick up the crib and take it back to the store. She even reached for the phone, but she couldn't seem to make herself dial.

If only...

She brought herself up short. There was no sense looking back. Mike Marshall, the love of her life, was in her past. They had made a rational, mature decision together to end the relationship nearly a year ago when he'd been offered an incredible job in San Francisco. A clean break, they had decided. No looking back.

Mike had always dreamed of the kind of opportunities this new company would give him. He'd craved the recognition it could bring him as an engineer, the financial stability of the salary a big firm could offer.

Jane's dreams were different, simpler—a home, a family, roots in a community where neighbors knew each other and cared about each other. It was almost the way she'd grown up, the way she wanted her own children to be raised, quietly and with a greater sense of stability in their lives than she had had with a father who'd always been running off.

Since Mike had gone, she'd told herself a thousand times that they'd made the right decision, the sensible decision. Love sometimes meant letting go. If they'd been meant to be together, they would have walked down the aisle years sooner, but Mike had always held back, needing the proof that he could support a family in a style his own background had never provided.

But Jane still cried herself to sleep thinking about him. Being sensible, she'd concluded, sucked.

Since he'd gone, she'd hidden her favorite snapshot of him deep in the bottom of her drawer, but every now and then she stumbled across it and each and every time it brought tears to her eyes. The sale of his old house, right next door, had made his move final and the permanency of it had left her shaken for months. Lately she'd told herself she was over him, that she *had* to be over him. But she wasn't, not by a long shot.

Once they had talked about a future, about having babies and growing old together, but that golden opportunity in California had been too powerful for Mike to resist. She wouldn't have let him turn it down, even if he'd wanted to.

And she hadn't been ready or willing to leave the town and the job that suited her so perfectly. Both of them had dug in their heels, unable to see any way to compromise. And so a relationship that had once meant the world to both of them had ended.

By now he'd probably found someone new, someone more suited to a big-city lifestyle, someone whose social life revolved around more than baby showers and picnics and an occasional movie. She hoped he had. She didn't want him to be as lonely and miserable as she was.

What if he was, though? What if he missed her as desperately as she missed him? If that were the case, though, wouldn't he have called?

No, of course not, she told herself, not if he took their agreement as seriously as she did. Not if that famous Irish pride of his had kicked in as viciously as hers had. When it came to pure stubbornness, they were a perfect match.

She opened the door to the spare room and stared at the crib again, imagining her baby there, hers and Mike's. A chubby, strong little boy with round cheeks and thick black hair just like Mike's. Or maybe a rosy-cheeked little girl with glints of red in her hair just like Jane's.

Had she closed the door on that dream too soon? Had she accepted Mike's departure too readily, conceding defeat when she should have been fighting tooth and nail to find a way to make it work?

Finding that crib at Annie's had forced her to face emotions she had convinced herself were dead and buried. If she still loved Mike as deeply as ever, didn't she owe it to both of them to see him again, to see if there was anything left now that he'd had a chance to test his wings in the kind of job and city he'd always dreamed of?

Spring break was just around the corner. So was Mike's birthday, though she'd always been more sentimental about such occasions than he had been. After she paid for the crib, her savings account was going to be low, but there was enough left for a trip to San Francisco without dipping into the rainy day money her mother's small insurance policy had left her. Could there be a better investment of her savings? She couldn't think of one.

Maybe they would fall in love all over again. Or maybe they would sleep together one last time for old times' sake.

Maybe by some glorious fluke they would make a baby, she thought wistfully. Okay, it was highly unlikely, but what a joyous blessing it would be! Whether their relationship resumed or faltered, she would treasure a child of theirs, raise it on her own, if need be.

The decision to go to San Francisco was made as impulsively as the purchase of that crib. It took an hour on the phone with the travel agent to nail down all the arrangements. By the time she was finished she was late for Daisy's shower.

The party was in full swing when she arrived, the laughter and teasing audible from outside. When she walked in, the group fell silent and stared.

"Where on earth have you been?" Daisy demanded, hefting her bulky figure from a chair and rushing over to hug Jane. "You're never late."

"We tried calling the house a half-dozen times but the line was busy," Ginger added. "Donna was about ready to drive over there."

"So? What happened?" Daisy prodded. "Don't tell me Mike showed up on your doorstep after all these months."

"Nothing like that," Jane said. "I just lost track of the time."

"You never lose track of the time," Daisy protested.

"Well, this time I did," she said, a defensive note in her voice that clearly startled them.

Donna, who'd known her since first grade, studied her intently. "Okay, maybe he didn't show up, but it has something to do with Mike, doesn't it? Did he call?"

"No, he didn't call."

"But it does have something to do with him?" Donna persisted with the unerring accuracy of such a longtime friend.

Jane wasn't ready to discuss her plans with anyone, not even her closest friends. She forced a brilliant smile. "Hey, forget about me, okay? I'm here now and I want to see the presents." She handed her own to Daisy to add to the pile beside her. "Get busy. You look as if that baby could pop out any second now. I want you to finish opening all these before it does."

With some reluctance, everyone finally turned their attention back to the gifts. Jane *oohed* and *ahhed* with the rest of them, but her mind was already somewhere else, in a city she'd never seen, with a man who was part of her soul.

Chapter 1

Engineer Mike Marshall had had more adventures than most men twice his age. Most of the riskiest had come in the past twelve months, since his move to San Francisco. Until today—his thirty-second birthday—it hadn't occurred to him to wonder why he was suddenly so willing to put his life on the line.

The truth was, he'd always been eager to take risks. As a kid, he took every dare ever offered. Now, though, he didn't even wait for the dare. If an overseas assignment for his company didn't satisfy his hunger for adventure, then he scheduled a trek up Mount Everest or a rafting trip on the Snake River. It had been months since he'd had a spare minute, much less a moment's boredom.

And yet, something was missing. He knew it, just

the way he knew when a design for a bridge or a dam wasn't quite right. He stared out his office window at the Golden Gate Bridge emerging from a thick fog and tried to put a name to what was missing from his life.

Not excitement, that was for sure. Every day was packed with it.

Not companionship. He'd met a dozen women, beautiful, successful women, who shared his passion for adventure.

Not money. His salary was more than adequate for his needs, more than he'd ever dreamed of making back in Virginia. For the first time in his life, he felt financially secure, able to support a wife and family if the right woman ever came along.

Not challenges. The partners in his engineering firm only took on the most challenging jobs.

What, then? What was the elusive something that made him feel as if the rest hardly mattered? What was behind this vague sense of dissatisfaction? It irked him that he couldn't pin it down.

To his relief, the buzzing of his intercom interrupted the rare and troubling introspection.

"Yes, Kim. What is it?"

"You have a visitor, sir. She doesn't have an appointment," she added with a little huff of disapproval.

Mike grinned. Kim Jensen was a retired army drill sergeant with close-cropped gray hair and the protective instincts of a pit bull. She maintained his schedule with the precision of a space shuttle flight plan. Flexibility was not part of her nature.

"Does this visitor have a name?" he asked.

"Jane Dawson, sir."

The clipped announcement rattled him as nothing else could have. His heart slammed to a stop, then took off as if he'd just been advised that it was his turn to bungee-jump from the penthouse floor of a Union Square office building. The reaction startled him almost as badly as the mere thought of Jane in San Francisco. Jane, who'd never flown in her life, had come clear across the country, out of the blue, with no warning? He had to see it with his own eyes.

"Send her in, by all means."

"Are you sure, sir? You have an appointment at fourteen hundred hours. Sorry, sir. I mean in ten minutes."

"Send her in," he repeated and stood up, wondering at the astonishing sense of anticipation that was zipping through him.

"Just plain Jane," as she'd been known a dozen years ago, was in San Francisco? The woman who'd vowed never to leave their small Virginia hometown had braved her first flight on a whim, just to say happy birthday, perhaps? The concept was so out of character he found it almost as impossible to grapple with as the design for a sturdy, yet inexpensive bridge in some third world country.

But unless he'd imagined Kim's announcement, Jane was here, on his turf, and his heart was beating as rapidly as it had the day he'd stolen his very first kiss from her. At the same time a long-missed sense of calm settled over him.

The door to his office opened, Kim stepped aside and Jane walked past her. His mouth dropped open. He'd known her his whole life and he almost didn't recognize her. Her old high school nickname was hardly appropriate anymore. There was nothing plain about the woman before him. She was wearing a lime green suit that flattered her coloring and slinky heels that flattered her long legs. Her hair was shorter, with a sassy, trendy cut that feathered against her cheeks, then skimmed to her shoulders in layers. The red highlights glinted brighter than ever. She looked more sophisticated than he remembered. Sexier, too. Then her familiar sweet, shy smile came and went and his heart flipped over, just as it always had.

"Hello, Mike. Happy birthday."

His own grin broadened. "I can't believe it. Come here, you."

He opened his arms and, after an instant's hesitation, Jane stepped into the embrace. When she was settled against his chest, her head tucked under his chin, the oddest sensation crept over him. It was as if he knew, at long last, what had been missing.

But, of course, that couldn't be. He'd put Jane Dawson firmly in his past when he'd made the move to San Francisco. He'd given her his word that the break would be clean and he'd kept it. With his parents dead, his brothers and sisters scattered and the family home sold, there'd been no reason to go home again. He hadn't looked back, not once. Well, hardly more than once.

He stepped back eventually and looked her over. "You look fabulous. Sit down. Tell me what you're doing in San Francisco. Is it a teachers' convention of some kind? Why didn't you let me know you were coming? How long are you staying?"

She laughed at the barrage of questions, the sound as clear and melodic as a bell. "Last question first. I'm here for a week. I didn't let you know because I didn't know myself until the last minute. Spring break crept up on me and I decided not to spend it cleaning the house the way I have every other year since I started teaching. This is pure vacation."

She regarded him uncertainly. "I hope you're not about to take off on an assignment or something. Will you have time to have dinner at least? We haven't missed celebrating your birthday together since we were kids."

"Dinner will be a start," he agreed, thinking of all he could show her in a week, imagining her excited reaction. That was the thing he had loved about Jane. She brought such enthusiasm to every discovery, whether it was finding an arrowhead in the clay banks of the Potomac River or seeing the first crocus pop up in the spring. It was the quality that made her such an excellent teacher. She was able to communicate that enthusiasm to her students.

She'd always been able to communicate it to him,

as well. Maybe that was why they'd been so good together, even though her pursuits were far more sedate than those he might have chosen for himself. Once they'd toured Stratford Hall, Robert E. Lee's birthplace, together. When she'd suggested it, Mike had shuddered at the prospect. He'd been barely into his teens and a whole lot more interested in playing ball than touring a musty old plantation.

Afterward, to his amazement, he'd felt as if he'd been caught up in the middle of an incredible family drama that had eventually played itself out on a Civil War battlefield. There was no denying that Jane had a gift for teaching, a gift for firing the imagination.

At the moment, with her looking the way she did, his imagination was taking off in a much more provocative direction, remembering the feel of her in his arms, the burning of her lips on his.

His intercom buzzed way before he was ready for the interruption.

"Sir, your appointment's here," Kim announced with a touch of triumph and the obvious expectation that he would promptly shoo his unscheduled visitor out of his office.

"Get him a cup of coffee or something and tell him I'll be right with him," Mike told her. He turned back to find Jane staring out the window, her eyes wide and shining with excitement.

"It's something, isn't it?" he asked, moving up behind her to gaze at the Golden Gate.

"Better than the pictures," she agreed. She turned.

"I can see why you were drawn here. The Golden Gate always did inspire you. Even when we were kids, that was your favorite picture in the encyclopedia. You must have sketched it a million times. Now it's right outside your window."

For a few weeks that had awed him, too. Then he'd begun to take it for granted, just as he once had the love of the woman standing here with him now. The sound of his buzzer reminded him that he had a prospective client waiting and an impatient secretary who wasn't likely to let him forget it.

He touched Jane's cheek with regret. "I do have to take this meeting. Where are you staying?" he asked. "I'll have Kim clear my schedule this week. I'll be by at six to pick you up."

"Are you sure? I don't expect you to drop everything for me."

"I'm sure," he said with no hesitation at all.

In fact, he hadn't been more sure of anything in a very long time.

Jane still couldn't believe it. Her first flight had been a real nail-biter even before the first pocket of turbulence, but it was nothing compared to walking into Mike's office, staring down that snippy, protective secretary of his, then actually seeing him again. She'd been stunned by the surge of old feelings, startled by an unfamiliar rush of uncertainty until she had seen the warm welcome in his eyes.

Now, a few hours later, she realized that their very

first date hadn't shaken her nearly as badly as dressing for this one nearly sixteen years later. Of course, she'd never before prayed so intently for a date to wind up in bed. For once in her life, she wanted to make something happen, to risk everything to make her dream come true. She'd been obsessing on having his baby ever since the possibility had first crossed her mind. She wanted desperately for it to happen, wanted him to want her as he once had. But as badly as she wanted his baby, she wanted him more.

Her hands shook as she fumbled with the clasp on the gold locket. Would he remember? Mike had given her the locket on her sixteenth birthday. His picture was still inside. Glancing in the mirror as the locket settled between her breasts, she wondered if it was the wrong touch. Was she counting too much on sentiment and old yearnings, instead of the here and now? If so, her presents were all wrong, too, chosen to remind Mike of all he'd left behind.

If only she could be cold and calculating, intent only on getting pregnant by a man who had once been her best friend, as well as her lover. But five minutes alone with Mike in his office had told her that, for better or worse, she was still in love with him. It remained to be seen how he felt about her or whether they would be any better at compromise now than they had been a year ago.

Her fingers faltered when she heard the impatient knock on her door. She almost dropped the tiny, very expensive bottle of French perfume she'd indulged in.

She managed one last dab of the scent between her breasts, then went to the door.

Mike never failed to startle her when he was all dressed up in a suit and tie. Used to seeing him in jeans and T-shirts for so many years or even in a dress shirt with the sleeves rolled up and his tie askew as he had been in his office earlier, she wasn't prepared for the full impact of a light gray suit, white shirt and teal-and-gray silk tie with Mike's dark hair and perpetually tanned skin. When she wasn't looking, the boy next door had turned into a sophisticated man. Odd how she'd never noticed that before he'd left, even though he'd been thirty-one by then.

His approving gaze swept over her, heating her flesh. An impudent grin spread across his face and the boy next door was back. "Did you buy an entire new wardrobe for this trip?" he asked.

"Of course not," she lied, unwilling to let him see just how much she'd invested in this supposedly impromptu visit. She wondered if he'd guessed that her new haircut and the glistening highlights were courtesy of a San Francisco stylist to the tune of over two hundred dollars. She'd turned pale when she'd seen the bill, but one glance in the mirror told her it had been money well spent.

"I've never seen that dress before," he insisted. "I definitely would have remembered."

"You've been gone a year. Naturally I've bought a few new things in all that time."

His gaze narrowed perceptibly. "Was the dress for a special occasion?"

Jane couldn't prevent the laughter that bubbled up. "Mike Marshall, you're jealous."

He looked appalled by the suggestion. "Don't be ridiculous."

"You are. You have never made such a fuss about my clothes before."

"Because you were always in sedate little outfits suitable for teaching fifth-graders," he muttered. He gestured toward the dipping neckline and clinging silk. "This is something else."

"Want me to change?" she asked.

"Oh, no. You can wear that dress for me anytime."

"Just not for anyone else."

"I didn't say that."

She grinned. "You didn't have to." She linked her arm through his. "Come on. Let's get out of here before you start getting ideas."

"Honey, if you don't want me getting ideas, you'd better pull a sweatshirt on over that dress."

Jane shook her head, deciding she liked this newly discovered power she had to turn him on. "Not a chance. I'm all dressed up with a handsome man at my side. I want to go out on the town. I'm not wasting a single minute of this trip. I want to see and do everything."

"Then we'd better get started. This isn't our hometown, where we could cover everything in a weekend. San Francisco will take a little more time to explore."

They started with dinner across the bay in Sausalito, followed by a stroll along Fisherman's Wharf and an Irish coffee on the waterfront. Jane fell in love with the twinkling lights, the riot of sights and sounds and smells. Questions tumbled out so quickly that Mike had a hard time keeping up with the answers.

It was almost two in the morning by the time they made their way, exhausted, back to her hotel. He paused at the door to her room.

"I should say good-night here," he said, his knuckles resting against her cheek as he toyed with a strand of her hair.

Familiar, never-forgotten sparks shot through her at his touch. "You should," she agreed, then stood on tiptoe to brush a kiss across his lips. "But I hope you won't."

"Jane—"

"Don't argue. Besides, I haven't given you your birthday presents yet."

It was exactly the right incentive. Despite his claims of indifference, Mike had never been able to resist a present. When they'd first met as kids, he'd been uncomfortable with the way her mom went all out on special occasions, especially birthdays. His own family barely acknowledged birthdays, maybe because there were so many of them and so little money for extras.

Jane had always treated Mike's birthday as if it were a national holiday. She'd baked a cake, found half a dozen small, special treats and wrapped them as if they were solid gold trinkets. She'd done the same this year. She'd even arranged for the hotel to deliver a birthday cake to her room while they were out. A bottle of champagne was on ice beside it. Mike stared at it as if she'd ordered a feast.

"How did you manage this?"

She grinned. "It is San Francisco, after all. Anything's possible. Isn't that what you told me when you were trying to convince me to move here with you?"

"I'll bet the cake's not my favorite," he said, already poking a knife speculatively through the thick coating of whipped cream frosting.

"Oh, but it is. Chocolate with raspberry filling," Jane confirmed.

He turned and smiled at her. "You're amazing."

"So you've always told me. I suppose I'll always have to go to extraordinary lengths to live up to my reputation." She opened a drawer and extracted three small, brightly wrapped packages. "These first, then cake."

As he always had, he opened the smallest one first. It was a gold key ring with a bright beach design enameled on it and Virginia written in bold red letters.

"Afraid I was going to forget home?" he asked, laughing.

She gazed at him, then said quietly, "I was afraid you already had."

His laughter died and his gaze locked with hers. "Never."

Jane swallowed hard, then looked away. She couldn't read too much into that, she didn't dare. "Open the biggest one next," she insisted.

"But I always save that for last."

"Not this year."

"Okay, okay," he said, picking up the flat, ten-by-twelve-inch package. As if to taunt her, he took his own sweet time with the ribbon and paper. When he finally had it open, she saw the heat rise in his cheeks as memories tumbled back. He glanced at her, his astonishment plain.

"It can't be."

"Oh, but it is," she assured him. "It's a picture of your car, that old blue convertible you loved so much." She paused, then added softly, "The one we made love in the first time."

"Where on earth...? I thought for sure this was on the junk heap long ago."

"Nope. I was walking through town one day and heard the sound of that engine—"

"Who could ever mistake that?" he asked, chuckling. "It sounded like a lawn mower on speed. The word clunker was coined for that engine."

"Maybe so, but that clunker still runs, and a teenager, one of Velma Scott's boys, has it now. He thinks he's the hottest kid in town."

"Just the way I did."

"You were the hottest boy in town," Jane said softly. "Anyway, I asked him if he'd take me over by the river and let me take a picture for you."

"I hope you didn't tell him why," Mike said.

She chuckled. "Didn't have to. He figured that part out all on his own. He said he remembered watching the two of us in that car when he was just a kid."

"Hopefully not while we were parked by the river."

Jane laughed at his horrified expression. "It was ten years ago when you sold it. He was maybe eight at the time. I doubt he was allowed out at midnight."

"Thank God for that." He ran his fingers over the glass as lovingly as he once had touched the finish on that beloved car. He met her gaze. "Thank you."

"You're welcome."

"Can I ask you something?"

"Sure."

"Why the trip down memory lane?"

She shrugged, trying to feign indifference. "I don't know. I suppose I was feeling nostalgic when I realized it was your birthday and it would be the first one in years we hadn't shared."

"Have you missed me, Jane? Is that it?"

She forced herself not to look away, not to skirt the truth. If ever an occasion called for honesty, this was it. "I missed you, yes. More than I'd imagined possible."

"Oh, baby," he whispered, gathering her close. "I've missed you, too."

He tilted her face up, then slowly—inevitably—lowered his mouth to hers. And with the touch of their lips, passion raged and a lifetime of memories came flooding back.

Chapter 2

No one back in Virginia would have called Jane plain if they could have seen her tonight, Mike thought as his touch brought color to her cheeks and a flare of heat to her eyes. He'd always thought she was pretty, but tonight he was certain he'd never seen any woman more beautiful.

Cupping her face in his hands and gazing directly into her eyes, he asked, "Are you sure? We promised we wouldn't do this again. You said—we agreed—it would only drag things out, complicate them."

"I haven't had a decent complication in my life in a long time now. I'll take my chances," she said, her gaze steady. "Please, Mike, I want you to make love to me again. I've missed being in your arms. I've missed the way I feel when you touch me."

"Like this?" he asked, caressing her. "And this?" His hand slid lower, caught the hem of her skirt and lifted it as he stroked the inside of her thigh above the sexy black hose she wore.

Her familiar whimper of pleasure was his answer. Teasing and taunting, he came closer and closer to the hot, moist place between her thighs, never touching it, until she was arching against his hand, demanding more. In bed, her natural shyness had always vanished. She let him know what she needed, provoked him into giving it to her, then shared every bit of her pleasure with him. She was doing the same thing now.

His own pulse was racing, his body hard, but still he concentrated on Jane. He took her to the edge, then retreated, until she was gasping and pleading with him to come inside her.

He wanted to. Oh, how he wanted to, but he hadn't come prepared. Making love had been the last thing he'd imagined them doing tonight, because they'd both so vehemently declared the relationship over. He'd figured he'd be lucky if she allowed him to steal the kiss he'd been wanting since she'd waltzed into his office earlier.

"Mike, please," she whispered against his ear. She reached between them, sought his erection and almost jolted him off the bed with her cleverly wicked touches.

"We can't. I don't have anything with me," he said, sorrier than he could say.

"It's okay," she insisted, arching against him.

He regarded her doubtfully. They'd never taken chances before. "You're sure?"

She shoved his clothes aside and feathered kisses across his belly, then lower. "I'm sure," she insisted, then touched her tongue to the tip of his arousal. "I'm sure."

Mike never questioned her sincerity after that. This was the first woman he'd ever loved, the woman whose body and responses were as familiar to him as his own. Urgency wiped out all rational thought as he stripped away his clothes and then the last scraps of hers. Her skin was hot and damp when he finally poised above her. Slowly, savoring every sweet sensation, he sank into her, sheathing himself in slick velvet heat.

For a moment that was enough, just being inside her again, just feeling the stirring of his body, the pounding of his heart. Then he wanted more, so much more. Jane's cries echoed in his head as each thrust went deeper and deeper, joining them in a frenzy that went beyond lust.

It had never been like this before. They'd never made love with such uninhibited abandon, as if each sensation were wild and reckless and new. No dare he'd taken since leaving her had been this exciting, this thrilling. Maybe he'd always held back something, knowing that one day the right job would come along and he would leave. Maybe she'd always held back, knowing she would stand aside and watch him go.

Now, though, it was as if they had reached that hurdle and pushed past it. Whatever happened to them, the chemistry between them would triumph. This was the proof of that. The past, the future, neither mattered. It was now, this moment they were living in.

Thinking of it, Mike smiled. Jane caught him. Entwined in his arms, their bodies slick with sweat, she tilted her head and assessed him curiously.

"Something about this amuses you?"

"It's you," he said at once. "You amuse and delight and thrill me."

"Prove it," she dared, wriggling her hips provocatively.

"You just wait," he taunted, rolling until he was on his back and she was astride him. "I'm going to let you have your way with me."

He linked his hands behind his head and leaned back against a pile of pillows. "I'm all yours, Janie."

Her eyes widened. "But—"

"Just use your imagination. Anything goes."

A grin spread slowly across her face. "Big mistake, Mike. I have a very inventive imagination and months alone to let it run wild."

To his astonishment and delight, she pretty much exhausted him proving it.

When they'd finally collapsed and were nestled in each other's arms again, Mike listened to the soft sound of her even breathing, then sighed. "Oh, Janie," he murmured. "How am I ever going to let you go a second time?"

He would have to, too. There wasn't a doubt in his mind about that. He loved San Francisco and his job, the life he'd built for himself, the sense of security that had been such a long time coming. And as much as he wanted to, he couldn't deny that Jane belonged in the town where they'd grown up. Her roots ran deep, her feelings for the place and her friends ran even deeper. In a few short days she would go back and he'd be left to make do with these new memories and a cold, lonely bed.

Waking up to find Mike still beside her, his breath on her shoulder warm, his arm across her middle heavy, Jane smiled contentedly. It wasn't over between them, not with such powerful chemistry exploding at the slightest touch. They had six more days to figure out a solution that would keep them together. She felt more hopeful than she had since the night he'd told her he was leaving.

"You look awfully smug," Mike murmured, his voice gravelly with sleep.

"Do I? Maybe that's because I actually managed to distract you not only from opening your third present last night, but from your birthday cake and champagne."

"And you consider that a coup?"

"I consider it a miracle."

"Where is that present?"

She shrugged. "On the floor somewhere, I suppose."

"I hope to heaven it wasn't breakable."

She grinned as she thought of what the box contained—glow in the dark condoms. They'd been meant as a joke...and as a last resort if the picture of his old car hadn't gotten him into bed. Mike was a healthy, virile male, unlikely to resist such a blatant message. And, as he'd said the night before, they'd never taken chances. She hadn't deliberately set out to take one last night. The condoms, she reassured herself, were proof of that.

Even so, she couldn't help whispering a little prayer that she had gotten pregnant. Not to trap him, never that, but to give herself the child she wanted so desperately. Mike's baby.

"Jane?"

"Hmm?"

"The present. It's not breakable, is it?"

"That's definitely something you don't need to worry about," she assured him. "These are guaranteed not to break."

"These?"

She scrambled off the bed and found the box, then tossed it to him. He shook it, obviously intrigued by the light weight. When he ripped off the paper and saw what was inside, he chuckled.

"Insurance?"

"There are twelve of them. As I recall, there was a time you would have considered that a dare."

He winked at her. "Still do. Order up a huge breakfast so I'll have the strength for it and we'll try to make a dent in the supply."

They saw very little of San Francisco that day or the next, but Jane couldn't have been happier. She had come to see Mike, not the city. This was the honeymoon they'd never had, the one she'd been envisioning since she first knew what the word meant. It didn't seem to matter that the wedding she'd also envisioned had never happened. If anything, their appetites for each other were more insatiable than ever. They talked, made love, ate, made love, slept and made love again. It couldn't have been more perfect.

On her fourth day in San Francisco, she awoke to hear Mike in the shower, humming an off-key rendition of an old Johnny Cash song. The sound was so familiar, had once been so much a part of her daily life that she had to remind herself sharply that it might be only temporary. Sooner or later they were going to have to talk about something besides what to order from room service and which color of condom to try next. She picked up the box and shook it. There were none left. That pretty much eliminated one of their favorite topics.

She slipped out of bed and crept into the bathroom. When she opened the shower curtain, Mike grinned at her.

"Lonely?"

She nodded. When he beckoned, she stepped under the shower. Mike's hands, slick with soap, began to explore. It took only a heartbeat for both of them to become as steamed up as the room and thoroughly aroused. Her body was sensitive to the slightest brush of his fingers. In the blink of an eye he was lifting her, guiding her until he was deep inside and her legs were wrapped around his waist, her back pressed against the cool tile.

"Oh, yes," she murmured, as the hot spiraling need slashed through her yet again.

Mike's head was thrown back, his muscles tensed as yet another climax tore through them both.

When the aftershocks were over, he released her slowly. Her body slid along his until her feet touched the tile floor. Jane was shaken by how quickly he was able to shatter her, how attuned her body was to his. She had always enjoyed sex with Mike, thrilled to his touch, but in the past few days, they had moved to some new level of neediness. She couldn't believe what he was able to do to her with little more than a slow, seductive look.

"I can't believe what you do to me," Mike said, echoing her thoughts, looking at her with amazement once they were back in the bedroom dressing. "We were always good together, but this..."

"I know. It's astonishing."

"Scary, too," he said.

Jane stilled, gazing at his reflection in the mirror in front of her. "Scary? Why?"

"What will happen when you go home again in a few days? This intensity isn't something you can just walk away from and forget." He studied her intently. "Or is it?"

So, she thought, they were going to have this conversation now. She'd hoped to put it off a little longer, hoped to have time to put her own feelings into perspective.

"What are you asking me?"

"I suppose I'm asking what happens next. Do you just go back home and pretend that this was just a romantic interlude, a spring break to remember, something you can tuck away in a mental scrapbook? Or does it mean something to you?"

Hands and knees trembling, Jane sank down on the edge of the bed. "Do you want it to mean something, Mike?"

He came and sat beside her and took her icy hand in his. "Yes, I want it to mean something," he said fervently. "I want it to mean that this time we'll figure out a way to make things work. I want our love to last this time. I want it to mean that you'll stay here and marry me."

Jane swallowed hard. It was what she wanted, what she'd prayed for...almost. "Here," she repeated, unable to hide the note of defeat that crept into her voice.

"Yes, here," he said, the old familiar defensiveness promptly coloring his words. "Why not here? It's a beautiful city. It's exciting. There are thousands of people who would give anything to be able to live here, especially in the style I can afford.'' He frowned. ''But you're not one of them, are you? You won't even give it a chance.''

''That's not true. I came here, didn't I? It's not entirely my fault that we've barely left the hotel.''

Mike sighed. ''You have a point, which is why I'm already dressed, instead of taking you back to bed again. I want you to see the city, see my place. I want you to meet my friends. I want to take you sight-seeing and shopping until you fall in love with it all the way I have.''

Jane's spirits sagged. Couldn't he see that she was in love with him? Wasn't that enough? Why did San Francisco have to be part of the bargain?

''Please,'' he said softly, as if he'd read her mind. ''Just give it a chance, keep an open mind. That's all I'm asking.''

It was only fair, she supposed. She reached up and touched his cheek. ''I'll give it a chance,'' she promised, then turned away before he could see the tears gathering in her eyes as she saw part of her dream already slipping away.

Chapter 3

Jane dedicated herself to getting to know San Francisco, to giving it a fair chance. Mike could see the grim determination in her eyes when she sat down with a guidebook over lunch on Fisherman's Wharf and chose the spots she wanted to visit. She mapped out a rigorous, dutiful schedule his secretary would have admired.

Once they'd started, though, her attitude began to change. As he'd anticipated, she was entranced with everything, almost despite herself. The transition over the next couple of days was slow, but unmistakable. She peppered him with more questions than he could answer, delighted in the strange and exotic food, the sight-seeing ride on a boat on San Francisco Bay, the opening day ball game he'd committed to attending with clients he couldn't offend. Jane charmed them and cheered as if she'd been a loyal Giants fan her whole life.

But there was no mistaking the sense that she was on vacation, enjoying an interlude, rather than settling into a new routine. Maybe that was his fault. Maybe he shouldn't have taken the time off. If he'd left her to her own devices, maybe she would have begun to adapt as if she lived there, instead of taking it all in as a tourist.

As it was, there was a sinking sensation in the pit of Mike's stomach as Sunday rolled in. He sensed that she would leave and nothing at all would have been resolved by this visit. He was at a loss over what else he could possibly do to win her over.

There was no question in his mind that their love was as strong as ever, even after a year's separation. The sex was extraordinary. Their thoughts meshed on so many topics, disagreements were rare. It was just that the one subject about which they disagreed was a doozy, the kind that could make or break their future.

They awoke at dawn on Sunday, this time in his bedroom, rather than her hotel. When he pulled her into his arms, when he made love to her, he couldn't hide the fierce desperation in his heart. It was in his every frantic, possessive touch, in every kiss.

And in hers.

When it was over and he held her, he felt the dampness of her tears falling on his chest and knew that he had lost the battle once more.

"You're going to leave, aren't you?"

"Of course," she said briskly, then added with a catch in her voice, "school starts again tomorrow. You knew that."

"It'll be out in June," he said, struggling to keep his tone even. "Will you be back then? Can't you at least give it a three-month trial run? You could move in here with me, really get to know the city. We could spend weekends exploring all of California. Don't we deserve that much?"

She looked at him briefly, then her gaze skittered away. "Maybe. I don't know, Mike. What would be the point? Your life is here. Mine's there. Teaching matters to me. My friends matter. And we can't do this to each other over and over again. It's not like this is around the corner from home. We can't exactly commute."

"There are teaching jobs here. You liked my friends. They adored you. Okay, maybe there's not the long history you share with Donna, Ginger, Daisy and the others, but these are good people, too. You loved the museums, the restaurants. I don't get it. What's the problem?"

Tears clung to her lashes. "It's not home," she said.

For her it was as simple—and as complex—as that. Anger ripped through him. Unreasonable fury stripped away any pretense of calm. He stood up and

began to pace. It was happening all over again. She
was throwing away what they had as if it had no
importance whatsoever. He tried telling himself that
she was throwing it away, not him, but it felt the
same.

"You could come back," she suggested tenta-
tively. "Obviously your company respects your work.
Maybe you could make some sort of an arrangement
with them. It would mean traveling, but you do that
now, right? You're not even in San Francisco most
of the time."

"That's not the point. This is where the headquar-
ters are, where clients meet with us. If I'm not underfoot, I won't be the one they think of when a big
job comes in. I'll get the leftovers. Then one day
they'll wake up and discover they don't need me anymore at all." He'd been through enough firings and
downsizings with his father to know what emotional
devastation that wreaked on everyone around. He
would wind up resenting Jane for having put him in
that position.

He and Jane had been over the same ground a hundred times before he'd left for San Francisco the first
time. Nothing had changed...in her position or his.
And it broke his heart.

If only this visit had gone badly, if only the feelings
had died. Instead they were stronger than ever. He
loved Jane. He wanted her as his wife. He wanted
their children. He just couldn't see any way to make

it work, not when she was so totally unyielding, not when he couldn't see any way to bend.

"We'd better be getting to the airport," he said finally. "You wouldn't want to miss your flight."

He refused to acknowledge the hurt in her eyes. It didn't make sense that they both had to be in this much pain. There had to be an alternative, one they hadn't thought of, but damned if he could see it.

They rode to the airport in silence. Inside the terminal, as she prepared to go to the gate, he pulled her into his arms and kissed her with a hunger that left them both shaking.

"I love you," he said fiercely, as if she needed the reminder.

"I love you," she whispered. "Will you call?"

He hesitated. "I don't know. I don't know if I can go through this again, if you should go through it again. We're just making each other miserable."

A tremulous smile quivered on her lips. "Only when we say goodbye. The rest is magic."

"But we seem doomed to keep saying goodbye," he told her with regret. "Maybe this should be the last time."

Tears spilled down her cheeks. "Or maybe we just need to learn to believe in the magic," she whispered, and then she was gone.

Maybe she was right, he thought as he watched her go. Maybe the magic would come through for them yet, but he was far too practical a man to count on it.

* * *

When the phone rang at ten o'clock on Sunday evening after she'd gotten home, Jane's heart began to race. It was Mike. It had to be. No matter what he'd said about making this latest goodbye the last, he hadn't meant it. He couldn't have. Her hand shook as she reached for the receiver.

"You're back," Donna said, sounding relieved. "How was your spring break? Was it wonderful? Are you going to tell me now where you went?"

"Not tonight," Jane said, trying to hide her disappointment at the sound of her best friend's voice. "I'm beat. It's been a long day."

"Are you okay? You sound funny."

"I'm fine, just a little tired."

"Then we'll go out after school tomorrow. Dinner's on me. Darryl's coaching Little League tomorrow night and I can't wait to hear all about this mysterious adventure of yours."

When Jane was about to beg off, Donna said, "No excuses. If you say no, I'll know something's wrong."

"Okay, fine. Dinner will be great." All she had to do was get through it without bursting into tears.

The next day after the last of the kids had cleared out and Jane had done every last bit of paperwork she could find to delay the inevitable, she looked up and spotted Donna in the doorway to her classroom.

"The kids have only been back one day. You can't possibly have any more papers to grade," she told Jane.

"No, I suppose not," Jane said with regret, glancing around just to be sure.

"Then let's get out of here. It's a beautiful day, or haven't you noticed?"

"I noticed." The damp morning fog had drifted away by noon, leaving behind a sky so blue it made her eyes ache looking at it. It reminded her of the days she'd spent in San Francisco.

"Where do you want to eat?" Donna asked.

"Doesn't matter. You pick."

"Emilio's, then. I'm in the mood for Italian with lots of cheese and garlic."

"And cholesterol," Jane teased.

"I lived on little more than trail mix for an entire week," Donna countered. "Darryl takes his camping seriously. I deserve real food."

Jane thought of all the excellent meals she'd eaten on her own vacation, every ethnic variety imaginable, each one more delectable than the one before. "Well, not me. I should be dieting for the next month."

Donna grinned. "Then you went someplace with terrific restaurants. Now we're getting somewhere."

Whey they arrived at Emilio's, Donna led the way into the restaurant and picked a table in the corner. "More privacy back here, so you can tell me all the details."

Emilio brought them both huge glasses of iced tea, took their orders, then vanished into the kitchen to shout orders at the chef, who also happened to be his wife.

"One of these days she's going to chase after him with a butcher knife," Donna observed, just as the debonair Italian came scooting back into the front.

"Maybe she just did," Jane said, chuckling at his chagrined expression as he retreated to his post at the door.

Her gaze was still on poor Emilio, when Donna asked casually, "How's Mike?"

Jane's head jerked around. "Mike? What made you bring him up?"

"That's where you went, isn't it? To see Mike in San Francisco?"

"Where would you get a crazy idea like that?"

"Oh, give it up, Janie. You've got that wounded look in your eyes again, just the way you did when you two split up last year. I take it it didn't go well."

"You're wrong."

"Wrong about where you spent spring break or wrong about how it went?"

Jane sighed. "Can't I have any secrets?"

"Not from me," Donna said easily. "I've been your friend for too many years now. Now, spill it. I want to hear everything. Is Mike spectacularly successful?"

"So it seems," Jane said with a trace of bitterness.

Donna stared. "Hey, what's that all about?"

"I'm sorry. I'm pleased for him, really I am. It's just that it would be so much easier if he hated it, if he wanted to come home again, but he doesn't. The job is a dream come true. He loves everything about San Francisco.''

''And you don't, I suppose.''

''It's a wonderful city. I had a terrific time,'' she claimed, but even she could hear that her tone was flat.

''But?''

''This is home.''

''Jane, aren't you being the teensiest bit stubborn?''

''Ornery as a mule, to hear Mike tell it,'' she admitted.

''Well, maybe you should give a little.''

''And do what? Go out there, marry Mike, then discover that I'm so homesick I can't stand it?''

''Were you homesick this week?'' Donna asked.

''Of course not, but it was just a week.'' She smiled. ''And Mike did keep me very busy.'' There was enough innuendo in her voice that no one could have mistaken her meaning, especially not someone as attuned to her as Donna.

''And you still walked away,'' Donna said with a shake of her head. She regarded Jane with a genuinely puzzled expression. ''Are you crazy or what?''

The pressure of the week in San Francisco, the still-unresolved conflict with the man she loved and now Donna's unsympathetic reaction were all too much. Jane snapped.

''How can you even ask me that?'' she demanded angrily. ''You of all people know what it was like in my family. My dad had the world's worst case of wanderlust. He took off whenever the mood struck him. When he was here, he felt trapped and we all paid for it with his foul moods. When he was gone, it was no better, because then my mom was miserable. I won't set myself or Mike up for the same kind of anguish.''

"Fine. I see where you're coming from, but have you ever explained all of that to Mike? Maybe he's never made the connection.''

"How could he not have made it? He lived next door. He saw it.''

"He was a kid," Donna argued. "Do you have any idea how oblivious kids can be? You should. You're a teacher. Besides, unless I miss my guess, you were as tight-lipped then as you are now. You probably never let him know what was going on.'' Her gaze was penetrating. "Did you?''

Jane sighed. "Probably not. I would have felt as if I were betraying my dad if I'd talked about it. In those days, I only wanted to please him so he'd stay.''

"Then tell Mike how you felt, why you're afraid going to San Francisco could turn out the same way. He deserves to know what's going on in your head. All of it. Right now he probably just thinks that he's not important enough for you to take a risk that seems perfectly reasonable to him. He's offered you marriage, right?''

Jane nodded.

"And you turned him down?''

"Yes."

"Again."

"Yes."

"Can't you see what that must do to his ego?"

"Yes, but—"

"But what?" Donna countered impatiently. "No excuses, Janie. You have to tell him everything or else close the door on the best thing that ever happened to you. In the end how happy will you be here if the man you love isn't in your life?"

"I thought you weren't all that crazy about Mike," she said, confused by her friend's sudden defense of him, this unexpected push into his arms.

"I wasn't, not when I thought he was the one totally at fault, but I'm seeing another side to this now. Tell him, Janie."

"There still won't be a way to compromise."

"Maybe there shouldn't be a compromise," Donna suggested carefully. "Maybe just this once you should give in and follow your heart. I know how much a home means to you, but that house of yours isn't a home, not unless you manage to fill it with love. Last time I checked the love you want is several thousand miles away."

"Why do I have to be the one to put everything on the line?" she asked plaintively. "Why is it my sacrifice to make?"

"It's not a contest," Donna countered. "If you look at it that way, you're both bound to lose. In this case, you're the one with the options. He has a job there that he can't equal back here, at least for now. You could teach there, as well as here. Mike's ready to make a home for you there. Isn't that really what you've always wanted—a house, kids, a man who really loves you?''

The idea was tempting. It always had been. ''He said the same thing,'' she admitted.

''Then maybe it's time you listened to him.'' Donna regarded her intently. ''Or is the real truth that he just doesn't matter enough?''

''How can you say that?''

''Because, sweetie, actions speak louder than words, and you're still here.''

Chapter 4

Mike wasn't going to call Jane. He made a solemn vow to himself about that. She was the one who'd walked away...again. The door to their future had slammed closed when she'd gotten on that plane.

It was amazing, though, how the color had gone out of his life when she left. San Francisco had had its own unique charm before she'd come. Now, having seen it all over again through her eyes, he should have been doubly enchanted by all it offered. Instead it felt empty and lonely and bland.

The excitement had gone out of his work, too. His boss had offered him a plum assignment just that morning and all he'd been able to do was nod and take notes on the details. The job meant spending two months in Canada planning a new bridge project. He should have been elated. Instead he saw it only as a way to escape the bittersweet memories San Francisco now held for him. Even at that, he debated turning it down. He'd promised his boss an answer before the day ended.

It was hard to believe that just over a week ago he'd been wondering what was missing in his life. Now he knew and he couldn't think of a single way to change things and get what he wanted, what he needed.

No, that wasn't entirely true. He could quit his job and go back to Virginia. Jane would marry him then, but he would wind up restless and bitter, just the way her old man had been.

Oh, he'd seen what a hell Johnny Dawson had put his family through, though Jane had done everything in her power to hide the dissension from him. For a long time he'd ached for the little girl whose life had been turned upside down every few months. He'd done as well as any kid could to offer the stability she didn't have at home. That's when the bond between them had been forged. He'd been so sure it would last a lifetime.

He'd seen the look in her eyes when he'd told her about San Francisco, the hurt and betrayal. At that moment, she had lumped him in with her father and that had been that. She couldn't see how different it would be for the two of them. He would have to travel, yes, but he would always come home. He would never leave her in any doubt about that, not the way her father had.

He wondered if it would do any good at all to tell her that, then concluded that it wouldn't. If she couldn't see it, then all the words in the world wouldn't convince her. And she wouldn't take the risk necessary for him to convince her with actions.

Which meant there were no answers, not now, anyway. He walked down the hall and told his boss he'd take the Canada assignment. He was on a plane the next day, grateful to be running from the memories that now haunted him everywhere he turned.

Jane hadn't needed the home pregnancy test or the visit to her doctor to confirm that she was pregnant. She had known it for weeks. Her body was as reliable as a clock. When she missed her period, there wasn't a doubt in her mind about the reason. Joy flooded through her, though, when the doctor actually said the words.

"You're going to have a baby," Dr. Laura Caine said. "Right after the first of the year."

Tears slid down Jane's cheeks. "You're sure? There's no mistake?" She didn't think she could bear it if she got her hopes up, only to discover there'd been an error in the lab.

"No mistake," Dr. Caine assured her. "I take it, despite the tears, that you're happy about this."

"Oh, yes," Jane breathed, cradling her stomach. "Oh, yes."

"There will be complications."

Jane's heart slammed against her ribs. "Complications? What sort of complications?"

"With the school. Parents might object to having an unmarried woman teaching when she's carrying a child."

"I don't care," Jane said, chin tilted defiantly. "I'll take a leave of absence, if I have to. I want this baby, Doctor."

"Can you manage a leave of absence financially?"

"If I have to," she said, thinking of the money her mother had left her. If ever there was a rainy day need for it, this was it. "You'll get paid. Don't worry about that."

"For heaven's sakes, Jane, I'm not concerned about your bill," the doctor said, clearly insulted. "I'm worried about the stress you'll be putting on yourself and the baby."

"Oh." She flushed. "I'm sorry."

"Don't worry about it. Look, if there's anything I can do to make it easier for you, if you need a letter for the school, whatever, let me know."

"Thank you."

"What about the father?"

"What about him?"

"Will you tell him? He could help out if you're out of work."

"No," Jane said quietly. "I won't be asking him for help."

That night, though, as she sat in the room she already thought of as a nursery and contemplated her wonderful news, an image of Mike kept intruding. He would be happy about this. She knew he would. And he had a right to know. Common decency told her that. It didn't have to mean marriage or child support or any of those things. He just had a right to know he was going to be a father.

It took her a week to work up the courage to call. When she'd left three unanswered messages at his apartment, she guessed that he was off on an assignment. She finally took a deep breath and forced herself to call his office, bracing herself for an inquisition from that ogre who answered his phones and guarded his door.

"Mr. Marshall is out of town," Kim told her, giving away nothing about his whereabouts.

"Can he be reached?"

"In an emergency."

"This qualifies as an emergency," Jane insisted. "Ask him to please call Jane Dawson as soon as possible. He has the number."

"I'll give him your message when I hear from him."

Jane lost patience. "Is that how you handle an emergency? You just sit around and wait for him to check in?"

"Those were his instructions."

Suddenly Jane was a twelve-year-old girl again. She'd fallen from a tree and broken her arm. She remembered desperately wanting her daddy, needing him, crying for him, only to be told by her mother that they had no way at all to reach him. It wasn't going to be that way for her child. She would see to that.

"Never mind," she said dully. "Don't bother telling Mr. Marshall I called."

That night, for the first time since she was twelve, she cried herself to sleep over a man who was too far away to care.

The Canadian project took forever, far longer than anyone had anticipated. Mike could have left someone else in charge once the work was underway, but his boss agreed with him that the client deserved Mike's personal attention. And Mike had no reason to go back to a lonely apartment in a city that had lost its luster. It was early December before he finally returned to San Francisco.

Spring, summer and fall had passed in a blur. Not a moment had gone by, though, that he hadn't thought about Jane. He'd missed her, longed for her and cursed himself for the weakness.

Obviously, though, she hadn't been thinking about him. If she'd called, Kim would have given him that message.

On his first night home, he knew he would be too restless to sleep. He drove straight from the airport to the office and found himself faced with a mountain of files and old message slips. He was about to toss the messages, when Jane's name popped out at him.

He glanced at the date: *May 27.* Cold fury ripped through him. Why the hell hadn't he gotten the message way back then? Why had it been left on his desk all these months?

He noted that Kim had first written "emergency" in the message space, then crossed it out and written, "never mind."

Dear God in heaven, what sort of emergency had there been? Why hadn't Jane been given his Canadian number at once? Oblivious to the hour, he called his secretary at home, waking her from a sound sleep.

"Kim, I'm at the office. There's a message here from last May from Jane Dawson. Why wasn't I told about this? She said it was an emergency. What kind of emergency?"

"Wait, let me think," she said, instantly alert. "It was right after you left. Oh, yes, I recall. When I told her you'd left instructions that messages were to wait until you called in, she told me to forget it. I should have just thrown the message slip away, sir. I'm sorry."

"No, what you should have done was give me the damned message," he shouted. "Never mind," he said, slamming the phone down, then dialing Jane's number. His heart pounded, thinking of her needing him and then being brushed off.

It had to be nearly dawn in Virginia, but Jane's phone rang and rang. Not even her answering machine picked up. At least the number hadn't been disconnected, he told himself, but that was small consolation.

He had a bad feeling about this, a very bad feeling. He called the airlines, then left the office. At home he heard three more messages from Jane, probably left months ago, as well. More panicked than ever, he threw some clean clothes into a suitcase and headed straight for the airport. He would be on the first flight out in the morning.

On the long drive from the airport to the riverfront town about eighty miles away, he told himself over and over that there was no reason to worry. Her answering machine was probably just broken. She'd probably just left the house earlier than usual that morning. He would find her at home when he arrived.

As he drove into town, he tried to see it through her eyes, tried to imagine it as a safe haven. True, the streets were clean and lined with large homes with gracious front porches. The old oaks were bare now, but in spring and summer their shade would provide welcome relief from the penetrating glare of the sun. Instead of being gray and choppy as it was now, the river would be a glistening blue.

The downtown section was barely more than a half dozen blocks of tidy storefronts and blinking neon signs. In summertime, the sidewalks were bustling with locals and tourists, but at this time of year, with the wind bitingly cold off the river, they were practically empty. One shopper, head lowered against the wind, rushed toward the blinking lights of the small gift shop, intent on Christmas shopping, no doubt.

Why didn't all of this beckon to him, as it did to Jane? It wasn't that he hated it or held bitter memories. Simply put, it had never been enough. It had lacked the opportunities he'd craved.

A few minutes later he was sitting in front of Jane's house, staring at the drawn blinds and remembering the first time he'd seen the little girl who lived there. She'd been his shadow from that first meeting.

He never even glanced next door at the house that had been his home for most of his life. He was too stunned by the bleak darkness of her house. There were no signs of life at all, no indication of Christmas preparations inside. Jane had always decorated and baked with a fervor for the holidays. That sick feeling in the pit of his stomach intensified.

What if something had happened to her? What if she'd been ill and needed him? A thousand *what ifs* ran through his head, each one worse than the one before.

The school, he thought finally. There would be answers at the school. He drove the few blocks without even noticing what he passed. He was tearing up the walk, when he ran smack into Donna Iverson exiting the building. He'd known her almost as long as he'd known Jane, but she'd never much liked him. Now she stared at him incredulously.

"Mike?"

He grabbed her shoulders. "Where is she?" he demanded, not even trying to hide his worry. "Where's Jane?"

He saw the caution spread across her face. "Dammit, Donna, tell me. Has something happened to her?"

"It's taken you long enough to get around to asking that question," she said heatedly. "It's been months since she called you."

"I just got her message last night. I've been in Canada for months. You have to believe me—if I'd known she was looking for me, I'd have gotten back to her." He ran his fingers through his hair as he thought of how Jane must have felt when he didn't return her calls. Compassion threaded through his voice as he imagined her pain. "She must have felt so abandoned when I didn't call."

"She did," Donna agreed, regarding him evenly, clearly not intending to give an inch.

He felt the need to defend himself to her. "But I didn't know she needed me. I swear I didn't. I would have called—hell, I would have been here—if I'd had any idea she needed me."

Something softened in her expression then. "You love her, don't you? You really love her?"

"Always have."

Donna nodded, clearly accepting it as the truth. "I thought so. I told her there had to be some sort of mix-up, some reason you hadn't called. I begged her to keep trying, but she refused."

"Then tell me where she is. Let me try to straighten this out."

"Come on over to my house," she said. "We need to have a talk."

He wanted answers here and now, but he could tell he didn't have a choice. Donna intended to do this her own way. He followed her to a small brick house with black shutters, went inside and accepted the cup of coffee she offered him. "You are going to tell me where she is, right?"

"After we talk. I want to be absolutely sure I'm doing the right thing."

Mike grinned despite himself. "I always knew I was going to have to ask permission to marry her. I never figured you were going to be the one I'd have to ask."

"Oh, there's a whole slew of us around here who care about Jane. You're just lucky I'm the first one you ran across. Darryl wants to cut your heart out."

She said it with such cold-blooded sincerity, he shuddered. "Then I'll be sure to steer clear of Darryl."

"Maybe not. I married him six months ago. He'll be home any minute now."

Mike had an image of Darryl Smoot left from high school. The boy had been as big as a house and mean to boot, at least on a football field. Off the field, he'd cultivated the same image, but the rumor had been that it had all been for show. Mike prayed that the rumors were true.

He and Donna were still skirting the subject of Jane's whereabouts when Darryl came through the door. He was still huge, but he was all muscle now and the scowl that spread across his face when he recognized Mike was intimidating enough to give Mike a few bad seconds. Then Darryl turned his back on him as if he didn't exist and gave his wife a re-sounding kiss.

"What's the story, sugar? When did he turn up?" He gestured in Mike's direction.

"He's looking for Jane."

Darryl turned a fierce look on him. "Maybe Jane doesn't want to be found, same way you didn't when she called looking for you."

"That was all a big mistake," Mike explained again.

"So you say."

"It's the truth, dammit. Just tell me where she is. Is she okay? What the hell is going on?"

Donna snagged her husband's arm, then shot a look at Mike. "Excuse us a minute, please."

He heard their whispered exchange outside the kitchen door, but he couldn't make out a single word. He guessed they were debating how much to tell him. If the circumstances had been different, he'd have told them what they could do with their games, but they were his best hope for getting at the truth in a hurry. If anyone knew Jane's secrets, it would be Donna. And like it or not, he'd rather tangle with her and

Darryl than try to get information out of the principal of Jane's school.

Finally, when he was about to lose it, the kitchen door swung open and Darryl came back alone. He held out a piece of paper.

"Here's her address." He positioned himself so he was in Mike's face, literally and figuratively. "You do anything to hurt her again and you'll deal with me. Is that understood?"

"Understood," Mike agreed, then moved around the man. When he was at the door, he glanced back. "I'm glad she's had you in her corner all this time," he said with absolute sincerity.

"Should have been you."

Mike sighed heavily. He could see Darryl's point. "Yes," he agreed without reservation, without even knowing what it was Jane had been left to face alone. "It should have been me."

Chapter 5

Jane had baked ten dozen batches of Christmas cookies since dawn. She'd only burned the first three dozen, trying to get the timing down in the ancient oven in the tiny furnished apartment she'd rented until the baby was born. The apartment itself wasn't bad, with its huge windows overlooking the river and its bright curtains and overstuffed furniture. The appliances, however, were a very different story. The stove was turning her holiday baking into an adventure.

She'd taken a leave of absence for an entire school year, rather than battle the board of education over her suitability to teach. She had enough money left from her mother's insurance policy to cover her expenses, including this apartment in a town just far enough from home to protect her reputation. Maybe it was a foolish, old-fashioned ruse, but she had to try to give her child a start that didn't include speculation about his or her paternity.

She had debated just staying in her own house and weathering the gossip, but in the end she'd concluded she and the baby would both be better off if they just turned up again in the spring. Maybe she was only postponing the inevitable questions, but she'd felt she would be better able to cope with them after she'd gotten through the pregnancy and had a healthy baby.

There was an ironic twist to her decision, of course. In the end, she'd done exactly what she'd refused to do for Mike. She had left the hometown she loved.

But it wasn't as if it was going to be forever, as it would have been if she'd married Mike. And she was still close enough to have lunch every couple of weeks with her friends. They met at a restaurant midway between the two towns, caught her up on all the news and brought her anything she needed from her house. They were scheduled to get together again on Saturday and she intended to have her usual packages of Christmas cookies ready for them since it was likely to be the last time she saw them before the holiday.

The apartment smelled of cinnamon and sugar and ginger and echoed with the sound of Christmas carols being played at full volume. In fact, the CD player was so loud, she barely heard the knock at the door. She turned the sound down, then listened just to be sure.

"Who on earth…?" she murmured, wiping her hands on a paper towel and grabbing the last batch of cookies from the oven before going to the door. It was probably a neighbor complaining about the volume of the music or her landlord coming to beg a couple of cookies. The man had an insatiable appetite for sweets and a constantly—and futilely—dieting wife who refused to bake them for him.

With her cheeks flushed from the heat of the oven and probably streaked with flour, Jane suspected she was quite a sight. Judging from the impatient pounding on the door, though, she didn't dare pause to make any improvements in her appearance.

"Okay, okay," she muttered under her breath, throwing open the door. Her mouth gaped. "Mike? How on earth did you find me?"

He shook his head, still staring. "Doesn't matter."

No, she supposed it didn't. The point was, he was here. She wasn't sure which of them was the most stunned. His gaze went from her face to her unmistakably huge belly in the blink of an eye, then remained there as all the color drained out of his face.

"You…you're…"

"I'm going to have a baby," she said, supplying the words that eluded him. She regarded him intently. For a rugged man, he looked awfully shaken. "You aren't going to faint, are you?"

"Of course not," he said at once. "But—"

"I think you'd better come in and sit down," she said, though that was the last thing she wanted. For months she'd dreamed of finding Mike on her doorstep, but the dream had eventually died. Now her own reaction was nothing like what she'd anticipated. She felt nothing, or so she swore to herself. She was just surprised, that explained the sudden racing of her pulse, the lurch of her heart.

To give herself a little time to gather her composure, she left Mike in the living room and went into the kitchen to pour him a cup of coffee and herself a glass of milk. She added a handful of cookies to the tray and carried it back into the living room. Mike still looked dazed.

"What? When?" he asked, apparently incapable of forming a coherent sentence.

If she'd imagined him sweeping her up and dancing around at the sight of her body swollen with his child, this stunned reaction would have been a serious letdown, but she'd stopped counting on anything from Mike Marshall. Still, she had no intention of lying to him.

"The baby's due in three weeks, right after New Year's. I got pregnant in April."

"April," he repeated, then his gaze shot to hers. "You mean?"

She tried not to be hurt that he hadn't guessed it at once. "Yes, the baby's yours, Mike."

The confirmation snapped him out of his daze. "Why the hell didn't you tell me?" he demanded angrily.

So much for the joy she'd hoped for. Jane stared him down, then said quietly, "I tried."

"Well, you didn't try hard enough."

"I left messages at your apartment," she said pointedly. "I called your office, only to be told you were away and weren't to be bothered. What more would you have had me do?"

"Write me a letter, keep calling." He ran a hand through his hair in a familiar gesture of frustration. "Dammit, Janie, you should have found a way."

"Did it ever once occur to you to call me?" she retorted. "You knew we'd taken chances. Maybe you should have been responsible enough to check to see if there were any consequences."

"So now it's my fault for not checking with you? Don't you dare try to pull that, Janie. You know perfectly well you told me there was no risk."

She flushed at that. "That's not exactly what I said," she argued, but without much spirit.

"It's sure as hell what you implied."

She couldn't deny that was exactly the impression she'd meant to give him. "Mike, it doesn't matter, not now. I'm having the baby in a few weeks. I don't expect anything from you. Not a thing. You're off the hook. You can hop the next flight to San Francisco and forget all about this."

He stared at her as if she'd lost her mind. "And what if I don't want to be off the hook? What if I want to be a father to this baby?"

She fought the little frisson of hope stirred by his words. He was just feeling territorial.

"Then we'll work something out," she said evenly. "I would never try to keep you from your child. That's why I called you in the first place."

"But you still won't marry me?"

"Now? Under these circumstances?" she asked incredulously. "No, of course not. A baby doesn't solve the problems we were having. It's just an added complication."

"That's how you view our child, as a complication?"

"No, never," she said fiercely. "That wasn't what I meant at all."

"What, then?"

"Just that it was difficult enough figuring out what to do when it was just the two of us involved."

"A baby should simplify it. We should both be thinking about what's best for our child."

"But we obviously don't agree on what that would be. We never have."

"How the hell do you know that? I only found out about this baby a few minutes ago. I don't even know what I think." He stared at her in frustration. "Jane Dawson, you are the most pigheaded woman I have ever known in my life."

"That kind of attitude will certainly win me over," she said dryly.

"I'm not trying to win you over. Obviously I've lost that battle. But I'll tell you one thing and make no mistake about it," he said, his voice climbing, "I am going to be a father to this baby and you can damned well get used to the idea."

"Well, that's just fine," she shouted back.

In the silence that followed, another CD slid into place on the player and the pure, clear notes of "Joy to the World" filled the air. Jane couldn't help it... she began to chuckle. When she glanced at Mike, she saw the fierce expression on his face begin to give way to a smile.

He sighed, then said softly, "Merry Christmas, Janie."

"Merry Christmas, Mike."

"Think we can discuss this rationally?" he asked.

"Maybe in the spirit of the season, we can try," she conceded, then gave a little gasp as the baby walloped her with a ferocious kick.

"What is it?" Mike demanded at once. "Are you okay?"

"It's nothing, just a little reminder that your kid's getting restless. The baby gets a little rambunctious around this time of day, probably because it's time to eat. A couple of cookies aren't going to do the trick."

"We'll go out," Mike said at once.

"I can fix something here."

"Do you have to argue about everything?"

She grinned. "Pretty much."

"Well, just this once give in gracefully, okay?"

His gaze settled on her stomach and a look of such yearning came over his face, that Janie felt something inside her shift. She had always imagined Mike look-ing at her with exactly that expression of awe when she was carrying his child. She had always imagined them sharing the wonder of it. Impulsively she moved across the room and stood in front of him.

"Give me your hand."

He stared at her. "Why?"

"Do *you* have to argue about everything?" she teased, echoing his accusation against her.

He held out his hand and she placed it against her stomach. The baby didn't disappoint her. The kick was another solid wallop. Mike's eyes widened and he stared at her incredulously.

"Oh, my God, that was him, her, whatever?"

Jane nodded.

"Do you know which it is?"

She shook her head. "I didn't want to know." The truth was it would have hurt too much to know if it was going to be the little boy she'd dreamed of giving Mike. She hadn't wanted to deal with that until she had to.

"It's a boy," Mike said with utter confidence. "If it's not, we're never going to have to worry about anybody messing with our daughter. She'll blow 'em away." His gaze on her softened. "You're okay? No problems with the pregnancy?"

"I'm healthy as a horse," she assured him.

"I want to know every detail," he said fiercely. "And I want to go to your next doctor's appointment with you."

Jane stared at him in shock. "You'll be here that long?"

"Honey, you couldn't get me out of town now if you wanted to. I'm here for the duration."

When she opened her mouth to argue, he cut her off. "Get used to it, Jane. I'm here to stay."

"But your job..."

"I've worked nonstop ever since you left San Francisco. I'm due for some time off. I'll call tomorrow and make the arrangements."

The thought of Mike being around for the birth of their child left her feeling shaken. If he stayed that long, if he took care of her as he obviously intended, if he reminded her of how deeply she loved him, how would she ever manage to say goodbye again?

Mike didn't sleep a wink that night. Only a part of his restlessness could be blamed on the too-short, lumpy sofa in Jane's living room. There hadn't been any question of him sharing her bed. When they'd gotten back from dinner, she'd walked into the bedroom and shut the door. A moment later she'd emerged and tossed some sheets and a pillow in the direction of the sofa. He'd gotten the message. What he hadn't gotten was a moment's sleep.

He was still wrestling with the idea that he was going to be a father. He and Janie were going to have a baby. The thought boggled his mind. Over dinner he had pumped her for every single detail of her pregnancy, trying to hide his resentment over having already missed so much of this miraculous process.

To think that she could have had this child and he might never have learned of it. The very idea of that made him so furious he wanted to break things. When he got past wanting to throttle her for not seeing to it he was informed, he thanked God over and over that she had decided to go through with the pregnancy. His next hurdle was to convince her to marry him so their child would bear his name.

He could hardly wait to hear the explosion likely to greet that plan. He'd spent the whole night trying to come up with the right words to convince her. In the end he'd concluded he would just drag her off to a church and let a minister persuade her that her child deserved to be born within the sanctity of marriage. He liked that. It was exactly the right button to push.

However well she might seem to be coping, it was obvious to him that she'd left her home because she didn't want the stigma for herself or her baby of being an unwed mom. That stigma wasn't likely to go away just because everyone back home missed the actual pregnancy. The only way to make things right for all of them was to get married. He just had to get the timing perfect.

Jane was a morning person. She always had been. He figured she'd be up with the birds, which meant he had to get busy. He dug around in the kitchen cupboards and came up with the best china the place had to offer. He found a couple of candles tucked in a drawer and put them in the middle of the table in the apartment's tiny dining alcove. Then he went to work in the kitchen.

He made biscuits and an omelet and squeezed fresh juice from the oranges he found in the refrigerator. He had coffee perking and a glass of milk poured by the time he heard the first stirrings in her room.

A few minutes later, she wandered into the dining area, barely covering a yawn. She stared at the fancy table and the huge breakfast, then sank into a chair.

"You've been busy," she said, regarding him warily.

"You told me to make myself at home. Do you want jam for your biscuits?"

"Yes, please." She toyed with the food on her plate. "Mike?"

"Yes."

"You can't keep doing this."

"Why not?"

"I'll be big as a barn."

"Maybe a bungalow," he said, grinning. "Never a barn. It won't matter anyway. I'll still think you're beautiful."

"That's only because you haven't seen my swollen ankles," she said, holding out her feet. She was wearing fluffy blue slippers. "Look. And this is at the beginning of the day. They'll only get worse."

"That's because you've been on your feet too much. That's going to stop, now that I'm here. You can keep them propped up."

"And do what?"

"Watch TV, read a book, crochet little booties."

"I don't think so."

"Jane, I intend to pamper you." He glanced at her plate. "Finish your omelet. The baby needs protein."

"How do you know?"

"I read that book you left by the sofa. Milk and protein for the baby's bones, plus plenty of fruits and vegetables."

She regarded him with amusement. "Mike, I'm eight and a half months pregnant. I know what to eat. I know how to take care of myself. If you're going to hover, you can leave now."

"I'm going to hover," he said, then added with a touch of defiance, "And I'm not going to leave. Get used to it."

Chapter 6

Mike was very big on routine. He always had been. Growing up in his household of rambunctious brothers and sisters, order and routine had been in short supply. He had always craved it. Jane suspected that was one of the reasons he'd been drawn to the calm and serenity in her house. Now he'd taken that need for order to new heights.

By the third day of his visit, Jane was fairly sure he'd missed his true calling…drill sergeant. When he wasn't stuffing her with food, promptly at seven a.m., noon and six with a couple of snacks thrown in at precisely two-thirty p.m. and eight, he was pushing the latest child care books on her to read. Judging from the stack he'd accumulated, she doubted there was a single title on parenting or prenatal care left in the local library.

And then there were the walks. Not the sort of strolls she'd grown accustomed to taking every afternoon, no. These were more like forced marches. By the time Saturday rolled around, she could hardly wait to get out from under his watchful gaze for a few hours while she met her friends for lunch.

When she appeared in the living room wearing her favorite maternity dress, the only outfit that didn't make her look like a blimp, he popped up out of his chair.

"Where are you going?"

"I'm meeting Donna and some others for lunch."

"Where?"

"At a little restaurant and craft shop in Lottsburg. I doubt you've ever been there."

He looked horrified. "But I know where Lottsburg is. It's on a back road in the middle of nowhere. You can't drive over there by yourself. I'll take you."

"Mike!"

"Stop arguing. I drive or you stay here."

"Dammit, Mike, I am not helpless."

"No, but the baby's due any second. What if you go into labor while you're on that country road all alone? Or what if there's an accident? The steering wheel could hurt the baby." He shuddered visibly. "No, I'm going and that's that."

"Mike, if you'd been this bossy when we were together, I'd have thrown you out on your ear."

"You weren't having a baby then," he said, as if

that were explanation enough for his overprotective-
ness.

Jane sighed and followed him to the car. "You'll
sit at a separate table," she informed him as they
drove.

"Whatever."

"In fact, you could wait in the car."

He grinned at her. "Don't push your luck, angel."

"Okay, a separate table will do."

Naturally, though, it didn't work out that way. All
of the women she knew were well acquainted with
Mike. They had all pretty much guessed that he was
the father of her expected baby, even if they hadn't
said as much to her face. The minute she and Mike
walked in the door together, the others crowded
around, assuming that his presence meant a wedding
was just around the corner. Jane guessed from
Donna's satisfied expression that she was the one
who'd steered Mike to Jane's apartment.

"Feeling smug?" Jane inquired, choosing a seat by
her friend.

"Hopeful," Donna replied. "He's still around.
That's a good sign, isn't it?"

"Depends on your point of view," Jane grumbled.
"He's fussing over me as if I were the first woman
on earth to have a baby."

"And your complaint about that is?"

Jane sighed. "It's not going to last. Sooner or later,
he will go back to San Francisco."

"You don't know that. He looks content enough to

me. This could be just what he needs to decide he wants to stay in Virginia.''

''He spends an hour or more on the phone to his office every day when he thinks I'm taking a nap. Doesn't that tell you something?''

''It tells me there are twenty-three hours he's devoting to you. Be grateful. Most husbands don't give their wives that much attention, ever.''

''You don't understand,'' Jane said. ''I can't let it matter. I just can't.''

''You still love him, don't you?''

''Yes, but...''

''Then use this time with him to come up with a workable arrangement.'' She regarded Jane slyly. ''Maybe you should think about the fact that you've been living away from home and away from teaching for months now and it hasn't been as awful as you feared it would be.''

''Because I still talk to all of you and see you. And at first I was so exhausted, I slept all the time. I wasn't awake long enough to miss teaching.''

''Honey, that's why they invented long-distance phone lines and airplanes. As for the exhaustion, wait till you have a toddler around the house.'' She patted Jane's hand. ''Think about it, okay? Promise me.''

Jane nodded. ''I promise.''

Donna grinned. ''Good. Now, then, let's get this party underway.''

''Party?''

"Annie?" Donna called. "Are you hiding back there?"

"I'm here," Annie called back and wheeled in a cart laden with packages as all the others shouted, "Surprise!"

"A baby shower. I can't believe it," Jane whispered, tears in her eyes. Mike made his way to her and put a hand on her shoulder and squeezed. She looked up at him and caught the way he was eyeing all the presents. She was probably going to have to fight him for the right to open them.

"After all the baby showers you've attended for the rest of us, it was the least we could do," Daisy said.

Jane thought back to Daisy's shower the previous March. That was the event that had triggered all of this. That was when she'd realized just how desperately she wanted a baby of her own. That was when she'd bought that wonderful antique crib from Annie.

It was also when she'd begun thinking of Mike again, wishing that they were together just like this. Well, almost like this. She'd hoped for a more traditional arrangement, but she was having his baby and he was here at her side. That counted for a lot.

As she opened the presents, *oohing* and *ahhing* this time over her own gifts, a feeling of absolute contentment stole over her. She wouldn't have done a thing differently, she realized now. Whatever difficulties lay ahead, she wanted this baby—Mike's baby—with all her heart. If she couldn't have Mike with her for the rest of her life, at least she would have a permanent reminder of the love they'd once shared.

When the last present had been opened, and the last crumb of cake had been devoured, she made a decision. She turned to Mike. "I want to go home," she whispered.

"Okay. I'll get all of this stuff in the car and then we'll go back to the apartment."

She shook her head. "No, I mean I want to go home, to my own house. I want to put these things in the nursery. I want to stay there. I want to spend Christmas in my own place, to be there when I go into labor."

He studied her worriedly. "Are you sure? You've gone to this much trouble to hide your pregnancy. Do you really want to go back now?"

"I'm sure. I don't want to hide out anymore. Will you come with me?"

"You know I will." He knelt down and brushed a strand of hair back from her cheek. "In fact, if you want we can stop at St. Mary's on the way and see about getting married."

"Married?" she said as if she'd never heard the word before, never heard him propose the same thing a dozen different times. Sneaking it in again now, when she was so clearly vulnerable, was a low-down, dirty trick. She wavered.

"If you won't do it for yourself or for me," he added, "let's do it for the baby."

She wanted to. Oh, how she wanted to, but a marriage that from the very start wasn't meant to last? Wouldn't that be worse than no marriage at all?

"Think about the baby," Mike persisted, when she remained silent, repeating a now-familiar refrain. "The baby deserves to have the father's name, my name. We've loved each other our whole lives. Surely we can do this one thing together for the baby we've created."

It was the right thing to do for the baby. Jane could see that. But was it right for the two of them? How much heartache could they bear? The time would come when Mike would leave. It was inevitable.

"Darling, stop thinking so hard. Stop trying to gaze into a crystal ball and figure out what will happen tomorrow or a month from now. Right now all that matters is the baby and what's best for his or her future."

He made his case passionately and persuasively. If he couldn't say the exact words Jane wanted to hear, if he couldn't promise to stay in Virginia, well, that wasn't the only thing that mattered under the circumstances.

"We can talk to the minister," she said at last and wondered if she'd just made the best decision of her life…or the worst.

It took some doing, but when Mike wanted to make something happen, he pulled out all the stops. By nightfall, they had moved Jane's belongings back into her own home, met with the minister and arranged for a quiet, private ceremony to take place two days before Christmas. Donna and Darryl had agreed to stand up for them.

On the morning of the wedding, they found the church already decorated for Christmas with huge baskets of poinsettias. The candles were lit, giving off a soft glow around the altar. Jane had bought a new, cream-colored silk maternity dress and shoes to match. Mike was wearing a black suit with a crisp white shirt and black tie.

Even though the marriage would be only temporary, little more than make-believe, Jane couldn't help trembling as she looked around at the beautiful old church. It was just as she'd always imagined her wedding would be, except in most of those daydreams she hadn't been almost nine months pregnant.

Just before the ceremony was to begin, Mike gave her a bouquet of a single white poinsettia surrounded by white roses and tied with white satin ribbons. He tilted her chin up and gazed into her eyes.

"Everything okay?"

Jane managed a wobbly smile. "Everything's fine," she assured him, thinking to herself if only...

If only it were for real, if only it were forever.

When the minister read the vows, she repeated them in a voice that trembled, while Mike's rang out clear and sure. It almost sounded as if he meant every word, but she knew better. This was for the baby, nothing more. Pride should have kept her from saying yes, but for once pride had mattered less than doing what was best for her child. And she would have a few days or weeks with Mike that she could cherish forever.

In a few weeks it would all be over, the baby would be here and Mike would leave. Her life would go on. Tears tracked down her cheeks as the minister pronounced them man and wife. Other brides had surely cried, she thought, but none from the sort of heartache she was feeling.

When Mike bent and kissed her and tasted the salty dampness on her lips, he regarded her with surprise. Instantly concerned, he whispered, "Oh, baby, it's going to be all right. I promise."

Jane wanted to believe him. He'd always made good on his promises. This one, though, seemed to be beyond his capabilities.

Donna and Darryl gave them a moment alone, then swept in and announced they'd arranged for a wedding lunch.

"That wasn't necessary," Jane said, touched by their attempt to make this occasion seem real and special, even though both of them knew the circumstances were anything but normal.

"Of course it was," Donna insisted. "Come on. We even have a limo waiting and sparkling grape juice in the back so we can toast the newlyweds on our way to the restaurant."

They were halfway to Fredericksburg when Jane's back began to ache. They were almost on the doorstep of the restaurant when the first contraction hit. She doubled over and clasped Mike's hand.

"Dear heaven, what is it?" Mike said, the color draining out of his face. "Janie, talk to me. What's wrong?"

When the hard grip of the contraction loosened, Jane managed a smile. "I'm not sure, but I'd say we got married in the nick of time. Unless I miss my guess, this baby's coming now."

"Now?" Three voices echoed with shock.

"Oh, yeah," Jane said as she was seized by another contraction.

Donna patted her hand as Mike guided her back into the limo. "Don't you worry about a thing," she told Jane. "The hospital's practically right around the corner and years from now you can tell your kid that he made the trip in a limo instead of an ambulance."

"As long as he's not delivered in the back seat of a limo," Jane said. She glanced at Mike. "How are you holding up?"

He swallowed hard. "To tell you the truth I'm feeling just the slightest bit superfluous. You're the one who's got to get the job done."

"Oh, no, you don't," Jane muttered. "You're not running off with Darryl to buy cigars or something. You're going to be in that delivery room with me."

"But I trained as your coach," Donna protested. "Are you sure you want to change at the last second like this? Does Mike even know how to do the breathing exercises?"

"Don't go getting territorial on me," Jane said. "You can coach. Mike can hover. It's something he does very well."

Darryl grinned. "I guess that leaves me to pace and buy the cigars."

The limo screeched to a halt at the emergency room entrance and Mike and Donna butted heads trying to be the first one out. Darryl took off out the other side. It was several seconds before anyone noticed that Jane was still inside.

"Hey, guys," she called out plaintively. "You can't do this without me."

Mike scooped her up and carried her inside. An orderly swooped down on them and took them straight up to labor and delivery, where less than two hours later black-haired, blue-eyed, David Michael Marshall entered the world screaming his head off to protest the indignity of it all.

By nightfall Donna and Darryl were gone and Jane and Mike were alone with their son. They regarded the six-pound-three-ounce baby with awe.

"How did we ever create anything so beautiful?" Mike wondered.

"He started out with a pretty decent gene pool on his daddy's side," Jane said pointedly.

"Better on his mother's."

"Do you want to hold him?"

There was no hesitation at all. Mike reached for him eagerly and settled into the rocker beside the bed. As Jane drifted off, the last thing she heard was Mike explaining to his son that he would always, always be there to protect him.

"You can count on it, son." He glanced at Jane. "So can you."

But she had already fallen asleep.

Chapter 7

Mike couldn't seem to take his eyes off of his son. From the moment he'd held the baby in his arms at the hospital, he'd felt an incredible mix of love and pride and joy. Nothing had prepared him for the overwhelming sense of protectiveness that had washed through him.

David was so tiny, so astonishingly fragile, yet the boy could bellow loud enough to be heard from the hospital nursery all the way to Jane's room. He was clearly going to be a kid who would make his displeasure known.

Staring down into that tiny face, Mike wondered if his father had felt the same way after the birth of each of his kids. It made him think about the way his father had struggled over the years trying to support his fam-

ily, trying to protect them, always falling just a little
short. He'd seen how defeated his father had looked
every time he failed to be promoted, every time another job ended.

Mike had watched, felt his father's pain and vowed
never to let that happen, to always go the extra mile
for his employers, to be so good at what he did that
he'd be indispensible. He knew that was what was
driving him now, that it was behind his refusal to give
up the opportunity he'd been given in San Francisco.
That job enabled him to give Jane and his son anything they wanted or needed. How could he walk
away from it?

And yet that job was the very thing that seemed
destined to keep them apart.

He sighed, glanced over at Jane and smiled. She
was finally asleep. She had shown amazing strength
and bravery in the delivery room. He'd been in awe
of her. She deserved to sleep for a month and he
intended to see to it that she got all the rest she needed
for as long as he could. He just wasn't sure how long
that would be.

He'd told his bosses he'd be back in San Francisco
after the baby's birth. He'd assumed that would be
sometime in late January. Since the baby was a few
weeks early, they would expect him sooner, probably
right after the first of the year.

He couldn't help wondering what Jane's reaction
was going to be when he said he had to go. He wanted
desperately for her to come with him, but nothing in

the past couple of weeks had indicated she'd softened her stance against leaving her home. And he knew that jobs as satisfying and challenging as the one he had in San Francisco were too few and far between to walk away from.

Was he being selfish to want to hold onto that kind of career satisfaction and financial security for his family? Or was it Jane who was at fault? One thing was for certain: Neither of them seemed willing to break the stalemate. Love, which supposedly conquered everything, couldn't seem to make a dent in this.

The door to Jane's hospital room opened and a nurse stepped in just as the baby began to whimper in his arms again.

"Just in the nick of time, I see," the woman said, reaching for the baby. "I'll take him for his bottle and put him down in the nursery so you and your wife can get some rest."

Mike relinquished his son with reluctance.

The nurse grinned. "Don't worry. I'll bring him back first thing in the morning. I promise. Believe me, you'll be glad you've had a full night's sleep tonight, once you get him home. This may be the last you have for some time to come."

Mike sighed when they'd gone. She had no way of knowing that his sleepless nights would be over in a couple of weeks at most. Then Jane would be left with the full burden of two a.m. feedings and pacing the floor with a cranky baby.

How could he let that happen? How could he possibly leave the two of them behind and go back to San Francisco? What kind of pleasure and satisfaction could he take from a job that had cost him his brand-new family? What good was financial security if it cost him the very family he was trying to protect?

He was still struggling with that when he realized Jane was awake, watching him. His mouth curved.

"Hey, you, why aren't you sleeping?"

"Where's the baby?" she asked.

"Back in the nursery, so you can sleep. The nurse suggests we both take advantage of the peace and quiet while we can."

"He's okay, though?" she asked, gazing worriedly toward the door.

"He's perfect."

"You're sure?"

"Janie, you saw him. He couldn't be healthier or more beautiful."

She struggled up. "I want to see him."

He recognized the stubborn jut to her chin and gave up the fight. "Let me get you a robe. Donna ran out and brought one back from the mall. She said you'd want to wander out of here in the middle of the night and you couldn't do it with your backside showing through that indecent hospital gown."

"I knew there was a reason she was my best friend."

Mike wrapped the robe around her, then tucked his

arm around her waist. "Ready? Do you want me to get a wheelchair?"

As he'd anticipated, she frowned at the idea.

"I can walk," she insisted, setting out a little stiffly.

Outside the nursery window, she scanned the bassinets until her gaze fell on their son. "There he is, Mike. Look, he's blowing little bubbles in his sleep."

"Just like you," he teased.

She regarded him with indignation. "I do not."

"Sure, you do. I was just sitting there watching you. You're both adorable when you sleep."

"Mike Marshall, you are a bald-faced liar."

He chuckled. "Okay, maybe I was wrong about the bubbles, but you do snore."

She swatted him. "You're just saying that so you won't feel so bad about the fact that I haven't let you in my bedroom."

"I was in your bedroom not five minutes ago," he reminded her. "That's how I know for a fact that you snore."

"If you want me to believe that, you'll have to tape-record it."

"Then you'll have to let me move into your room with you. It could take several nights to get convincing documentation."

"Oh, no, you don't. If you can't get it in one night, right here in the hospital, then it doesn't happen."

"Come on back to bed. I'll get one of the nurses

to come in and witness it firsthand. Will you believe an impartial observer?''

''Not likely,'' she said, after taking one last look at the baby. ''You can charm those women into saying anything you want them to. I saw you wheedle a dinner tray out of one of them.''

''That was for you,'' he protested, walking her slowly down the hall. ''I knew you had to be starved.''

''The point is you were able to get your way, even though it was way past dinnertime.''

''If I'm so good, how come I can't talk you into coming back to San Francisco with me?''

For just an instant, he thought he saw pure longing in her eyes, but then it was gone. She crawled gingerly back into the bed without answering.

''Jane?''

''I can't,'' she whispered. ''I want to, but I can't.''

''Couldn't you just give it a try?'' he pleaded. ''Maybe for a few months? They're not expecting you back at school this year anyway, right? Come home with me and see how it goes. Let me give you the perfect life we always imagined we'd have.''

A tear spilled over and washed down her cheek. Mike relented. ''Never mind. It's not the time to talk about it.''

''I'm sorry.''

''Don't be,'' he said, trying not to blame her for feelings that were so entrenched they might never get past them. He tucked the covers back around her, then brushed a kiss across her forehead. "Get some sleep."

Her eyes drifted closed, then struggled back open. "Mike—"

"Hush. It's okay."

"No, you don't understand. I just wanted to say thank you."

"For what?"

"For being here. For my baby."

"Our baby," he said fiercely. "He's our baby, Janie."

But she was already asleep.

The baby's homecoming was as triumphant as if he'd been royalty. It might not have been marked by media attention, but all of Jane's friends were there when Mike drove up.

Inside, Jane found the house decorated for the holidays and the nursery filled with all the supplies the baby could possibly need. Everything was perfect, or would have been if she hadn't had this sick feeling that it was all about to end. She forced a smile when Donna came over with outstretched arms.

"Let me hold my godson," she said.

"Don't go getting any ideas," Darryl warned, coming up behind her. "We've agreed to wait another year."

"I know. That's why I need to hold this one as much as Jane will let me," Donna said.

Mike joined them. "Hand him over," he said. "You'll get your turn when I'm gone."

Jane felt the salty sting of tears at the reminder that this whole homecoming was bittersweet. It marked a new beginning for her and the baby, but the clock was already ticking toward the end of her brief marriage to Mike. No doubt he'd want to set a divorce in motion before he left. What was the point of staying married when there was going to be an entire continent between them? The baby carried his father's name and that was what this whole sham of a marriage had been about in the first place.

Suddenly she couldn't bear it another minute. She ran from the room. As she let the kitchen door slam behind her, she was dimly aware of Mike's muttered curse, then pounding footsteps chasing after her.

"Jane!"

He caught her heaving shoulders and turned her around. "Oh, baby, don't cry. Dammit, I keep getting it all wrong."

She looked up and caught the tormented expression on his face. "It's not you. It's us. One minute I can almost believe that all of this is real, that we really are a family, just the way I always dreamed we would be. The next I realize it's make-believe."

"It's not make-believe," he said. "It doesn't have to be. I love you, Janie. And you love me. I know you do."

"Yes," she agreed, her voice ragged. "But that

doesn't change anything. You're going to leave. You have to do it. I understand that.''

He stared deep into her eyes. "Do you? Do you really understand it?''

She nodded. "Yes, but I hate it, Mike. I really hate it.''

He gathered her close. "I know, baby. I know. It's just like it was when your dad used to go away, isn't it?''

Startled, she met his gaze. "You know that?''

"Well, of course. Remember, I was the one you used to run to every time he'd go. Not that you ever talked about it, but I could see the hurt in your eyes, the fear that he wouldn't come back. I hated him for doing that to you.'' He sighed. "And now I'm doing the same damned thing. Telling you I love you one minute, then saying goodbye and walking out the door.''

He tucked a finger under her chin and tilted her face up. "There's one difference, though.''

"What's that?''

"You can count on me coming back.''

Hope stirred inside her. "You'll be back?''

"Whenever I can. Our boy is not going to grow up wondering if his father cares about him. It may not be a perfect arrangement, but I promise you we'll make it work.''

Something died inside Jane as she realized what he meant, that the separation would go on forever. "I guess we'll be no different from a million other divorced couples," she said bitterly. "Shipping our child back and forth on a plane."

He stared at her. "Who said anything about a divorce?"

"You did."

"No, what I said was we would make this arrangement work."

She stared at him, appalled by the suggestion. "You expect me to just hang around here, waiting for the moments you can spare us? I don't think so, Mike Marshall. I do not intend to live my life in the same sort of emotional limbo that my mother did. Go or stay, it's your choice. But let me be very clear about one thing, if you go, it will be the end for the two of us. I'll file for divorce the day you get on the plane."

She whirled around and went back inside, making very sure that she was always in the middle of a throng of friends, so Mike couldn't challenge her about her threat. She knew that a confrontation was inevitable. She couldn't ask her friends to hang around all night to prevent it, but for once she felt she was in charge of her own destiny.

If Mike chose to go—and she told herself she was prepared for that possibility—then he was the loser. There would never be anyone who could love him as she did, never be anyone to compare with his firstborn son. Her life was here, and so was his, if only he could recognize it in time.

Chapter 8

Christmas came and went, then New Year's. On the second day of January, Jane was sitting in the nursery rocking the baby, when she caught a glimpse of Mike in the doorway. She could tell from his expression that the time had come and he was going to say good-bye. Tears flooded her eyes and streamed down her cheeks. He saw them and was by her side in an instant.

"Janie, don't cry." He pulled out a handkerchief and dabbed at the dampness on her cheeks.

She shrugged off his touch. "It's okay. Just roller-coaster hormones."

"Is that all?" he asked, watching her worriedly.

She forced a smile. "Of course." She met his gaze evenly. "What about you? You seem upset."

"We can talk about it later." His gaze settled on his son. "How's my boy doing?"

"Your boy has a full tummy and is sound asleep," she said. "I should put him in his crib, but I love sitting here holding him in my arms and rocking him. I still can't quite believe he's real."

A ghost of a smile passed over Mike's face. "Yeah, I know what you mean."

"Want to trade places?"

"Sure."

He said it so eagerly that she laughed. "Here, then. I'll go do the latest mountain of laundry. I never imagined that a guy this little could generate so many dirty clothes."

Mike traded places with her, settling Davey against his chest and humming to him. She would have given anything for a picture of the two of them, but her camera was out of film. They'd gone through three rolls in the past week and she'd neglected to pick up more. She'd have to remind Mike to get some when he picked up the prints later.

Unless he was going to leave before that. That was what he'd been about to tell her. She was sure of it. She wouldn't cry when he said the words. She wouldn't. Why make it harder than it had to be? They'd both known this day was coming.

But knowing it intellectually and facing it were two very different things. She listened in dread for the sound of his footsteps coming from the nursery. When he finally walked into the kitchen a half hour later, she was dry-eyed.

"We need to talk," he said, gesturing toward a

chair. When she was seated, he asked, "Want some tea?"

Jane shook her head. Her stomach had knotted the moment she saw him. Tea wouldn't help. Nothing would.

Mike sat down opposite her and drew in a deep breath. "I'm leaving tomorrow."

Even though she'd anticipated the words, shock rippled through her. "I see."

"But I have a request before I go."

She regarded him warily. "What kind of a request?"

"A few days back you threatened to file for divorce the minute I left. I'd like you to wait."

"Why, Mike? Why wait?"

"Because I don't think we should throw our marriage away like this."

"We're not throwing it away," she said angrily. "It never had a chance."

"And whose fault is that?" he demanded, then closed his eyes, visibly struggling for calm. "I'm sorry. I know it's not your fault or mine. This goes deeper than pure stubbornness. I know that, too. We both have reasons for feeling the way we do."

"Reasons that won't change over time," she said. "We were apart for a whole year and nothing changed."

"Because neither of us made the effort."

"What's different about now? What kind of effort are we supposed to make?" she lashed out. To her shock, she thought she saw tears in his eyes.

"Please, Janie, don't write us off yet," he pleaded.

"There has to be some way to make it work. I have to leave here believing that."

"I wish I could say I agreed with you, but I don't. Some impasses just can't be broken. Why prolong this?"

"Because we made vows," he said fiercely. "Despite the circumstances, those vows meant something to me. If they meant anything at all to you, then you have to give us more time." He gazed at her intently. "Did they? Did they mean anything at all to you?"

"You know they did," she said in a whisper. "They meant everything."

He stood up and gathered her into his arms. "Then you have to wait. Don't file those papers, Janie. Please."

Engulfed by the pure masculine scent of him, surrounded by his heat and his strength, she couldn't have refused him anything at all.

"I'll wait," she said at last. "For whatever good it will do, I'll wait."

If there was any shred of hope at all for the three of them to be together always, she would cling to it.

In the middle of March, Jane had a call from the principal of her school. The teacher who'd taken over her classes was ill. The principal wanted to know if there was any chance that Jane could come back to finish out the school year.

"Of course," she said eagerly. Staying home was driving her batty. Davey didn't need her attention every second. And if she was going to be a single working mom, the sooner she set the pattern for it, the better. "When do you need me?"

"Monday will be fine."

"Thank you. I'll be looking forward to it," Jane said. Only after she'd hung up did she realize that in accepting the job, she was conceding that she would never leave home to join Mike.

Donna stopped by later that afternoon. "I hear you're coming back to work on Monday."

"The grapevine in that school always was remarkable."

"What's Mike going to say about it?"

"Mike doesn't have anything to do with it. He's in California. I'm here. I always intended to go back to work. This is just a little sooner than I planned."

"But you still haven't filed for divorce and neither has he. Shouldn't you talk this over?"

"No. It's only a matter of time. We talk almost every day but nothing's really changed. He keeps holding me to the promise I made before he left, that I wouldn't file for a divorce until we agreed that there was no chance we could make it work."

"Is he coming back any time soon?"

"He hasn't mentioned it and I haven't asked."

"Do you miss him?"

Jane sighed. "My heart breaks every time I hear his voice. I want him here with me more than anything in the world. And I know it's crazy, but I think Davey misses him, too. He's been fussier since Mike left, as if he knows he's lost someone important."

Donna regarded her sympathetically. "I hate this. I really do. You two belong together."

"I always thought so," Jane agreed. "But maybe Fate had something else in mind."

Jane went back to work the following Monday and quickly settled back into a routine that had once been as familiar to her as breathing. Because it was such a small school, she already knew many of the kids in her class. The substitute teacher's gradebook and detailed progress reports on each student filled in what she didn't know.

By the end of the first week, she felt as if she'd put her life in order and resigned herself to the idea that Mike would never be a part of it. She even dropped by Annie's Baby Boutique after school on Friday just as she had before she'd gotten pregnant with Davey. Now, though, she could shop to her heart's content for her own child.

At home, the minute she stepped inside, she sensed that something was different even before she spotted the pile of suitcases in the hallway. Her heart slammed against her chest, then began an unsteady rhythm.

"Mike?" She hurried down the hall toward the nursery, knowing instinctively that was where he would be. "Mike?"

He was in the rocker with the baby in his arms. The sight of the two of them made her breath catch in her throat.

He glanced up. "Hey, pipe down, will you? I've just gotten him settled down."

"And what have you done with the baby-sitter?"

"Sent her home. The kid and I don't need any help."

She grinned at him. "Is that so? Did she, by any chance, feed and change him before she left?"

"Of course."

"No wonder you're so confident, then." He did look confident, too. He also stared at her as if he couldn't wait to devour her. She felt the heat of that look all the way across the room.

Finally she dared to ask, "How long will you be here?"

His gaze locked with hers. "For good."

This time she was pretty sure she stopped breathing altogether. "For good?" she repeated in a shaky voice. "Why? How?"

"Later," he said. "Right now, how about getting over here and giving your husband a proper welcome-home kiss?"

Dazed, Jane crossed the room and bent down to brush a quick kiss across his brow.

He scowled at her. "You call that a proper kiss?"

She grinned. "That's exactly what I call it—very, very proper."

"Then I guess what I'm after is something else entirely." He reached up and curved his hand around her neck and drew her back down. When their lips were barely a hairbreadth apart, he paused. "I love you, Janie."

And then he kissed her and there was nothing the least bit proper about it. In fact, the kiss devoured, sending heat and need flooding through her. When he finally released her, she frowned at him.

"You'd better have meant it," she said.

"Meant what?"

"You'd better be staying for good, because I'd have to slug you if you were kidding around."

"No kidding," he vowed. "In fact, I think I'll just put Davey here in his crib so I can take his mommy to her bed and prove just exactly how serious I am."

The minute he had their son settled in for his nap, he turned and the fire in his eyes set off butterflies in Jane's stomach. When he swept her into his arms and headed across the hall to her room, she pushed aside every last reservation she had and let the sensation of being in his arms overwhelm her.

Explanations, everything could wait until later, she thought as she gave herself up to the tender glide of his hand over her flesh. His caresses, the heavenly feel of his mouth on her breasts, the wicked demand of his fingers probing her moist, secret places, all of it carried her off to a place where everything was perfect and love was eternal.

Slick fire raged between them as their bodies joined. Each thrust lifted her higher until she was crying out for release, crying out for Mike, then shuddering as he took her over the top and beyond.

Tears streamed down her cheeks when it was over, tears of joy, but Mike stared at her with concern.

"Janie, what is it? Did I hurt you?"

He started to move away, but she held him tightly. "No, please. It's just that we've never made love like this before. It's never felt like this."

"Like what?"

"Like the start of forever." She searched his face. "That is what it meant, isn't it?"

He brushed the damp tendrils of hair back from her cheeks. "Yes, that's what it meant."

She sighed then and fell asleep. For the first time in months, she slept peacefully.

Mike stared down at the woman in his arms and wondered how he could ever have convinced himself to leave her. This was where he belonged. It had taken some ingenuity on his part and a whole lot of understanding and cooperation on the part of his bosses, but he'd finally found a way to get back to her.

Jane sighed contentedly and opened her eyes. She reached for his face and touched her fingers to his cheek, then smiled.

"You are here. This is real."

"It's real."

"You aren't going back to San Francisco?"

"I'll have to go occasionally, but this will be home."

"You didn't quit your job?"

"I threatened to." He described the scene in which he'd told his bosses that he was going to have to make the most difficult—most impossible—choice of his life. "Then I offered them an alternative. I suggested we open an East Coast office. We're getting more and more business on this coast anyway. It made perfect sense."

A smile of pure joy spread across her face as she grasped the implications. "And it made perfect sense to put you in charge of it," she guessed.

"That's pretty much it. The office will be in northern Virginia, but the commute's workable. Once in a while I may have to stay over up there if a meeting's going to run very late, but they'll be paying me enough that we could even get a small apartment if we wanted to." He grinned at her. "Our own private little love nest."

"Now that's an interesting spin to put on a place you'll need because you're tied up in business meetings," she teased.

"I figure that's only one use we can put it to. Once we have a bunch of kids underfoot, we're going to need a little privacy every once in a while. We can go to the Kennedy Center, have a late-night supper, then spend all night making love and come back to our kids like a couple of rejuvenated newlyweds. What do you think?"

She knelt on the bed beside him and peppered his face with kisses. "I think that you are the most inventive, smartest man on the face of the earth. You've done the impossible."

He traced a line from the pulse at her throat down between her breasts and on beyond. "Just wait till you see what I can do with the possible," he said.

The first sparkle he'd seen in ages lit her eyes. "Dare you to show me," she said at once.

So he did.

* * * * *

MEN at WORK

All work and no play?
Not these men!

July 1998
MACKENZIE'S LADY by Dallas Schulze

Undercover agent Mackenzie Donahue's
lazy smile and deep blue eyes were his best
weapons. But after rescuing—and kissing!—
damsel in distress Holly Reynolds, how could
he betray her by spying on her brother?

August 1998
MISS LIZ'S PASSION by Sherryl Woods

Todd Lewis could put up a building with ease,
but quailed at the sight of a classroom! Still,
Liz Gentry, his son's teacher, was no battle-ax,
and soon Todd started planning some
extracurricular activities of his own....

September 1998
A CLASSIC ENCOUNTER
by Emilie Richards

Doctor Chris Matthews was intelligent, sexy
and *very* good with his hands—which made
him all the more dangerous to single mom
Lizette St. Hilaire. So how long could she
resist Chris's special brand of TLC?

Available at your favorite retail outlet!

MEN AT WORK™

HARLEQUIN®   *Silhouette*®

Look us up on-line at: http://www.romance.net   PMAW2

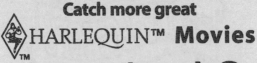 

THE TALLCHIEFS

the beloved miniseries by
USA Today bestselling author

Cait London

continues with
RAFE PALLADIN: MAN OF SECRETS
(SD #1160)
Available August 1998

When takeover tycoon Rafe Palladin set out to *acquire* Demi Tallchief as part of a business deal, Demi had a few conditions of her own. And Rafe had some startling secrets to reveal....

> "Cait London is one of the best writers in contemporary romance today."   —*Affaire de Coeur*

And coming from Desire in **December 1998,** look for **The Perfect Fit** in which *Man of the Month* Nick Palladin lures Ivory Tallchief back home to Amen Flats, Wyoming.

Available at your favorite retail outlet.

Silhouette®